THE GRUB RIDER

A KEYSTONE RANCH STORY

THE GRUB RIDER

JAMES C. WORK

FIVE STAR

A part of Gale, Cengage Learning

GALE
CENGAGE Learning·

Farmington Hills, Mich • San Francisco • New York • Waterville, Maine
Meriden, Conn • Mason, Ohio • Chicago

Copyright © 2017 by James C. Work
Five Star™ Publishing, a part of Cengage Learning, Inc.

LIBRARY OF CONGRESS CATALOGING-IN-PUBLICATION DATA

Names: Work, James C., author.
Title: The grub rider / James C. Work.
Description: First edition. | Waterville, Maine : Five Star Publishing, [2017] | Series: A Keystone Ranch story
Identifiers: LCCN 2016041926 (print) | LCCN 2016051416 (ebook) | ISBN 9781432833954 (hardcover) | ISBN 1432833952 (hardcover) | ISBN 9781432837020 (ebook) | ISBN 1432837028 (ebook) | ISBN 9781432833909 (ebook) | ISBN 1432833901 (ebook)
Subjects: LCSH: Frontier and pioneer life—Fiction. | Ranches—Fiction. | BISAC: FICTION / Action & Adventure. | FICTION / Westerns. | GSAFD: Adventure fiction. | Western stories.
Classification: LCC PS3573.O6925 G78 2017 (print) | LCC PS3573.O6925 (ebook) | DDC 813/.54—dc23
LC record available at https://lccn.loc.gov/2016041926

First Edition. First Printing: April 2017
Find us on Facebook– https://www.facebook.com/FiveStarCengage
Visit our website– http://www.gale.cengage.com/fivestar/
Contact Five Star– Publishing at FiveStar@cengage.com

Printed in the United States of America
2 3 4 5 6 7 21 20 19 18 17

THE GRUB RIDER

CHAPTER ONE

"I'M ON MY WAY TO THE KEYSTONE."

"I'd like to stay and work for you some more," Gabe told the homesteader, "but y'see, I'm on my way to the Keystone. Keystone Ranch. Up north a ways."

"Let's get movin', Plug," he told his horse as he rode away. "Y' know what Plato says. A horse isn't a horse until it's doing what horses are born to do. And there sure weren't much for a horse to do around that place."

Gabe topped the rise and twisted around. He rested his hand on the cantle. The sod house with its thin string of chimney smoke, the cowshed, and the pole barn seemed squat and low and temporary. The place was struggling to grow but seemed destined to melt back into the sod.

Gabe felt guilty leaving any of the homesteaders at the mercy of the high plains where they would watch their vague dreams wither, then freeze, then blow away. But he also felt guilty for staying when there was barely enough food for a family. Some were trying to raise cattle or horses. Others pinned their hopes on wheat and hay. Still others huddled in little towns where a few struggling stores lined the single street and a handful of families kept poultry or a few dairy cows.

That was the trouble with riding the grub line. The isolated homesteads, the latchstring ranchers who really needed help but who could only pay with meals. Pretty soon even his meals put a strain on the place and the grub rider needed to drift on. And he really wanted to help, wanted to help everybody he came across. Gabe was naturally helpful, and a cheerful young lad whose mother had raised him on a steady diet of books, boundless optimism, and respect for his fellow man. But a week in a frontier settlement could make his eyes glaze and the corners of his mouth turn down. He understood that the towns and farms represented hope and freedom to people. But it always made him gloomy to see them struggling just to make it through another season.

"The best you can do," Thompson the blacksmith told him, "is keep your eyes open and learn. Remember everything and move on. All right to look back. The main thing for *you*, young Gabe, is to keep going forward."

So keep going is what he did.

Listening to Evan Thompson, the blacksmith, was like getting talked to by your old grandfather—if you talked back, you didn't know what would happen. The blacksmith had mysterious ways and knew mysterious things. He knew, for instance, that Gabe's mother had told Gabe it was time for him to leave home and seek the Keystone. To look for a life farther west. Perhaps it was no more than an easy supposition on Thompson's part; most mothers of young men who kept outgrowing their pants probably said the same thing. Go west. Go east, go north, but just go. Go find somebody else to feed those two hollow legs of yours.

The blacksmith knew all the places Gabe had worked along the way. He knew how Gabe earned a few weeks' wages substituting for a horse wrangler who had a busted leg. The wrangler had learned the hard way not to ride a loose *latigo* on a green bronc, at least not while the law of gravity was still in effect. The blacksmith knew Gabe was a "swamper" at the Big Griddle Ranch. The Big Griddle had a good-size milking parlor and someone was needed to shovel aromatic muck from a clogged drainage ditch. He got two dollars for that job, plus his grub and a place to throw down his bedroll. Moving on, he slept in a widow's woodshed and earned a few days of chuck fixing her roof and fences. When the work ran out, she introduced him to the town baker who had a contract to supply bread to the grading crews working for the railroad. So Gabe helped him build a new brick oven and hauled loads of firewood from the hills.

The baker knew the blacksmith.

"See those hinges on m' oven? 'Twas Evan Thompson hammered them out for me. Know what he did? Didn't seem to make any sense. Told me to give bread away. He's tol' me to take fresh bread out t' the gang foreman and give it t' him for free. Darned if I didn't get a contract t' bake for the whole bunch! Now I need more help just t' keep up."

A couple of dollars from the baker, a couple of weeks of food and shelter for himself and the horse, and Gabe was back on grass again, pointed north by west like before.

"Sorry there's no more work," they would say.

"That's fine," Gabe would reply. "Y'see, I'm on my way to the Keystone, north of here."

"Well, Plug," he would say to the horse, "let us see what we find farther on."

Everywhere they went Gabe found someone who needed help. None of them could afford to pay wages for very long. "Good help is shore hard to find" was the refrain he heard over and over. "Yup, good help is shore tough to come by." It was true. They needed strong unmarried men, but most men of that particular description couldn't be bothered with ordinary jobs. Such men were usually dead set on being cattlemen. Or if they couldn't be cowboys, they wanted to become free trappers or prospectors.

"Too many men try to live by following their natural bent," Gabe said. "Plato said that."

Too many young men thought their natural bent lay in being drovers, wranglers, hostlers, punchers, or just "hands," and figured any kind of work that involved saddles and six-guns was preferable to any labor requiring carrying a shovel or wearing an apron. Some wanted so badly to be cowboys that they fell into the company of men who talked them into rounding up livestock they didn't exactly own.

Gabe wasn't interested when a drifting band of dark-looking men asked if he was good with his gun. He didn't mind helping out at the dairy—except that he couldn't tell what language the Swiss dairyman was shouting in—nor did he mind the hard-sweating toil of working for a well driller. The Swiss and the driller needed help. Gabe needed food. Enough said.

The worst job? Probably those manure-clogged drainage ditches. No, now that he thought it over, probably not. The very worst was working for the charcoal burner. Gabe met the charcoal man a couple days after the blacksmith's camp and he had never seen such dirty work in all his young life. He chopped down trees and sawed logs until he was pouring rivers of sweat. Then he snaked the logs to the stacks until his feet were sore and twisted from bashing over logs and rocks all day, and his hands were blistered from holding the lines of the team. Then, after the logging and hauling, there was the charcoal burning where the choking smoke never let up and a man never could be clean of black soot.

But he wasn't afraid of work no matter how hard or how dirty, because it was taking him to the Keystone. Other grub riders drifted from ranch to ranch or trail herd to trail herd where they would ask for a job but settle for a meal; Gabriel Hugh Allen, however, knew where he was headed. Knew his goal. He was headed to find out who Gabriel Hugh Allen was. His mother told him he'd find out when he got to the Keystone Ranch, just as his older brother had once done.

"So . . . you saw me there, did you, Ma?" he teased, grinning at her. "At this Keystone Ranch place? You never been there, so did you have a vision or something? Is that how you know I'll find myself there?"

"You're not so big I can't still whop you with the laundry stick," she replied. "You know what I mean about finding out who you are. And another thing. Along the way and when you get there, you use the name Gabriel Hugh Allen. Don't tell anybody your real name nor who your family is, not until you're somebody. You'll know when."

Strangely enough, the blacksmith told him the same thing.

"What plan, once you arrive the Keystone?" Evan Thompson had asked him.

"How did you know I'm headed for the Keystone? Don't tell me you saw me there too?" Gabe replied. Seeing as how his joke didn't work any better with the blacksmith than it had with his mother, Gabe got serious.

"I plan to ask for work, like I always do," he said.

"Work's to be had everywhere," Thompson said. "Don't need go all the way up there."

"To the Keystone? Sure I do. I'm told it's a special place."

"You think so? Probably because your brother was there, but he's long gone. You won't tell them who you are?"

"Should I?"

"No. Not why you go there. Your mother said what to you?"

"Time for me to be somebody," Gabe said. "Somebody with my own name. A name people will respect. Ride for the Keystone brand. Get a reputation. The Keystone is special. If Mother said so once, she said so a dozen times."

Their last afternoon together, Evan Thompson poured him a beaker of sweet warm wine and invited him to sit by the forge.

"I knew the brother," the blacksmith began. "His name gets you a job at the Keystone. Instant. Times hard, money scarce.

Pendragon could sign you on for your brother's sake. But don't take advantage. Show you're worth wages."

"Good advice."

"More. Watch and remember. Keep that six-gun out of sight. Make yourself useful. Ordinary chores and keep your eyes open."

"That how I get hired to punch Keystone cattle? Be useful and harmless?"

"Don't even expect cowboy work. Not that quick. You're going there and make a beginning."

"Well, you know what Plato said. A good beginning is half the work done."

"Listen close," Thompson said. "Listen and remember. Take any work. A chance to be Keystone rider will come at midwinter. Watch for when days stop getting shorter and begin the other way. When that time comes, Pendragon must grant favors. A big party for neighbors. When the sunlight starts to last longer, watch for him to gather his neighbors to him. Then ask him for the favor. For the boon. Listen to me now: *this* is what you must ask of Pendragon . . ."

What Evan Thompson told Gabe to ask for didn't seem to make much sense. But he would remember.

As he had done so many times and in so many places, Gabe turned in the saddle, rested his hand on the cantle, and looked back. Evan Thompson was loading the wagon, carrying the huge anvil cradled in his arms as easily as a new lamb or a sack of oats. The blacksmith didn't need extra help. He had his wife and a son strong enough to pump the forge bellows. He had another helper, a youth who was the size of a dwarf. He carried water and wood and tended to the teams.

Eben was his name. Gabe didn't know it, but he was to be seeing Eben sooner than he thought.

Gabe pointed Plug in the direction Thompson told him to go. He slept that night in scrub timber. The following day he came to the charcoal burner's encampment. The weather turned chilly the very day he began to work at the charcoal burner's trade and a light snowfall made skidding the logs easier. But the footing got treacherous. The stacks of smoldering wood kept the camp warm. Most of the time it was hard to breathe for the smoke, but at least it was warm.

After a couple of miserable weeks, Gabe strapped his bedroll behind the saddle.

"Sorry to leave you," he told the charcoal burner, "but y'see, I'm on my way to the Keystone."

He came across a miner blasting away at quartz outcrops. After a week of blisters and poor food, Gabe asked the miner to point the way to the nearest town. It was Salt Creek, where an ailing storekeeper offered Gabe a few weeks of work and a place to sleep.

"Just open the place up an' get a fire goin' of a mornin'," the man said, and coughed. "Once it warms up, I kin come down an' sit in my chair with a blanket by the stove while you tend the counter and fetch things fer people. Nuthin' to it."

Gabe hesitated. He had only stopped to buy some work gloves, but when he saw the hand-lettered sign saying "help wanted" he asked about it out of force of habit.

"I need to warn you," Gabe said, "I'm not looking for permanent work. I'm heading for the Keystone Ranch. Don't want to be late getting there."

"Hell," the storekeeper wheezed. "You're nearly there already. It's jist west of here. You kin be there in less than a day's ride. I only need y' for a week or so, till I'm feelin' stronger."

"In that case," Gabe said, "you've got yourself a clerk. I'll get my gear and put Plug in the stable down the street."

"Don't let that livery bastard talk y' into workin' for him," the man said. "He loves t' get cowboys who'll haul hay and shovel horse manure for chuck. Help's hard t' find around these parts."

"I'll be back," Gabe promised.

He was as good as his word. And he stayed until the storekeeper got better. The store was far from being busy, except when the supply wagon came to town and had to be unloaded, so Gabe found time to do a few other things he'd been meaning to do, such as writing a long letter home to his mother. That's when he got the idea of drawing a map to show her all the places he'd traveled . . . the homesteads, the Swiss dairy with the cows, the prosperous Big Griddle Ranch, the forest where the charcoal burner worked, and the clearing where Evan Thompson was camped. He drew the rivers and hills as he remembered them. He liked his map so much that he made himself another copy to carry in his saddlebag.

"I guess I'm gonna live," the storekeeper said one day.

Gabe had been sitting in a kitchen chair on the porch of the mercantile, tilted back against the wall. He was soaking up the warmth of the sun, looking up and down the street, watching horse turds thaw.

"That's good news," Gabe smiled.

"But I guess I ain't gonna need yore help from now on," the storekeeper continued. "Can't really afford t' pay y' no more wages."

"That's good news as well," Gabe said. "It's time Plug and I headed on out to the Keystone."

"An' if they don't hire y'? Back to ridin' the grub line?"

"Maybe not," Gabe grinned. "Maybe so, but maybe not."

Gabe was more than a little puzzled about his reception at the Keystone Ranch. At the first gate he met a cowboy sitting a flashy pinto.

14

"Yep, this is Keystone land all right," the cowboy said. "If it's work you're lookin' for, I expect you've come to the right place. If you're the right man, that is. You just ride to the main house. Up this road another mile. If you're hungry, stop at the bunkhouse kitchen. It's right close by the main house. You'll be just in time, I expect."

The pinto cowboy kept smiling a big friendly smile all the time he talked, and it made Gabe nervous. With his fancy clothes and fancy gun rig and big sombrero, he seemed a little too slick.

Gabe rode on and soon met two cowboys driving a loaded hay wagon. He asked how far it was to the main house and whether the Keystone was doing any hiring. Like the flashy cowboy on the pinto, these two were as nice as could be. "Sure!" one said. "Couldn't of timed it better. If you're hungry, stop off at the bunkhouse kitchen. Ol' Lou Barlow, he's the cowboy cook. He'll do you right."

"Gracias," Gabe said. "Giddyup, Plug. I don't know what they're all bein' so nice about, but we might as well find out."

The road led straight to an imposing two-story ranch house where it took a bend to the right and led around behind the big house. That's where the stables would be, as well as the kitchen door and this "bunkhouse kitchen" the men mentioned. They had seemed pretty eager to get him to stop at the bunkhouse kitchen.

The other kitchen, the one attached to the big house, was a one-story addition with a sloping roof. Ordinarily, Gabe wouldn't have thought much about it, except he noticed there was no smoke coming from the kitchen chimney. There was plenty of firewood stacked outside the door, and a coal shed handy with a neat flagstone path leading to it. But the kitchen looked deserted.

Gabe used one finger to push back the brim of his Stetson. A big house with no cooking going on.

He swung Plug's head toward the long, low bunkhouse where the chimney had plenty of smoke coming out. White smoke, the kind a cook makes when he's firing up kindling wood in preparation for a coal fire to bake biscuits and such. Gabe was particularly partial to biscuits. And such.

Gabe tied Plug to the hitch rail and walked into the kitchen.

"Good evening," Gabe said to the back of the man in the apron shaking down the clinkers. The man turned and glowered.

"Who're you?" he demanded.

"Name's Gabe. Gabriel Hugh Allen. A couple of your cowboys said there might be some sort of work hereabouts."

"Sent you on in, did they?"

"That's right."

"I'm Lou," the cook growled. "Lou Barlow. You picked a good day to git here. Y' hungry?"

"Somewhat," Gabe said. "I haven't eaten since last time."

"You look skinny enough, that's for sure," Lou Barlow said. "How many times do you have t' stand up before y' make a shadow?"

Lou Barlow gestured at the long table and pointed to the hat pegs along the wall, which Gabe took as an invitation to hang up his hat and sit down. Before long, he was face to face with a thick slice of beef, drowned in pretty good gravy, and a half-dozen biscuits. Lou brought a mug of coffee for himself and sat down on the bench opposite Gabe.

"The other hands, they et some time ago," he explained. "Gone off to do real important stuff. Leastways, that's what they keep tellin' me."

This was puzzlement number two. Gabe had never heard of a ranch cook, especially a bunkhouse cook, who would offer to feed a man after the supper dishes were washed. Any cowboy who came in late had to rustle his own chuck. And he'd damn better stay out of the cook's way. And what kind of "important stuff" made all the ranch hands vanish after evening supper? They ought to be sitting around comparing belches and picking their teeth with slivers.

"Awful nice of you," Gabe said over a mouthful of biscuit and gravy.

"Think nuthin' of it," Lou said.

"I would be glad to pay for my supper," Gabe offered. "Or maybe there's something you need done. Firewood, maybe? I'm a pretty fair hand at just about anything."

"Well! Now, that's real nice of y' to ask, it truly is," Lou said. "Fact is, there is one little chore. It's up to the big house. But it's too late t' start now. Plenty of time tomorra. When you're finished inhaling that beef, you probably oughta take your horse over t' the stables. You'll find hay. I hope he don't eat like you do. Then get one of the boys t' show y' a bunk."

Gabe did just that.

The stable hand showed him where to hang his saddle. A cowboy sporting a huge black mustache grinned and chuckled as he took Gabe to the bunkhouse and showed him where to toss his bedroll. Two more hands sat by the heater stove, one of them weaving reins out of horsehair, and they looked at Gabe and grinned broadly. Their whole aspect reminded him of the evening he arrived at the Big Griddle and asked if there were any chores he could do in return for a meal or two. The Big Griddle cowboys made him feel real welcome. As it turned out, there was a power of cow shit that had needed shifting, and Gabe was the answer to their prayers.

"It's a good cook you've got there," Gabe said, stepping up to warm his hands at the little potbellied heater.

"He'll do. He's grumpy, but ain't they all?"

"He's clean, that's the main thing," the other cowboy added.

"Grumpier now that he's havin' to cook for the big house."

There was a period of polite silence. Gabe watched the man weaving horsehair.

"Gonna make me a headstall, too, once I finish with this," he volunteered.

"I noticed the kitchen up there was empty," Gabe ventured. "Did the house cook quit, or something?"

"Well," said the weaver, "not yet. In fact, that's the problem. No. If Mary gets mad and quits, life 'round hereabouts won't be worth a plug nickel. She's the house cook. Nossir. We do *not* want that to happen. Don't need ol' Barlow gettin' *his* hackles up, neither. Nossir. God, I pity any man the boss sends over there! That Mary, she's likely t' rip inta him like a she-grizzly."

"Send a man?" Gabe asked. "Send a man to do what?"

"You'll sleep better if y' don't know," the cowboy said. " 'Cause I got a strong feelin' it's gonna be you."

CHAPTER TWO
KITCHEN HELP

Art Pendragon squished the last dab of mashed potatoes into the tines of his fork and wiped up the last speck of gravy. Across the table, Gwen applied a corner of her napkin to her lips and set the napkin next to her plate.

"Mighty good," Art said.

"Yes, it was," Gwen replied.

They both looked up as the kitchen door opened, expecting to see the hired girl coming in to clear the dishes. But it was not the hired girl who came in. It was the cook. Herself.

Art winced and braced himself. For the past week, ever since that careless kitchen boy collapsed the kitchen stovepipe and let loose an avalanche of black, greasy soot all over her floor and tabletops, having Mary appear in the kitchen doorway was something not to look forward to.

Things seemed to be improved this evening. Mary was calm and poised. She carried a fresh pie, which she set on the table while she fetched three plates and forks from the sideboard. She even smiled as she sat down and cut into the pie.

"Happier tonight, Mary?" Gwen asked.

"The pie smells wonderful," Art said. "So," he added tentatively, "so, are you still making do with the bunkhouse kitchen?"

"I should say not," Mary said, handing him his plate. "But it's no thanks to those yellow-livered so-called 'hired men' of yours. *My* kitchen is operating proper now, so it is."

"Somebody fix the stovepipe? Who fixed it?"

"It was none of your fearless riders, I can tell you."

"We can't really blame them," Gwen said. "Not after the way you treated that poor boy who knocked the stovepipe down. Chasing him out of the house like that."

"And clear off the ranch!" Art added. "You did tie a can to his tail! He was last seen makin' a beeline for town. They said he was runnin' so fast, he was only hitting the high spots."

"Two days that boy cost me!" Mary huffed. "Didn't it take the whole of two days for me and the girl to clean the soot off everything? Two days! And we've still got the curtains to wash."

"It's fixed now?" Art said. "The flue is drawing all right, stove works fine?"

"Thanks to that nice young man, the new one. Just imagine that cocky Pinto Kid, thinking to himself he was playing a funny trick on a stranger—*and* on me as well—sending him to my kitchen door to ask for chores and a meal, and myself with a cold stove and just havin' cleaned the remains of soot and filth all over everywhere. Your bunkhouse bed-pressers were hangin' around outside hoping they'd see me chase him across the yard with the broom. Or better yet, they probably hoped to see him try and clean that flue pipe and end up covering my kitchen with soot all over again."

"Didn't happen that way?" Art asked, his pie-laden fork poised in air.

"I should say not. Didn't I warn him about the boy who tried to clean out the stovepipe and brought the whole shebang down around our ears? Well sir, the new fellow he studies on it real close for a few minutes, then asks the girl for two flour sacks and two gunnysacks. Then he took the doors off the range. Puts doors, lids, shaker, and all in gunnysacks and takes 'em outside. Puts ashes and sand in the sacks, jounces them up and down and sideways awhile, and brings 'em back so clean and shiny I was that amazed at it."

"Hmmm," Art said, chasing the last crumbs of pie on his plate.

"And then, with all the doors off, didn't he get both his arms into the range there and fasten a damp flour sack over the openin' where the pipe comes down. After that, he's out in the road, pickin' up all these little stones and pebbles. Then he finds himself the ladder and a stretch of rope and presently he's up on the kitchen roof. Directly the girl and me hear rumblin' noises in the flue pipe, and presently he's back down to collect the bag of soot and put the doors back on. Left my range clean as a whistle, and not a fleck of soot did he drop on the floor or anywheres. Not a fleck."

"He sounds like an ingenious young man," Gwen said. "Did you say he was just passing through?"

"He's ridin' the 'grub line,' is what those steer chowsers of yours call it. Grub. If I catch one of them calling my cooking 'grub,' there'd be the devil to pay, let me tell you."

"I don't doubt it," Gwen said, smiling over at Art.

"And didn't that same young man fix the fancy patented milk cooler doohickey you bought us, Mr. Pendragon?"

"Fix it?"

"None of your boys knew why it wouldn't lift the milk cans up out of the coolin' water like it's supposed to. That cowhand calls himself Link tried to fix it and ended up tippin' a whole cream can all over the spring cellar floor. Said the elevator gimcrack was jammed or broken. I told this 'grub rider' he'd have to make do with water beside his meal, seeing as how the patented thingus was broke and I'm not strong enough to hoist the milk cans outa it. 'Let me look at it,' says he, right sharp as you please, and 'there's your problem, somebody's fastened that cross arm backwards t' where it oughta be' and quick as a wink he had it fixed."

"I'd like to meet this prodigy," Art said, dropping his napkin beside his plate and rising from his chair. "He still around?"

"I'll send the girl to find him."

Mary collected the supper plates and disappeared back through the kitchen door, humming just a tiny bit of tune as she went. Wouldn't it be nice if Mr. Pendragon could see his way clear to hiring her a man to help around her kitchen? The girl was fine, as girls went, but when it came to hauling firewood or carrying the big tubs of wash water—or wrestling with milk and cream cans, come to that—a strong young man would be ever so much better.

And this one so nicely spoken as well. It was plain as the nose on your face that his old mother had taken pains with his educating.

Gabe entered the main house and found Mr. Pendragon in his office—which doubled as a study and general hideaway—frowning over a pair of oversized leather-bound ledger books.

"Gabriel Hugh Allen," Gabe said, offering his hand across the desk.

"Art Pendragon," Art said, taking notice of the strong grip in those long fingers.

Gabe looked around at the maps and ledgers that filled the bookcases and overflowed onto desk and table. Running a spread the size of the Keystone Ranch must involve more paper and ink than it did men and horses.

"Mary tells me you're a grub rider," Art began.

"Yes, sir," Gabe said. "Sometimes it turns out to be more riding than grub. I've been out on the grass for about a year now. But I've learned a lot of jobs. Met an interesting mix of people."

"Wyoming Territory is never short on 'mix' when it comes to people," Art said. "We got all kinds. You headed anywhere in particular?"

"Here."

"Here?"

"Yes, sir."

"If you came all the way here in hopes of a job, I need to tell you right up-front that there aren't any," Art said. "We just aren't taking on any new help right at the moment."

"Yes, sir."

"Things are a little tough. Well, you already know that. From riding the territory, I mean. You've seen all the good men out of work. Plenty of jobs waiting, but no money for salaries. Cattle prices are way down. That dry, cold winter nearly wiped us out. I'd like to help you, but trust me, I've already hired every good rider I was able to. A lot of them are men who worked for my neighbors and got laid off. Or else they were men we knew pretty well."

"Yes, sir."

"You're sure welcome to a bunk and meals, though. We can find chores or something for you. I know you'd want to work it off. You don't look like a man who takes kindly to charity."

"I appreciate it," Gabe said.

"All right, then," Art said, picking up his pencil and turning his attention to the ledgers. "You're more than welcome to stay a few days, if you want."

"Mr. Pendragon?" Gabe asked.

"Yes?"

"I was told about a custom you had. Granting favors? What the old writers called 'boons'?"

"Word gets around. Who told you about that?"

"A blacksmith. A big man. Seemed to just suddenly appear one day."

"Evan Thompson," Art said. "He does that. Comes outa nowhere, I mean."

"That was his name. Thompson. He said to ask you for a

boon favor."

"Did he? Well, if Thompson sent you, that changes the situation. But I don't know where Thompson thought I'd come up with the wherewithal to hire another hand."

"I think he was aware of that," Gabe said. "He told me to ask you for three favors. In lieu of being put on the payroll. He said something pretty odd, too. He said it's not midwinter, then he said to ask when the time was right."

"Sounds odd, but not for him. Did our blacksmith say what these three favors are supposed to be?"

"Yes."

"You know they have to be something I can actually do. Nothing unreasonable. I can't nominate you for territorial governor, or give you a homestead or anything like that."

"A year of board and someplace to sleep," Gabe stated. "That's the first favor."

"That's it? What else?"

"Right now, that's it. Grub and a place to throw my bedroll. I'll work in return. One year."

"Grub riders generally stay a day or two and move on. The boys aren't goin' t' like it much, a grub rider hanging around for a whole year. What did Thompson say is supposed t' happen at the end of that year?"

"That's when I ask you for two more things," Gabe said.

"What are those, then?" Art said.

"Rather not tell you what he said, not right now. Because I don't really understand it. But the blacksmith, he said you could grant them. And I could do them. After a year."

Art stood up and put out his hand.

"Thompson's word is good enough for me," he said. "I trust him. He can be mysterious as hell sometimes. Most of the time, now I think about it. All right then, you've got yourself a 'boon.' You go hunt up Lou Barlow. He's the bunkhouse cook."

"I met him," Gabe said.

"Tell him I said to give you a place to sleep. You can eat with the hands at the bunkhouse."

Art went to the calendar on the wall and circled the date in heavy pencil.

"One year."

"And then I'll ask for the next two things," Gabe said.

"Done."

Art Pendragon watched Gabe walk out of his office and across the big room beyond. *So,* he thought. *The blacksmith again. Evan Thompson sent this kid. I wonder what Thompson sees happening after a year is up?*

Lou Barlow sputtered and grumbled, then limped up to the main house to make sure the kid had told the truth. Mr. Pendragon had promised a year of free meals. A year! Then Lou stopped in the kitchen and heard Mary and her hired girl laud his fine manners and his eagerness to be helpful, and, well, it was just the final damned straw. Here's the drought, rustlers and squatters and all, good cowboys out of work, and along comes this green kid and gets taken in like he was an orphan or somethin'. Well, Lou groused, he might have to feed him, but he sure didn't have to live with him.

"He ain't sleepin' in my bunkhouse!" he sputtered to Mary. "My boys come in all tuckered out and saddle-sore from workin' hard all day, an' the last thing they need is t' see that kid sittin' on a bunk where a *real* Keystone rider oughta be. He'll take his chuck with us, like Mr. Pendragon says, providin' he turns up on time. But he ain't sleepin' with us."

Gabe didn't mind throwing his bedroll down on the back porch, or in the hayloft, or anywhere dry and out of the wind. Lou used him pretty hard the first few weeks, setting him to split cords of firewood, or having him haul ashes to dump in the arroyo, where the slightest breeze sent clouds of ash flying up to cover him from head to toe. Sometimes Lou told him to mop the bunkhouse floors when they didn't need it, or sent him all the way to town on some errand that seemed pointless. As the early dry spring turned into a muddy May, Lou had him building a boardwalk so the "real" cowboys wouldn't track in so much mud. And Gabe slept in the loft over the stable until one night when the rain came through the shingles and soaked him and his bedroll. The next morning, Mary heard him sneezing and coughing.

"You'll catch your death, you will," she said. And she went to speak with Mr. Pendragon.

Her idea was twofold. Mary wanted the nice young man to have better sleeping conditions than Lou Barlow was giving him, and she wanted him to do more work in her kitchen and less work at the bunkhouse. She had come up with a way to do it. Art Pendragon approved, although he would have preferred to stay out of the situation altogether, and two mornings later, Mary's girl brought Gabe to the kitchen.

"Look here," Mary said.

She led him to the corner behind the cookstove where she drew aside a curtain and showed him a tiny alcove. There was a narrow folding bunk and a nightstand with an oil lamp on it.

"This was built as a pantry," she said. "But as you can plainly see, 'tis done all wrong. Too warm on account of being near the stove, and too much out of the way, all at the same time. It's just the most unhandy place you can imagine for keepin' things I need every day. Now, you go get your things and move in."

Gabe started to say he didn't need a place nearly so tidy and warm, but Mary flapped her apron at him.

"And did you hear me askin' you for an argument?" she said. "Get your things. And don't think it's any big favor you're getting, neither. In return, I'm expectin' you to be up at first light to get the stove going for me. That'll be your job from now on. And you'll keep the heater tank filled as well."

So Gabe had a better place to sleep, and another chore to do. Now when he walked into the bunkhouse for his meals, he caught even more of the cowboys' barbs and humor. As he spent more time doing chores for Mary and fewer chores for Lou, the distance between himself and the Keystone riders increased. Sometimes they would be gone a week at a time, returning with hair-raising stories of fighting rustlers or chasing stampeding cattle. One day, a rider came pounding in with news of a holdup in Salt Creek. Quicker than you could believe, Mr. Pendragon was on his horse, his Colt on his hip and his Winchester tied to his saddle, calling men by name and urging them to hurry. Gabe stood in the doorway in his flour sack apron, a serving dish forgotten in his hand, watching Keystone cowboys tighten cinches and swing up into their saddles, setting their jaws toward the trail of the robbers.

When they returned, they told of whizzing bullets and wild chases across treacherous country, of men "holed up" behind walls where they had to be "smoked out" with gunfire. The Keystone men recounted every lamed horse, each broken strap and cartridge misfire; they told of cold nights and hot days, of bad water and frightened settlers. Gabe brought great bowls of beans and huge platters of biscuits and listened to the stories. After the washing up was done with, he went back to his cuddy behind the stove and dreamed of being one of them.

"Y' seen where he sleeps?" a cowboy quipped one day. "Mary, she's got him bunked behind her stove like a pet cat."

" 'Member that old dog they used t' have up at the house?" the Pinto Kid said. "He slept there, too. There, or else right under the stove."

"Nice ol' dog," Link said. "Good ol' yellow dog."

"What was his name?" Gabe asked.

27

"The dog? They called him Ranger," Link said.

"But not 'cause he did any traveling!" Dick Elliot grinned. "That old dog, he never ranged anywhere except to his food bowl. Or outside once in a while to pee. They called him Ranger 'cause he spent all his time sleepin' next to the range!"

And now it was Lem's turn to laugh uproariously at something he had just thought of. Lem was the bunkhouse joker.

"We'd oughta be calling him Gabe the Ranger," Lem laughed, wholly pleased with himself. "Yessir. A regular man of the range, that's him! What do y' say?"

"Whatever keeps your spirits up," Gabe smiled. "You go right ahead."

Gabe shrugged off the jokes and went on doing his best to be useful. By the time spring had a good hold on the land, hardly anyone took notice of a lean young man in a white flour sack apron peeling potatoes, lugging wood, or sweeping a porch.

The skies over Wyoming Territory gave up their rains exactly twice in June. In July, only one rain came to spatter the dust and turn roads and trails to mud for a few days. The summer heat dragged on and on, and the grass turned brown as moldy straw. Keystone riders found themselves pushing the herds more frequently now, often moving them from a range after only a few weeks of grazing. By September, when the herds should have been slowly moving back toward the home ranch, they were widely scattered throughout the foothills and across the high prairie country.

Rustlers became more daring, quick to take advantage of the widely dispersed herds. Before long, Art was getting messages from as far away as Green River and Pikes Peak that bunches of steers carrying the Keystone brand were seen penned up at railroad yards or mixed in with trail herds headed toward the Mexican border.

Link took four men and packhorses and started south with

orders to find Keystone cattle and recruit men along the way to head them north again. Will and Lem set out for Green River country with a spring wagon and four more men, and Art expected they would be out there into the winter, rounding up Keystone stock.

Gabe carried coffee and pie to Art's office one day. He found him pacing the floor, muttering to himself. He had the map of the hill country tacked to the wall.

"Is something wrong?" Gabe asked, setting the tray on the desk.

"Damn right," Art scowled. "More of the same."

"The same? Rustling, you mean?"

"That's what I mean," Art said. "They're taking more chances now. Dick just rode in with the news that a gang grabbed off the red herd I've been saving to breed next year. A hundred head or more. We're thin on men, but I've got to get after them. Dammit."

"Is there anything I can do?" Gabe said.

Art stopped pacing and looked at him.

"Matter of fact, yes. You can cook, can't you?"

"Yes."

"All right. Then get down to the bunkhouse and tell Lou I want the chuck wagon fixed up for you to drive, the small one. He'll know what to stock it with. Have the hostler get a team ready and check the tack and running gear. By the time it's set up, I'll have some boys picked out and ready to ride. We're going after those cattle thieves. Nobody steals from the Keystone."

Orders were shouted. Horses whinnied to one another. Cowboys strapped on chaps and stuffed boxes of cartridges into saddlebags. One after the other they swung up into their saddles and moved off down the road until the last rider was racing at the gallop to catch up with the departing cloud of dust.

Gabe clucked to the wagon team and slapped the leathers

along the horses' backs.

"Step up! Go boys, step up now! Get along!"

Once the chuck wagon was going along at a decent pace, Gabe relaxed on the seat and pushed his hat back on his head. He held the lines easily, casual as a man driving to a picnic. He whistled snatches of an old Irish air. He was to follow the tracks of the Keystone posse until sundown or thereabouts when he would unhitch, set up camp, and get supper ready for the riders.

The scouts sighted the red herd on the third day. But the cattle thieves also saw the scouts. Realizing they were being pursued, their first thought was to find some place they could hole up. They began to push the herd as fast as it would move, two men riding ahead to search for some place in the rocks or gullies that could serve as a fortress.

"Good canyon ahead!" one of them shouted.

Even better, there was a deep gorge off to one side where they could hide the whole herd. A couple of men with rifles, he figured, could hold the mouth of the gorge against a small army.

"Hell, once we get in there we can hold 'em off till they get tired and hungry and go home!"

There ensued two long, hot days of doing nothing. The rustlers were caught in a box. They could leave their horses and climb out on foot, but that would be tantamount to suicide. Art Pendragon's riders would hunt them down like so many coyotes. On the other hand, they were safe where they were; Art wouldn't risk sending men into the canyon so long as the entrance was guarded by concealed men with rifles. It was a stalemate, a standoff.

"No steer is worth a cowboy's life," Art said.

Art was anxious to be back at the Keystone. He had six men with him—seven if he included Gabe—which left the main ranch short-handed. Six men and himself, sitting on their butts for two days looking into the mouth of a box canyon.

"Tomorrow we've gotta get in there," he said. "Maybe get up the ridge behind them and pick off one or two."

But Gabe had another idea. He had just dished up supper to the men sitting around his cookfire.

"Why not go back to the ranch?" he said. "Leave two men here. And me. Before you go, blockade the opening to the gorge. Maybe roll those rocks down from the hill there. Use the horses to drag logs and build a good wall. Three of us taking turns standing watch could keep them penned up in there."

"Then what?" Art grinned. "You all just sit here until winter? And hope they'll starve?"

"Nossir. Penning them in gives you the advantage of time. You return to the ranch. Get the men rested up, then send some of them back here. I imagine our cow-thieving friends will be pretty easy to coax out, given a few more days. No need for all of us to stay here."

"The kid's makin' a good case," Dick said. Tom Whistler said the same thing.

"Dammit," Art said. "I'd love the chance to shoot a rustler. But Gabe does make sense. I can do a lot more back at the Keystone than I can sitting here."

And so it was settled. Dick, Tom, and Gabe would stay behind and make sure the rustlers couldn't get out of the canyon. Art and the others would return to the ranch.

What happened after that became the stuff of many a yarn-swapping session. The first to tell the story was Dick Elliot, after the red herd was back safely on its range and the rustlers were jailed.

"Well," Tom said. "You gonna tell us what happened, Dick?"

Supper was over. The boys had gathered around the bunkhouse stove to hear the story.

"Well, didn't our pot-walloper read it right!" Dick said. "It went slick as a new maverick. Them hot days we had sure helped. First thing we did was build a good solid fence across that canyon. Instead of trying to get 'em to come out, we walled 'em in, hah! I snuck up along the ridge and spied on 'em every day, and every day you could see 'em trying to figure some way to get their horses up out of that little tiny canyon."

"What good did it do?" the Pinto Kid asked. "To wall them in, I mean?"

"Good? Hell, ol' Gabe had it figured. Those boys—there was four of 'em—they're stuck in that little ol' canyon with scarce a flat spot t' lie down in. And they gotta share it with a hundred beeves! Hungry, thirsty beeves! Day and night, those animals keep on bawlin' and bellowin' fit to be tied. You ever been penned up with a hundred head of cattle? Whooeee! Some of them steers got mean toward the rustlers' horses, too. And of course they're browsing all the grass down short and leaving big piles of nice fresh cow shit everywhere."

He paused and helped himself to the coffee pot.

"Gabe here, he just goes on fixin' meals for us, calm as y' please. One of us stands guard all the time, watching that barricade. 'Just wait,' he says. 'Just wait.' And by an' by, that rustler bunch made their last mistake. You tell me now. You're starvin' in a place like that. You're really gettin' hungry. So, what do you do?"

"Easy," said the Pinto Kid. "We beef out one of those cows."

"Right!" Dick exclaimed. "Just right! So you shoot yourself a cow. *Now* you got to bleed the thing, and there's the smell of blood everywhere keepin' the other cattle stirred up and wide-eyed, not to mention the horses. Y' get your steak dinner all right, but after a day or two under that hot sun, the carcass of that ol' cow starts to stink something fierce."

The cowhands smiled knowingly at each other and nodded. Crowded into a gorge with a bunch of cattle, then the smell of rotting meat in the air. Damned discouragin' is what it would be. That grub rider had a good head on his shoulders.

"Well," Dick went on, "here's one cowpuncher what wouldn't have missed it for the world. By an' by here comes Mr. Pendragon and a fresh posse up the trail, and here we come down t' meet him, bringin' with us four disgusted cow rustlers with their feet hogtied under their saddles. We was makin' them do the herdin', us two guardin' 'em with our rifles, and ol' Gabe there on the seat of his chuck wagon bringin' up the drag with another rifle."

" 'What happened?' Mr. Pendragon asks Gabe."

" 'Oh,' says he, just as sweet as y' please, 'I guess they just decided to come out of there on their own. They just give up, for some reason.' Hah! What a deal! Beats all heck outa swappin' lead with 'em and then havin' to bury the bodies, let me tell you. They just flat got so tired, hungry, and smelly they decided to quit."

When Gabe helped serve breakfast to Mr. and Mrs. Pendragon and their guests the next morning, Art looked at the young man with new interest.

"Thanks for your help with the rustlers," Art said.

"You're welcome," Gabe said.

"He seems like a nice young man," Gwen said after Gabe had returned to the kitchen. "A shame you can't find him a better job than being a cook's helper."

"Dear, I'll let you in on something," Art said as he passed her the syrup. "In a couple of months, our cook's helper is going to ask me for another favor. Evan Thompson told him what to ask for."

The blacksmith's name made Gwen pause.

"Mr. Thompson?" she said. "I wonder what it will be?"

"No way of knowing," Art said. "Something unexpected, I'll lay you a wager on that."

"Something unexpected," Gwen said. "Yes, something unexpected."

Chapter Three
THE LADY'S LADY

Early, early morning. No longer night, not light enough to be called day. There was a thin haze of fog lying on the ground, a rare thing in the dry air of Wyoming. Not a thick, soaking fog, not a fog to hide the grass and low-growing bushes; in Wyoming ground fog is thin and mysterious, a wavering mirage of mist that hangs on the sage like rags of a gossamer gown. It floats into gulches and gulleys, losing itself among the rabbit brush.

Gabe rose while it was still dark, shivered into his clothes, dashed cold water on his face and combed his hair by the light of his candle, then built the morning fire in the stove.

His first chore after breakfast was to kill and pluck three hens for supper.

"Three? Company coming?" he asked Mary.

"So we do hear," the cook replied. "A rider came in last night to say we should expect a lady and her servant sometime today. Now listen: after you killed those hens, you take them on up the hill a ways for the pluckin'. I don't want feathers blowing all over my wash yard, you hear?"

"Yes, ma'am," he said, grinning.

So Gabe found himself out away from the buildings, standing alone with thin wisps of ground fog rubbing against his boots, holding a dead chicken as he looked away along the road. It was far too early in the morning for visitors to be arriving at the Keystone; the ranch hands had just barely begun their morning rituals.

But what he did see, as he stood plucking feathers and staring into the distance, was a mirage. A living, moving mirage coming out of the mist. An apparition so realistic and sudden that the half-stripped chicken slipped from his grasp unnoticed and thudded into the dirt unheard. Gabe raised both hands to shade his eyes. Riders coming in! Riders pounding toward him at a fast gallop, yet making no sound. Five or six abreast, they charged like cavalry gone mad. They raged over the hill, quirting their horses hard. Their hat brims were flat against the air and, although their mouths were open and gaping like men shouting and whooping as they rode, there was no sound to be heard. No thunder of hoofbeats, no voices, nothing. Nothing at all. Gabe couldn't tell if they were touching the ground or floating over it, yet on they came, a ghostly legion of gray-shirted riders on foam-flecked mounts. A pageant of phantom men and animals rose and swelled and swayed in eerie unison, the horses shoulder to shoulder, the riders mutely shouting and using their quirts with a vengeance. And yet it was silent. It was stampeding toward him without even the sound of wind.

Gabe dropped to his knees. His mind understood the spectacle was unreal, yet in his heart he was certain that his end had come. In another moment the wave of running horses and shouting men surely would sweep over him and pound him into the cold, damp earth. But as quickly as the apparition had appeared, it vanished. Where the squadron of riders had been, now there was only gray sky, the same featureless sage hill as before, and the same quiet of the morning's light mist. Gabe blinked once, twice. As he rose to his feet and bent down to retrieve the hen, he looked toward the hill where the charging band of riders had been.

Coming toward him was a small person riding on a small mule. The figure waved a greeting, as if he knew Gabe, and as he drew nearer Gabe did recognize him. It was the blacksmith's helper, the dwarf-like Eben.

The scene would have caught the imagination of a newspaper cartoonist. Over here was a miniature mounted cowboy, scarcely topping out at four feet in physical altitude, decked from head to toe in cowboy attire. From boots and chaps to sheepskin coat and Stetson, he looked every inch a cowhand. But there weren't that many inches to him. He rode straight up and relaxed, the posture of a man who has spent most of his life sitting in the saddle of a cow pony, yet in this case the cow pony was a mule of almost comical dimensions. One might take it for a burro.

On the other side of the cartoon tableau stood Gabe, also wearing a broad Stetson. Gabe was attired in a homemade apron fashioned from two flour sacks that still bore the name and symbol of the flour mill. His left hand was partly raised, for he had automatically begun to wave back to the visitor. In his right hand he held a half-plucked chicken by its well-wrung neck. His mouth was partly open, but no words came out.

"Hullo, Gabriel!" Eben greeted him. "A nice little mist we're havin' this morning!"

"Eben?"

The little man could see Gabe looking past him, trying to see if Evan Thompson was somewhere in his wake.

"He's set up the forge just outside of town," Eben volunteered.

"Oh."

"Sent me to tell you!"

"Tell me? Tell me what?"

"That it's time. Mr. Thompson says, 'your time is upon you.' He says to me, 'the boy's iron is in the fire ready for the anvil!' "

"Huh?" Gabe said, not yet certain he wasn't talking to a phantom.

"The first year is up, Gabriel!" Eben laughed. "Haven't you kept track of the days? Remember what he told you to do next."

"This visitor they're expecting . . . is *that* the one Thompson told me about?"

"Indeed!"

"But I can't go anywhere. I'm too ragged for travelin'. Old Plug has been off his feed lately, too. I don't even own a pair of pants that aren't patched. Nor a rifle. I had to borrow one to go chase rustlers a while back. No, I couldn't ride off looking like this."

"And why do you think I'm here, then?" Eben laughed again. "You pluck your chickens and go about your business. You'll know when the time is right to ask Pendragon about those next two boons. You'll know. Leave me to manage the rest, Gabriel."

The dwarf turned his small mule northward and in the next minute he was gone.

For nearly a year Gabe had waited, uncertain what Evan Thompson intended for him to do and yet trusting in the blacksmith's advice. He had made no progress toward becoming a rider for the Keystone brand, none at all. But he had been patient. He had endured the cowboys' jokes and Lou Barlow's thousand unkind acts, and now it seemed his final hour of trial was close at hand. If this was the day the blacksmith foretold, never again would he have to peel a hundredweight of potatoes for Lou, nor haul sacks of coal, or clean ashes from the stove, nor mop the kitchen and bunkhouse. Ol' Lou would have to do his own fetch and carry from here on. Served him right. Probably the most disagreeable man Gabe had ever met.

The young man who had gone up the misty hill as a kitchen jack and step-and-fetch-it boy returned with chin held high and chest full of hope. He believed he was facing the end of his servitude and the beginning of a proud time. In a patched apron and carrying three dead chickens, Gabe strode down toward his future.

Gabe had a few days of servitude left. Mary asked him to

wait on the table for her while the visitors were there. She scrounged up some relatively new trousers for him, along with a starched shirt with a boiled collar. She made him shave and trim his hair. All so he could carry tureens of soup and stew and platters of meat from the kitchen to the table in the big dining room. The good thing of it was he could stand by the sideboard, ready to refill a water glass or fetch more rolls from the kitchen, and listen in on the conversation. During the first meal it was all polite observations about weather and cattle prices and the condition of the roads, but at supper on the second day, the lady visitor began spelling out the reason she had come to the Keystone.

At the head of the table sat Art Pendragon. Mrs. Pendragon presided over the other end. On Mr. Pendragon's right hand sat Link Lochlin, the Kansas cowboy who was top rider of the Keystone and probably the most respected, most feared shooter in the territory. Next to him was Bob Riley, an equally respected top hand and a Keystone foreman. Like Link, Pasque, Kyle Owens, and the Pinto Kid, Bob Riley was a man for whom other men stepped aside.

Near Mrs. Pendragon sat a quiet, modest man of middle age who had been introduced as "Dobé" Adams. He was the visiting lady's driver, bodyguard, cook, hostler, and general factotum. He didn't look like much of a bodyguard, not to Gabe at least. He looked more like a bookkeeper. He dressed more like a dude or a whiskey drummer.

The lady who sat at Mr. Pendragon's left hand was Mrs. Lynette Townsend, and don't you forget it, thank you very much. Brown was her color and brown was her disposition. Gabe first saw her when she stepped down from the three-inch spring wagon—after waiting impatiently for "Dobé" to lock the brake, wrap the lines, and hustle around to offer her his arm—and she was wearing a rich brown traveling cloak with black fur collar.

In the trunks, which Gabe helped haul upstairs to the guest room, she kept an apparently inexhaustible supply of other brown clothes. Even her white shirtwaist was brown.

"So, Mr. Pendragon," she said at the second supper, "you say you have not heard of our tormentor, this Karl Rothaus? Unfortunate, most unfortunate. However, should you have heard of him, you would certainly have sent your men to deal with him. And long before this."

"No, never heard of him. What is it he has done, exactly?"

Her two brown eyebrows arched upward as if she thought the legendary lord of the Keystone enterprise was questioning her veracity. Or that it was only for her to mention to him that a man needed hanging, and he would see it carried out without delay.

"What has he done?" The lady Townsend looked at Gwen Pendragon. "What has he not done?"

Well, Gabe thought, standing by with a pitcher of water, Plato did say something about questions being the best answers. Or was it answers lead on to the better questions?

"I shall not recount his other transgressions, only those which affect my benefactor, my lady Surrey."

"Surrey?" Gwen asked politely.

"Lady Catherine Surrey," explained the lady Townsend. Gabe marveled that she could pronounce words so clearly despite the fact that her thin upper lip seemed to be glued down tight to her teeth. It never moved when she spoke.

"Lady Surrey inherited title from her father, who had scarcely established his seat in this wild country before falling victim to some rampant illness and fever. I blame the water, of course."

"Oh, of course," Gwen said. "One has to be so careful of the water out here."

"The earth upon Lord Surrey's grave had hardly settled when the difficulties began. In very short order, it was discovered who was behind them. All of them. Karl Rothaus."

"And he is . . . ?" Art Pendragon said.

"A tyrant. A plague. An enormous man with no morals and few scruples. In the guise of 'neighbor' and 'protector' of my innocent lady, he gathered most of her cattle into his own herds. He explained that it would relieve her of the trouble of watching over them and would insure a better price for them at market."

"Sounds suspicious to me," Art said.

"He lured her best workers with promises of doubled wages. He has put a fence around one of my lady's principal water supplies and has diverted the water to his own use. Oh, the list of offenses goes on and on, I assure you. With his great size and savage brutality, he intimidates all those who come near him. Even his own employees are afraid to leave him."

"This lady," Art said. "You said her name is Lady Surrey? She hasn't been hurt, has she? Is she in danger?"

"No. However, she is a prisoner. She was taken from her own *hacienda*. I was allowed to leave—together with our trusted servant Mr. Dobé—only on the promise that I would return within the fortnight. Ostensibly, I am journeying to the city to purchase certain female necessities. Undergarments and the like. The ogre would never permit her to venture from his house, nor does he permit visitors. His hope, you see, is to gradually ingratiate himself until the day she accepts him as a suitor. He has acquired much of his own vast estates through illegal means, mostly intimidation and bribery, but he is anxious to gain title to Surrey Ranch. And gain the favors of my lady along with the land."

"So you're saying . . ." Art said.

"That he holds her prisoner and intends to marry her."

"What a horrid man," Gwen said.

"Indeed," sniffed their guest. "Horrid, indeed. As horrid as

41

he is huge."

"After supper," Art said, "I got a map in the study. You can show me where the Surrey Ranch is. Maybe we can decide what to do."

" 'Maybe'?" she said. " 'Maybe'? I was given to understand you will do whatever is necessary! I traveled a great distance, and at great discomfort, to arrive at this particular time exclusively because I have been told of your annual disposition of benevolences!"

"Sorry?" Art said. "I dispose of what?"

"Your tradition of granting assistance to those in need. At this time of year."

Gabe was all ears. He was listening so hard he nearly missed Mrs. Pendragon's signal to begin clearing away the dishes so dessert could be served. The new visitor had come to the Keystone for a boon! Just like Evan Thompson said she would!

"I see," Art said.

"I should hope so," replied the lady Townsend. "I should most certainly hope so. I wish to return without delay, accompanied by a contingent of your cattle employees sufficient to intimidate Mr. Rothaus, restore my lady's livestock to her, and secure her land against further outrages. Tell them to bring a very stout rope with which to hang him, for he is twice your size."

Gabe carried dishes to the kitchen and helped Mary carry two pies and a stack of dessert plates back to the dining room.

Art was explaining how things were.

"We're stretched awful thin," he said. "There's hundreds of men out of jobs. Some get desperate and start to throw a pretty wide loop. Then with this drought going on, we have to push the herds farther and farther out just to find enough grass, which makes them easier prey for these rustlers. If I was to send a dozen men with you—which seems like the least it would take—or even a half-dozen, why, I might as well kiss most of my cattle goodbye."

"Kissing cattle. What a repulsive image," the lady said. "I know nothing about cattle persons and 'wide loops,' but I remain adamant. My lady needs assistance and your reputation renders you honor bound to provide it. I shall not leave until I have your assurance. If there is some kind of ceremonial bowing and scraping to be performed, I trust you will explain what it is I must do. Otherwise, you know our need, and we know your reputation."

Art finished his pie before saying anything else. Chilly silence hung over the table. His mood, Gwen noticed, had quickly gone from that of cheerful host to beleaguered defendant. He reminded her of a badger trapped in his burrow by a wolf.

"Maybe you didn't understand our predicament," he said. "Right now I don't have a single man on the place that isn't essential. Without my men, I lose the cattle. And without the cattle, we lose the Keystone. Then we can't help anybody, anywhere. It's a hard, hard decision for me. It could bring down the economy of half the territory."

The lady merely sniffed and looked away.

"If I can ask," Art said, "who exactly was it told you about my solstice tradition?"

"A priest," she replied. "An itinerant priest of rather notable stature."

"Tall, was he?" Art said. Then he turned to Gwen. "Father Nicholas," he said.

"It must be." She nodded.

Must be. If it wasn't that blacksmith telling out-of-work kids to go to the Keystone, it was that darned priest sending needy widows to his doorstep. How two homeless men like Evan Thompson and Father Nicholas could cover so much territory, Pendragon had no idea.

With dessert finished, he and Lady Townsend examined the large map on the wall of Art's study. After a moment, she pointed to a certain spot.

"There," she said. "Surrey Ranch."

Later in the evening, after the lady Townsend and Dobé had gone up to their rooms, Gwen looked in on Art. He was still in his study, slouched back in his big leather chair staring at the map. As he heard the rustle of her skirts, he uttered the first words since Lady Townsend had pointed out the location of the Surrey Ranch.

"Good damn lord holy Jee . . ." he began.

"Art! Don't you *dare!*"

"Look!" he exploded. "You look where she says that place is and tell me if it don't make you want to swear! Good hell on wheels! I'm supposed to send how many men way out there?"

"Art, you settle down! Surely it's not that bad."

"Bad? I can't even figure out how in hell—'scuse me—she and that Dobé character got here! You're looking at darned near two hundred miles of lawless country! Road agents, range tramps with nothing to lose, landowners going broke and shooting at anything that moves, not to mention towns and gangs of men with guns. Anybody I'd send out there would have to fight every inch of the way. Out of a dozen, there's bound to be one or two that wouldn't come back. Keystone tradition or no Keystone tradition, this Surrey woman will just have to hold on until something better can get organized. Maybe I could get the governor to send some troops or something."

"That doesn't sound like you, my love."

Gwen reached across the desk to dim the lamp.

"Out of here," she ordered. "No more sitting in here worrying about things, not tonight. You come out to the fireplace, and I'll get Mary to fix you some warm milk or maybe some chocolate. You can take your boots off and relax awhile before bed."

He followed her, but not without turning once to look back into the gloom at the big map on the wall.

"Holy Jesus," he said under his breath.

The same scene was set the following evening. The same faces around the supper table, the same polite conversation during the meal, the same polite effort to put off talking about the troublesome topic until people were finished eating.

As Gwen and the guests moved toward the great room for their after-dinner coffee, Art took Gabe by the elbow and led him aside.

"Everything all right, Mr. Pendragon?" Gabe asked.

"That depends on your definition." Art smiled. "I just wanted to check something with you. Lou Barlow tells me you got another horse. According to him, a little dwarf kind of character brought you a pretty nice-looking mount today."

"That's right. His name's Eben. The little guy, I mean. Not the horse. Eben works for that blacksmith, Evan Thompson. He says the horse is a loan, along with saddle and bridle. And the Winchester."

"Thompson again. Thompson wanted you to have a new outfit? I sure wish people would tell me what's going on, just once in a while. Anyway, I wanted to warn you that Lou's none too happy about another horse in the home stables, eating more hay. And he's worried you'll spend more time taking care of two horses and neglect your chores."

"I'll be careful," Gabe said.

"Your year of free meals is about up," Art said.

"I know."

Back in the great room, Gabe built up the fire, then went for the coffee tray. By the time he returned, Mr. Pendragon and the lady Townsend were hot into the subject of what to do about the giant, Karl Rothaus.

"Now, Mr. Pendragon," she was saying, "how long until you can gather your forces? During my walk today, I counted eight very able-looking men. We shall need at least a dozen. It is imperative I start for the Surrey Ranch before the week is out."

Art Pendragon sighed a deep sigh and took the cup Gabe offered him.

"The plain truth of the matter is, Miss Townsend, I still can't see my way clear to send any men at all, not just now. But I'm expecting a message from one of my foremen any day now. With any luck, he's on his way back with a herd of stolen cattle. When he and his men get here, maybe we can send a half-dozen to help you. But I need at least a dozen hands just to keep the home ranch running. Now, last night Gwen and I were talking about the possibility of asking the territorial governor to send some troops—"

Lady Townsend came out of her chair as though someone had stuck a buggy spring up her backside. Her man Dobé was so taken by surprise, he nearly dropped his coffee cup.

"Mister Pendragon!" she began. "This cannot be possible! I cannot believe you are refusing your aid to a woman in distress! I will not waste another moment trying to persuade you to do your duty, and I certainly question the reputation of the Keystone enterprise. We shall pack tonight and depart at first light. It seems I shall have to depend upon hiring mercenaries to deal with Mr. Rothaus. One hears there are these 'gunfighters' to be had almost anywhere in the region."

"Don't let's be too hasty," Art said. He urged her back into her chair. "The kind of men you mean would only shoot you and take the money. Like I said, if you'll wait a few more weeks, we can possibly put together a decent posse to look into your mistress's problem. Or talk to the governor."

"Mr. Pendragon?" Gabe interrupted.

Art turned to look at Gabe as though he had forgotten he was there in the room. The lady looked surprised that Gabe could speak.

"Yes?" Art said.

"I'll go."

"You? You and who else?"

"Just me. I'll ride along back home with the lady and see what I can do. You can spare me."

"Out of the question."

Art braced himself for what he knew was coming next.

"But you owe me two more favors," Gabe said. "You said so yourself."

"Damn it. And this is one of them?"

"Yessir. I want you to give me this job of helping Lady Surrey. I'll just start getting my kit together so's I can leave. My year here is up."

"No!"

It was the lady Townsend who spoke. Her face was livid and her voice became shrill.

"No! It must be one of the Keystone riders! I want the one you call Link, not this, this . . . kitchen boy! Send Link, or I go alone!"

"You're determined to leave?" Art asked. "Not stay until I can organize some men from town, or from other ranches?"

"I cannot delay any longer," she said with a sniff. "Even if I must go alone, I must go."

"All right," Art sighed. "I don't know why you want Link in particular. But if you've got to leave, I'm sending somebody with you. That's my final decision."

Art turned to the young man.

"Gabe. Soon as you've helped Mary clear up the dishes, you start packing up. Use your old horse for a pack animal, and ride the new one the blacksmith gave you."

Gabe nodded.

"Get going, then."

From the kitchen Gabe heard the lady Townsend exploding. She could not believe what she had just heard. A kitchen servant! A mere menial, someone fit only to wash dishes and carry firewood? She asked for Keystone champions to ride to her lady's aid, and Mr. Pendragon—the famous Mr. Pendragon—would send a dishwasher? It was the final insult. It was the end of the Keystone's reputation for justice and protection of the innocent.

With tightly clamped lip, she spat out a litany of abuse. It was arrogance, dereliction, cowardice, self-interest . . . She framed each term into a sharp-edged accusation to shoot like arrows into Art Pendragon. Her thin lip trembled with frustration. She could not return to the Surrey without at least one of the Keystone riders. When she finally ran out of invectives to hurl at the master of the Keystone, her thin hands were clenched into knots until her nails threatened to draw blood from her palms.

Red-faced and trembling, she swept from the room in a flurry of petticoat and brown skirt, followed by Dobé Adams. Art stomped into his study to stand grimly staring at the map. He remained in that position, arms crossed and jaw set, until Gwen came to him with a comforting, understanding smile, and a large whiskey.

"What else could I do?" Art said.

"There's nothing else you can do, darling."

"But Gabe! He's not ready to go up against the man she describes."

"My love," Gwen said, "it's not the first time we've had these strange encounters. You know that. It's like there's a sort of fate driving our lives. Every time it happens, one of your young riders has drawn the straw. There was Link, then Will, then Pasque and Kyle. I've watched you each time you saw one of them ride out alone. Now it is Gabriel's turn. If Evan Thompson says this is to be the young man's quest, you cannot stand in the way."

Art looked into her eyes and understood.

"Another thing," she added. "She and I chatted a few times—woman to woman, you know—and something about her story doesn't quite ring true. Why would a horrible man like Rothaus allow her to go for help? Why isn't she more anxious about Lady Surrey, whoever that is? She doesn't seem like a lady's maid to me. Or any kind of servant. Who is she, really?"

"I don't know," Art said. "Maybe the blacksmith Thompson knows. All *I* know is I'm going to need another whiskey."

CHAPTER FOUR
LOU BARLOW AND LINK

During Gabe's year in the kitchens, Lou Barlow seldom missed a chance to make life hell for the boy. Gabe wanting to be a Keystone rider increased Lou's ire fourfold; Lou had himself been a rider, albeit for another ranch. Then old age and a bad accident reduced him to wrangling beans for cowpunchers.

Every day he stumped back and forth behind the long benches, reaching between men to ladle out soup or slam down another platter of bread. Hardly a meal went by when Lou did not interrupt their conversation to let them know he could still ride and shoot and fight as well as any of them. Any of them except Link. He was careful not to compare himself with Link. Then along comes this skinny kid riding the grub line. The kid not only wangled a free bed and meals, but started right in by showing up his betters. Always finding clever ways of doing things. And he wanted to be a Keystone rider.

Lou liked to send Gabe out to do some meaningless chore and then harp at him for not being where he was needed. And there was the constant teasing about Gabe "livin' with the women" up at the big house. Most of the cowhands looked the other way when Lou was abusing Gabe. Among the unwritten commandments of bunkhouse living was "Thou Shalt Not Upset the Cook." Having a cook get mad at the outfit was bad enough, but an outfit without a cook was in trouble. No man wanted to be the cause of Lou Barlow's displeasure. The kid could take it. It seemed better to ignore it than suffer through a month of salted coffee, burnt bacon, tough bread, and gristly stew.

Link Lochlin was the only man who took Barlow to task. Although he felt sympathy for the cook, he didn't much care for his high-and-mighty attitude. Link especially didn't like to hear Lou bragging about how good he had been. Even more than that, he objected to any man lording it over another man without cause.

"No matter what you say, the kid has sand," Link told Lou. "He puts up with a hell of a lot from you and never says a word. A lotta men would give up and walk out on y'. Instead of griping how much time he spends at the house doin' for Mary, why don't y' try being nice to him? Maybe he'd feel more like workin' for you if you'd treat him better."

"I got advice for you, Lochlin," Lou Barlow replied. "You oughta try keepin' your nose outa my kitchen business. Try spendin' more time in the saddle and less time lecturin' people what don't need it."

"I'm just sayin' some of the boys don't like t' see you raggin' Gabe like you do."

"Whatta ya think you'll do about it?" Barlow sneered.

The air turned cold at the question. Many a man had issued the same challenge and found himself squinting down the business end of Link's .45 Colt's revolver.

"Piece of advice for y'," Link said in a quiet voice. "Don't y' ever ask me such a thing again."

Link went outside. A couple of the boys were lounging against the sunny side of the bunkhouse. Their big dumb grins showed they'd been eavesdropping.

"When are you intending to shoot the cook?" the Pinto Kid politely inquired. "I'd like to know so I can get ahead on my eating before we bury him."

"Maybe Link could talk Mary into taking Lou's place after

he shoots him," Will Jensen suggested. "Link's a wizard when it comes to women."

"I'm afraid we're stuck with him," Link said. "But you boys know how these things go. They always have a way of workin' themselves out. The things a man does always seem t' come back on him sooner or later. Every dog has his day."

"Did Plato say that?" the Pinto Kid smiled. "About the dog, I mean?"

"Nope," Link said. "Come to think of it, I don't even know what the hell it means. I'm not a hundred percent sure who Plato was, neither."

Lou Barlow's abuse of Gabe continued. Some men noticed that he did less of it when others were around, Link in particular, but it still went on. The bunkhouse cook also picked on the newcomer, the little dwarf-like Eben. Eben responded by sitting at the far end of the long table at meals and letting the cowboys pass food down to him, then vanishing as soon as chuck was finished. He slept in one of the outlying sheds and mostly stayed out of Lou's vicinity. He consoled himself in the knowledge that his torment wouldn't last a whole year the way Gabe's had.

When Gabe hit the trail on his way to help the beleaguered lady, Eben would go with him. And he was ready to go. He kept the blacksmith's extra saddle horse in the pasture nearest the buildings. He kept the saddles and bridles at hand and conspired with Mary to be ready to fill a food pack for them at a moment's notice. Eben talked the hostler out of two panniers and a packsaddle, which he padded and adjusted to fit on Plug.

The dwarf and the grub rider were ready to go. More than ready.

Early on the morning of the lady Townsend's departure, Lou sent Gabe all the way to a far end of the main place to find out if a particular patch of wild rhubarb was ready to be cut for pie.

Lou knew it was still too early for rhubarb; he merely wanted to get Gabe tangled up in the thickets of gooseberry and bramble currant that grew around the patch. He hoped to see the kid come straggling home late in the afternoon all scratched up and dirty right before Mary wanted him to serve at the table. It made Lou chuckle to imagine the sour look on Mary's face when she saw her pet pot-walloper looking like he'd been drug through a patch of cactus.

It was a tired Gabe who came walking back to the cookhouse late that afternoon. He looked like he'd been in a fight with a wildcat and the wildcat had come out on top. Eben found him at the horse trough getting cleaned up.

"She's gone," Eben said.

"How's that?" Gabe said.

"That lady. And her man, Dobé. They pulled out at first light this morning. The noise of their buggy going past the shed woke me up."

"Then I'm leaving first thing tomorrow," Gabe said. "Can you get that horse ready? Give him a good feed, water him well, then tie him in the corral for the night."

"I'm coming, too," Eben said.

"Thought you might. We'll need to get grub together and fix up a packsaddle so old Plug can carry our bedrolls and gear."

"Already taken care of."

"Good. Then I'll find out which way that lady headed, and we'll hit the trail first thing tomorrow. In fact, now that I think of it, once we get going I'll probably ride on ahead alone. By traveling light and fast I can probably catch her up. No offense, but your little mule and that packhorse'll slow me down considerably. I'll catch her and make her stop until you get there."

"All right," Eben said. "That sounds best."

★ ★ ★ ★ ★

Early the following morning, Lou Barlow was in his room yawning and scratching himself and pulling up his suspenders when he heard the corral gate bang against the barn. Then he heard the clop-clop of hooves heading toward the road. He blew out his lantern so he could see out the window, and there was Gabe riding away on that new horse, followed by the damned midget on his midget mule, leading another horse loaded down with a pack.

"Runnin' away, eh? Probl'y stealin' food, to boot. Damn good riddance t' both of them."

As soon as Barlow had the stove fired up a night guard came into the cookshack for a cup of coffee.

"Sit," Lou commanded. "This here coffee's gonna take a minute since I had t' build up the fire m'self. That damn kid run off about a hour ago. Probably left the stove cold up to the big house, too."

"No, I saw smoke comin' out the chimney. I saw Gabe, too," the guard said. "I was on the west gate. Here he come, all slicked up an' wearin' his best shirt and pants and carryin' a Colt at his hip. Said he was on his way to help that lady that was here."

"He's *what*?"

"He's gonna go help that lady, the one with the buggy. She was mad as a hornet when she pulled out. Gabe, he said somebody has to go after her. 'Uphold the Keystone name,' he says. That new little guy, he went with him."

"Uphold the horseshit!" Lou sputtered. "He ain't supposed t' uphold nuthin' 'cept a ashcan! Kitchen help don't just up an' go ridin' off the ranch in help of nobody! I knew there'd be trouble after Pendragon let him go with that posse. It jus' put ideas in his head. Now he thinks he's some kind of gunslick hero. Dammit! We'll be the laughin'stock of the whole damn territory, once it gets out we're lettin' drifters an' grub riders do our fightin' for us! Plus that, I got me a whole load of chores waitin' for that whippersnapper, dammit. Goin' off t' 'rescue' that uppity damn woman. He ain't no rider."

Muttering and cussing, Lou lifted a stove lid and banged it down while he stoked the fire, then banged the lid back into place. He slammed the coffee pot down and stormed over to the cupboard for his sourdough crock, but before he could begin making breakfast, his anger became too much for him. Throwing his apron on the floor, he limped back to his room and dug through an old trunk to find his gun belt and sheepskin coat. Pulling on his beat-up hat, he limped off toward the corral, barking orders for the hostler to saddle him a horse.

"And be sure there's a lariat tied to the saddle," he shouted. "I'll drag that son of a bitch back here by his damn neck if I have to. Thinks he's a rider. Goddammit, I'll show him a rider."

It caused quite a stir, the ranch cook suddenly galloping off that way and leaving the boys with no breakfast. But they had their own work to do, so they pitched in and fixed themselves eggs and sourdough griddle cakes. They left the dishes in the washing-up tub as usual, although it looked pretty doubtful whether Gabe would ever come back to wash them. Then each man went to tend to his own particular chores.

All except Link.

Link stood on the cookhouse porch, leaning against one of the roof posts and looking off down the road. After a few minutes, he went around to the corral and asked the hostler to saddle one of the night horses while he went to get his coat and saddlebags. He did not hurry, for Link Lochlin was a cool and deliberate man. He was careful to tie down the saddlebags. He checked the saddle girths, flipped the reins over the horse's head, and stepped into the stirrup.

"Looks like we're in for a sunny day," he said to the hostler as he swung into the saddle.

"Yep. Probably kinda cool. Like yesterday."

"I suppose so," Link said. "See ya."

"See ya."

He set his hat the way he liked to wear it. He opened the loading gate on his Colt .45 and spun the cylinder, then holstered the gun, waved goodbye to the hostler, and rode away at a smooth trot.

About a mile ahead of Link, Lou was pushing his horse pretty hard, giving the animal an earful of what he was going to do to Gabe when he caught up to him. But he caught up with Eben first.

"You git yourself and that sawed-off mule the hell back to the ranch!" he ordered. "And you take that packsaddle back where y' found it, and put the stuff y' stole out where I can check it over. I'll make sure y' brought it all back. You're lucky I don't take the hard end of this lariat to you right here and right now! Now git!"

Eben watched Lou trot on past him. The small man smiled to see the old cook's butt bouncing up and down on the leather, taking a beating from the horse's jogging gait. Up and down, up and down, slamming into the saddle with every other step of the horse. Eben kicked his heels into the mule's flank and followed after.

It wasn't much longer until Link came up behind him. Link seemed amused by the morning's turn of events and didn't even mention the packhorse or Gabriel's sudden departure from the ranch. He rode along with Eben awhile, asking about the blacksmith and how he was doing, where he had been camped when Eben last saw him, that sort of thing. Then, real casual, as if they'd just run into each other in town and stopped to chat for a moment, Link took his leave.

"Guess I'd better catch that cook up," he said. "So I'll see ya."

"See ya," Eben said.

It was maybe an hour later when Eben saw them again.

The sun had just risen high enough to warm his back when he spotted Link sitting his horse on top of a rise just ahead of him. The cowboy motioned for him to come ahead.

"They've been like that about a quarter of an hour," Link said, pointing toward a big grassy clearing in the sagebrush. In the clearing, Lou and Gabe were sitting on their horses watching one another.

"That's sure one crafty kid," Link said.

"What are they doing?"

"Lou's tryin' to rope him. Figures to make good on that threat he made and drag Gabe back to the kitchen. Or so I'd guess. Watch how the boy moves, real slow and easy. He keeps the horse's head up and facin' Lou so the loop won't get him without getting the horse, too. Look how he moves. See that? Just moves a little at a time, always on the off side of Lou's horse. Lou can't get a good throw that way, see? Lou might be a cook, but he remembers bein' on a horse that spooks to the right. Yessir! If he flips that lariat loop wrong that cow pony's gonna spill him. I rode that one not long ago. Made the mistake of taking off my Stetson so as to wipe my brow. Pony saw that shadow out his right-hand eye and started sunfishin' something awful. Spooked the hell out of him."

Lou and Gabe circled slowly. Gabe grinned his familiar grin and moved his horse to match Lou's moves. Lou's throwing arm was getting tired and his legs were cramping up from using his knees to guide the horse. He was tired and impatient, and Gabe knew it. Gabe knew the cook's horse the same as Link: the animal was touchy on the right-hand side, likely to shy at anything sudden or strange. Gabe could see shoulder muscles twitching when Lou leaned too far to the right. Probably been whipped on that side or maybe a mountain lion jumped him once.

"Well," Gabe said, speaking softly to his own horse, "we need to be gettin' this medicine show started, I guess."

He signaled with rein and heel.

Lou Barlow responded by turning his own horse a little. Now the animal was standing right where Gabe wanted him, where sunlight made a reflection on his spooky eye and made it hard for him to see anything but movement. The horse's eye swiveled back: it didn't like the glare. When Gabe saw the flicker of white in that eye, he pretended he was making a break for the sagebrush. Lou whipped the lariat across the saddle to toss the loop.

But the loop never left his hand. His horse shied at the shadow of the rope and up went its front feet. Off into the grass went the bunkhouse cook, still clutching hard to the rope as if somehow it might save him from falling. But it didn't. He sat down on the ground with a *thumppfh!* that knocked the wind out of him.

Lou gasped and wheezed to get his breath back again. He felt the loop of Gabe's lariat settling over his shoulders. The lasso tightened. Gabe's horse backed up and braced its feet to keep the rope taut. Gabe jumped out of the saddle and ran down the rope, lifted Lou's revolver from its holster, and emptied the cylinder.

When Link and Eben rode up, they smiled to see the cook trussed up in his own rope and Gabe coiling his lariat. He hung it back on his saddle, then inspected the cook's old gun belt. He removed the cartridges.

"Six extras? That's all you got?" Gabe said. "When was the last time you fired this gun, anyway?"

"Damn grub-ridin' saddle tramp," Lou yelled. "Locklin! You get me outa this! I'm gonna kill this kid, and nobody's gonna stop me. You too," he spat at Eben. "I told you t' get on back to the ranch, and now yer gonna git the same. Now, untie this rope!"

"Maybe it'll get untied," Gabe said. "And maybe not. I'm sure not gonna trust you with a loaded gun right now. We need t' get rid of these cartridges of yours. You figure Mr. Link here is a pretty good shot, am I right?"

"Best in the territory, you bastard. Pendragon's top hand, the best. But he won't need no gun to kick your ass all the way back to the ranch for this. Lemme go!"

"Better stop struggling," Gabe suggested. "Now pick a number. One to three. If I toss these cartridges of yours out there into the grass, how many you figure Link can hit?"

"How the hell do I know? Lemme loose! Link, you kill this kid and lemme go!"

"Figure he can hit more'n me?" Gabe went on. "C'mon. How many more would you say he could hit? One, two, three? You're always sayin' how I can't do anything. Think I can shoot against Mr. Link?"

"Go to hell!"

"All right, then," Gabe said. "Let's do it this way. If Link can hit three more than me, then you get your gun, your horse, and you're free to go. If he can hit two more than me, you get your horse and you go. If he's only one better than me, you walk home."

"Go to hell."

"Feel like doing some shooting?"

Link looked down at the handful of cartridges.

"Sure."

"So things'll be fair, I'll get back up so we're both on horseback," Gabe said.

He dropped the cartridges into his pocket and mounted his horse.

"Ready?" Gabe said.

"Any time," Link smiled.

"Lemme loose!" Lou screeched.

Gabe took a handful of cartridges and hurled them away into the grass.

Gabe aimed and fired. "One!" he said as one of the brass cartridges exploded.

"And one for me," Link said, blasting a second cartridge.

"Two for me!" Gabe said, shooting again. Then, "three!"

Link's Colt barked twice more, then again, and he claimed two more hits. But Gabe's aim was truer than Link's. When Gabe's six rounds were gone, there was nothing to be seen of the targets except the holes in the grass upon which the dust was already settling. Some had exploded. Others had just caromed off into the brush.

"Three more than me," Link smiled. "Somebody taught you how to shoot. Fact is, I've only seen one other man shoot like that. The way you do it. Both eyes open, gun held low. We had a Keystone rider and he shot just like that. Called him Pasque."

"Maybe we had the same teacher," Gabe said. He was dying to tell Link the truth about the man called Pasque, but he had to hold his tongue. His mother and the blacksmith both said so.

Gabe dismounted and shoved Lou Barlow's empty gun back into its holster before untying the rope and letting him go.

"You didn't pick a number, Lou," he grinned. "Anyhow, I'm gonna do you a big favor. Eben, why don't you switch your gear from your little mule to this good Keystone horse of Lou's? We'll make better time if you got somethin' a little taller to ride on. Lou can ride the mule back to the ranch. I'm sure he'll see to it that he's well taken care of."

"I'll see to it," Link said.

Link studied Gabe's face. The kid's way of holding a Colt. That grin of his. The way he outsmarted the cook. He was beginning to get an inkling of who this "Gabe" *hombre* really was. In fact, the more Link studied on it, the more certain he was. He didn't know why Gabe had been working in the kitchen, but he knew he had the makings of a top hand, a top rider.

Link dismounted to undo one of the silver Keystone *conchos* tied to the skirt of his saddle. All Keystone riders had them, either on the saddle or on the headstall. Unlike ordinary leather medallions, these silver ones were made in the shape of a keystone. The edge was stamped with a braided rope design with the letter K carved in the middle.

Link put the *concho* in Gabe's hand.

"This just might come in handy somewhere down the road," he said. "A lot of men recognize it. Tie it to your saddle thong when you get a chance."

"I appreciate that," Gabe said. "Thanks. I'll take good care of it."

"And I'll tell Mr. Pendragon you're riding for the Keystone now, in case somebody wants to know. You figure you got enough ammunition, food?"

"I imagine so," Gabe said. "Thanks."

"Send word back, if y' can," Link said.

"If I can," Gabe said. "If that lady Townsend person doesn't kill me before the rustlers do. She's gonna be none too happy about having a grub rider escort."

There was a sound of snorting and swearing. The two riders looked back to see Lou Barlow huffing and puffing away on the small mule, bouncing with every step the mule took and cussing with every bounce.

"I'd better get after our cook," Link smiled. He put a foot in the stirrup and swung his leg over the saddle. "If I don't cool him down, there's gonna be a powerful lot of indigestion around the Keystone."

"Thanks for the shooting contest," Gabe said. "Next time we'll use bigger targets."

"Next time I won't miss." Link laughed.

"I'd better be getting after the lady and her buggy driver," Gabe said. "Eben, let's go."

Mounted on a full-sized horse, Eben looked taller and more important. And now there was a whole new aura about Gabriel Hugh Allen. He had increased in stature. He seemed enveloped in a kind of haze that was not caused by the dust or heat waves beginning to shimmer up from the sage.

Chapter Five
THE TWA TRAPPERS

Gabe had ridden less than a mile when a change in the buggy's tracks told him the team was being pushed to move faster. Their hoofprints were sharper, with more dirt thrown to the side. The buggy wheels were scattering sand and dirt on the turns. He put his horse into a fast lope until he spotted the buggy. When he caught up with it, the lady was turned on the seat to watch the trail behind. Dobé was sitting all tensed up, leaning forward with the lines between his fingers. He had the team going at a brisk pace, trying to eat up miles without exhausting the horses.

Gabe came abreast of the buggy with his big grin on his face. "Are you late for a meeting?" he smiled.

"Didn't you hear those shots?" Dobé said. "Oh, you must have. Not far behind us! Rustlers or renegades, I think. Shooting it out with some poor traveler. Did you see anything? We heard lots of shots!"

"So that's the problem!" Gabe said. "Now that you mention it, there were four rather rough-looking gentlemen back there. They were certainly on your trail. I sorted them out. They won't be bothering you at all."

"Oh, dear," said Dobé. "I still don't like the sound of it."

"It's all right. I'm here now," Gabe said. "I'll watch the back trail for you."

Gabe grinned amiably, but the lady Townsend only tightened her thin upper lip and gave a loud sniff.

"I do not know," she said, "why you persist in following us! It really is intolerable to have a . . . a common laborer behaving as if he were some sort of law officer or hired detective. If you think I will offer you food or money to accompany us—you!—then you are greatly mistaken."

"I wouldn't think of asking for a thing, ma'am," Gabe smiled. "I've got Eben and a packhorse coming along with food and gear. Won't trouble you at all. And as soon as I've settled Mr. Rothaus's hash and rescued Lady Surrey I'll be gone and you'll never see me again."

"Oh, my!" she said with a little snorting sound. "Aren't we confident, though! And yet we still carry the odor of the kitchen about us and our hands are still chafed from washing other people's dishes. Tell me, will you wear your apron when you confront Mr. Rothaus? Will you threaten him with your basting spoon?"

Gabe chuckled.

"First, I guess I'll find out what kind of *hombre malo* he is. Some men you just don't need to dress up for. Some men can be whipped with just a word or two and y' don't even need to take off your hat. For others you need to hunt up the biggest club you can find. There's a few who just need shootin'. We'll see which kind he is. Mr. Rothaus, I mean."

"I know what kind he is, and I certainly know what kind you are," the lady Townsend snapped. She looked straight ahead.

"You are a ladle washer, a potboiler, a common dishwasher. I made an exhausting journey to the Keystone for a posse of their famous riders, and not only am I dismissed, but I find myself being followed home by the kitchen help. Let me tell you one thing, mister cook's helper: should you persist in trailing after us, you will regret it. If you encounter Mr. Rothaus you will find him terrifying. You couldn't look him in the face, not for all the bacon you have ever fried."

"All this chat about kitchens and bacon makes me remember

my stomach," Gabe said. "I hope Eben and the packhorse catch up with us directly. I could do with a bit of supper."

Dobé had calmed the team into a walking pace. But suddenly he threw his arm out and pointed at a clump of cedars.

"Indians!" he shouted, reaching under the seat for the shotgun with one hand while flapping the lines with the other. Gabe spurred his horse forward to the edge of the trees, drawing and cocking his Colt.

"Outa there!" he commanded.

The creature that emerged from the covert did have the appearance of a savage tribesman. Question was, what tribe? For that matter, what century? The hat seemed to be the carcass of a dead skunk hollowed out and jammed down over his skull, caveman fashion. His face was all hair, curling and twisted and the color of an unusually robust carrot. His trousers could have been made of leather, originally, possibly mastodon hide, but now looked like two tubes of grime held up with a belt made of twisted intestines. Beneath the leather coat, which he probably wore open for ventilation rather than appearance, Gabe could see the remains of a gingham shirt laid over a pinkish garment that might once have been part of a long red union suit.

Gabe was primarily interested in the fine Sharps repeater the man carried, as well as the long knife hanging in a deep sheath from his belt.

"Better throw that down," Gabe said, gesturing his Colt toward the rifle.

"Nae," spoke the leathern image. "Gi'en what's just happened, I'd sooner die w' m' gun in m' hand."

Gabe relaxed. "And what would that be?" he asked. "What's just happened, I mean."

" 'plain ye're nae one of them," the man said. "Not w' sich a lady and buggy and all. Besides, Willis and me saw this same lady and buggy pass by here a week or more back. In a rush, they were."

"Who's this 'them' you're hunting?" Gabe asked.

"They're a different ilk altogether. Renegades, half-breeds, I'd say. Crawlin' vermin, the lot o' em."

"Care to talk about it?" Gabe said, lowering the hammer on his Colt.

"Nae much ta tell," he said. "Me an' m' partner have a wee bit o' house yonder, off nigh the rye there. If y' squint, y'll jist make out the chimney smoke. Trappin's our game, but we've got a wee herd of fine horses t' boot. Breedin' 'em for sale. And didn't we think t' move them t' better grass this very mornin' when out pops this band o' heathen highwaymen and takes them all?"

There was a sound of gunfire among the willows a half-mile away, down along the twisting course of the "rye" the trapper had mentioned.

"Och, he's kilted!" the trapper moaned. "Oh, m' poor faithful partner. They've done for him now. I told him not t' go after them, but would he listen? Now he's kilt."

"Stay here with this lady," Gabe ordered. "Dobé, you and this . . . gentleman . . . see about doing whatever you can to fort up somehow, in case they come back this way. And don't waste any time."

Gabe galloped along the faint track, not really a road so much as two wheel ruts, until he discovered an open trail leading down through the willows to the riverbank. A gunshot directed him to where he found another leather-clad trapper. This one was hunched down behind a fallen cottonwood reloading his single-shot rifle.

"Where are they?" Gabe asked.

The trapper looked up, astonished at the rider's sudden appearance. Then he gestured downriver. Gabe swerved around the log and forced the horse through the brush, absorbing the punishment of the willows whipping at him.

Two men of unrivaled ugliness suddenly jumped from their hiding place and presented guns.

"Throw down!" Gabe shouted. "Both of you!"

But both men cocked the hammers instead. For Gabe, it was enough of an answer. He said nothing more but let his Colt take up the conversation, at the conclusion of which one of the gargoyles lay on the ground with his eyes turned up as if they were trying to look at the .44 caliber hole in his forehead. The other brute was dragging himself into hiding, his shoulder shattered.

A movement caught Gabe's eye. He rode toward it to discover two more ragged individuals attempting to force a small band of fine-looking horses into the river.

"Hold up, there!" Gabe called. "There's a man back there who wants to see your bill of sale!"

The first horse thief was near the edge of the water. He spun around, obviously intending to leap for cover over the riverbank. Gabe's shot caught the fellow square in the left buttock, and the thief's revolver went flying into the river. Off balance from trying to grab his wound with both hands, the man followed his gun over the edge. There was a resounding splash. At this point, his partner came to the conclusion that flight would be better than fight, but failed to remember that a bullet can outdistance a running man.

Gabe did not try to gather the stolen horses, but rather reloaded his Colt and made a few wide sweeps through the willows in case there were more renegades in hiding. He rode back toward the trapper, who was sitting on the log with the muzzleloader cradled in his arms. Gabe looked down into the face of the first dead man. It was dark and twisted with evil.

"Skinner Cole," the trapper explained. "A bad one, he was.

Been known to flay the men he's killed. Ye're better off not knowin' what they say he's done to some lassies, now."

"A face only a mother could love," Gabe said. "Particularly if she was blind in both eyes."

"Grit McByre," the trapper said, standing up and proffering his hand.

"Pardon?" Gabe said, reaching down to shake hands.

"M' name, mon. Grit McByre. I take it ye've met m' partner yonder."

"We were just getting around to names when the trouble began," Gabe said. "I'm Gabriel Hugh Allen, generally known as Gabe."

"A good Scots name, is Allen. That human specimen ye met yonder, thae one wi' a dead skunk on his head is Mr. Willis. William Willis."

Grit McByre drew an antique percussion pocket revolver from his belt and checked the caps. He thumbed back the hammer of his rifle and checked that cap as well.

"I've a bit o' tidying up tae do," he said. "Your help's welcome, should ye care t' jine me."

They first went in search of William Willis, who took the news of his partner's survival with typical Scots emotional enthusiasm.

"Jus' as well ye're still alive," he said. " 'Tis your turn at fixin' the supper tonight."

Willis announced he would lead the lady and buggy to the "wee bit o' house," while Grit and Gabe set out into the brush along the river to take care of the "tidying up." Grit prowled the undergrowth afoot while Gabe rode in zigzags, looking for any lurking horse thieves. Finding none, Gabe dropped a loop on the corpse with the hideously ugly face and dragged it to a washout some considerable distance from the river, where he shoved it up under a cut bank and then caved the bank in on it.

Instant burial. Back at the river, he found Grit tying another corpse to a driftwood log, using the thief's own belt and pants for the lashing.

"In case there's others o' them downstream," he explained. "It'll be just a wee hint tae them t' take a care who they rob."

The one whom Gabe had shot in the hindquarters was nowhere to be seen, but signs indicated he had already drifted downriver. Grit set off downstream, just in case, and after a quarter of an hour Gabe heard the distant "boom!" of a large caliber rifle. In another quarter hour Grit returned.

"Find him?" Gabe inquired.

"Aye, facedown and caught up on a snag. Next bit o' high water should float him."

"Shoot him?"

"Nay. He's done for. Nay, the shot y' heard was the last one o' the gang. Came for me while I was studyin' on the floater. So, there's that bunch all shined up and sent home to their Maker. Now . . . if ye were tae gie me a hand in collectin' yon horses, there might just be a wee nip o' whiskey in it for you back at the house."

In calling their bachelor dwelling "a wee bit o' house," the trapper had been exercising the Scots talent for modest understatement mentioned earlier. The "hoose," as the two highlanders pronounced it, was in actuality both large and elaborate. Each man had his own sleeping and reading room, while they shared a commodious living and cooking area complete with pantry. Large river rocks had been used for the lower part of the walls, the upper half being made of carefully fitted logs. High shelves of halved logs protected their dozens of books from hungry vermin.

While Gabe, Eben, and Dobé saw to the feeding and comfort of the horses and the unpacking of necessities, the "twa" bachelor Scots tended to the lady Townsend. She was supplied with a room of her own—Grit would share with his brother for the night—together with clean blankets, towels, and a ewer of hot water with which to remove the road dust. Grit waxed rather eloquent concerning the "battle" in the willows as he brought the blankets, water, and towels to the lady's room. He described the fate of each of the evildoers, and he did not spare to ascribe much of the credit to the tall Keystone boy and his deadly Colt's revolver.

"Yon Hawken o'mine shoots square, y' ken. But 'tis a rare talent for a man tae hit a runnin' target wi' a handgun. From off a horse. Aye, your lanky friend is a man tae be reckoned wi', for fair."

"He is not my friend," the lady corrected him. "And as for his personal qualities, I believe your people might employ the term 'lusk' in describing him."

McByre laughed heartily at that, partly because he thought the lady was joking with him. She was not.

"Aye?" he said. "Lusk? I've nae heerd that word since takin' my leave o' me mother's knee. Bein' of a poetic nature, her phrase for me was 'lazy layabout lusker.' "

The trappers Willis and Grit repaired to the washstand behind the cabin where they cleaned and combed themselves into a semblance of presentability before setting about cooking supper for their guests. They laid the table with such dinnerware as they possessed, and Grit knocked on the bedroom door to announce that all was ready. He went outside and repeated the summons to Eben and Gabe. The lady Townsend gracefully accepted the chair at the head of the table. But when Gabe started to occupy the bench immediately to the lady's left, she objected in the strongest terms.

"Mr. Willis!" she said to her host, who had put himself in

charge of serving supper. "Mr. Willis! Surely you do not intend for me to sit next to kitchen help?"

William Willis looked about in a bit of confusion, for of all the people in the room, he was most likely to be called kitchen help.

"I'm nae wi' ye, I'm afraid," he said.

"This spit-turner here," she said. "This man, whom your partner esteems so highly, is no more than a kitchen servant from the Keystone Ranch. He is not even a member of my party. Mr. Dobé here is my assistant and good right hand; this one they call Gabriel has merely tagged along after us, for some reason, dragging that unfortunate small person with him. Please be so good as to set that man's plate at the far end of the table. He carries a strong smell of the kitchen about him, and it puts me off my appetite."

Gabe smiled and took up his plate and hardware and moved down to the farthest corner.

"It seems a poor way to treat a man who has protected you from a bunch of outlaws," he said, but not in an angry way.

"Oh?" the lady said. "Oh? As it happens, Mr. Keystone cook's helper, one of our hosts was good enough to give me a rather full account of how you went about your 'protection' business. Am I correct—is Mr. McByre correct—in saying you actually shot two men in the back?"

Gabe winked at McByre. "The one was running into the brush," Gabe said. "If he'd gotten to cover and turned with his gun, I'd have been a clear target for him. Being on my horse and all, you know. As for that other spoiler . . ." he looked at McByre again. ". . . I didn't exactly shoot him in the *back*. Lower down, if anything."

"And this is considered fair play among the Keystone men? What about shooting a man between the eyes when you could have just as easily wounded him and let him live?"

"Ma'am, had you seen that face of his, you would understand. I did start to aim for his gun arm, I really did. But looking into that face, the thought flashed across that a broken arm would hardly stop him. It was like facing Satan himself. What was needed was a quick, clean dead shot. So he wouldn't get up again, you see."

William Willis served the soup and passed the bread, and conversation about killing ended right there. Until supper was over and the dishes cleared, the lady Townsend contented herself with talking to Willis and to Dobé, seated on her left hand, while Gabe, Eben, and McByre chatted quietly at the other end of the board.

" 'Tis a fair ripper ye've got there," McByre whispered to Gabe.

"Let's say she's been disappointed lately," Gabe said. "She faces a big responsibility. I can't say I blame her, getting me instead of the dozen Keystone riders she asked for. Or Link, the man she really wanted."

"Aye," McByre said. "Still, she needn't act like the great laird's lady around here. She's the sort o' gentry we thought tae leave behind us in auld Caledonia."

"You're fortunate," Gabe said, smiling his familiar smile. "Tomorrow you two will be quit of her, but Eben and I will have to go on quite a ways more. With her as company. Think on that."

"Speaking of which," McByre said, "I'd better put ye on guard. From here, ye ken, the road takes 'ee over a hard, high pass yonder or else down along the wee rye till 'ee come tae a broad river."

"With the buggy," Eben asked, "which way's best?"

"Oh, the river way, lad. 'Tis the only way, with a buggy. There's a good crossing of it, just upstream from where the rye joins. The only crossing for miles. Trouble is, there's been word come up tae us that it's bein' held against travelers."

"Held?" Gabe said. "You mean someone will keep us from crossing?"

"Aye. Three men an' huge, so 'tis said. Brothers, 'tis said. They've thrown up a shanty and fenced the crossing. They call it a 'tariff' on it, but it's nae mair than highway robbery. *And* it seems they take cattle from those as don't have coin. They've a goodly bunch of cows, and them not cowboys."

"What are they, then?" Eben asked.

"Robbers. Huge and towsy, as I said. Ye'll be well advised tae find how tae hide any o' your valuables from them."

"Is there any way to go around them?" Gabe asked.

"Provided the river's not up, as is generally the case of it, ye'll be able tae swim the horses and float the buggy. It's nae deep there, and the bottom's of rock. 'Twas me, I might spy them out and find a time when they'd be asleep or lookin' after their cattle and kine. Sneak over without they're knowin', 'tis what I'd try."

"Maybe stampede their livestock," Eben suggested. "We might cross the river while they're busy rounding them up again."

"That could be a plan," Gabe agreed. He looked down the table to where the lady Townsend was chatting with Mr. Willis. "Then again, since I'm such a murderous back-shooter, I might just assassinate all three of them in their sleep, burn down the shanty, and steal all their goods."

Eben laughed, and so did McByre.

"Nae, 'tis a daft way t' think, laddie!" McByre said. "Ye'd first want tae steal the goods before firin' the shanty! Otherwise ye'd be grandly disappointed in your loot, it bein' all burned tae hell."

Up at the far end of the table the lady and bachelor trapper paused in their conversation. She glared at them suspiciously, wondering what the three were laughing about.

Chapter Six
THE SWITZERS THREE

Gabe needed a map.

William Willis was eager to provide verbal directions for the next leg of the lady's journey; the problem lay in the fact that he gave these directions with more enthusiasm than clarity. The Scot's peculiar Highland vocabulary left Gabe in some considerable uncertainty as to what lay ahead, so he asked Willis to sketch it on paper instead. Gabe hoped the map picture would be worth at least a hundred Scots words, if not a full thousand.

Willis turned out to be a good cartographer when it came to indicating hills, rivers, and buildings. His terminology still required extensive translation.

"Hoose," as Gabe already realized, meant the house. The "rye" was the small stream running past the trapper's place and down the narrow valley. The "wee mow" referred to a line of small trees along the rye, mostly cottonwood. Following the wee mow they would eventually come "up ahint" a good-sized "brae" the shape of a "bicker" turned upside down. Upon reaching this bowl-shaped hill, he said, they should stop and send someone to scout ahead, for "nae mair" than twa miles distant was the river where the three cattle thieves extorted payment from anyone who wanted to cross over.

"A sma' word more," Willis said as Gabe folded the map and put it in his chaps pocket. "Watch y'rsel' should 'ee come on one o' them alone, for ye maunna think he'll ken what ye say tae him in English. There's ain th' one who speaks ooor tongue, and he's nae sae glib wi' it. 'Tother two don't speak English atall. They've got a gab that's fu' fremit."

" 'Fremit'?"

"Aye! Foreign! Difficult tae understan', y' ken."

"Aha," Gabe said. "So I'd be better off to pull my Colt and throw down on any one of them I come across. I shouldn't depend on being able to talk to him."

"Aye. So I just said."

"So you did." Gabe laughed. "So you did."

The lady Townsend was impatient. They thanked the trappers for their hospitality and set off. The lady still was not pleased to have Gabe along. However, Dobé was pleased enough for both of them. Gabe decided he and Eben should ride a half-mile ahead of the buggy and keep an eye out for trouble. He told Dobé they would make a stop at the round "brae" so he could scout ahead and figure out what to do about crossing the river.

"I almost wish we had taken the northern way, the way we came to the Keystone in the first place. We skirted the pass that man was talking about. It was long and tiring, but it seemed safe," Dobé said.

"You never know," Gabe said. "Might run into almost anything anywhere. Don't worry: we'll get past these three thieving brothers."

It was a cold camp they made in the north shade of the lumpish hill, but there was a seeping spring for water and plenty of fallen cottonwoods, which could be dragged together to make an enclosure. Gabe saw to the comfort and safety of his charges, even though it meant more jibes and remarks from the lady about being a mediocre camp servant. Then, with more than an hour of light left, he rode out to do his scouting. But he did not follow the stream; he thought he might learn more about the robbers and their river crossing if he went around the hill the other way. Enter through the back door, so to speak.

Before he had seen any sign of the bandits who held the river crossing, he encountered their herd of pilfered livestock. It consisted of nearly four dozen cattle of various breeds and various brands. They were browsing in an open meadow as large as the Keystone's outer horse pasture. Gabe concealed himself in the trees and watched them, taking note of the different brands. At least a dozen were Keystone cattle. It seemed unlikely that the three thieves had ridden all the way from here to Keystone territory; they probably "liberated" the steers from other rustlers attempting to cross the river. Grazing alongside the Keystones was a number of pale-colored cattle ranging from blond to almost silver, all bearing a brand like an inverted T with a gate next to it, inside a box.

T-Gate Box brand? He had never heard of it.

A sound caught his attention. He peered out through the branches at an unusual spectacle. Not unheard of, but unusual. He had only witnessed it once or twice in his entire life. A man milking a range cow.

The tall blond man rode out of the trees on the other side of the meadow. He rode in among the cattle and singled one out. He dismounted before tossing his rope on the beast, something else Gabe had seldom seen anyone do, and led it to a small tree. He snubbed the rope around the tree and pulled the cow tight to it. Then the blond man went back to his horse, lifted a bucket from the saddle horn, and proceeded to do his milking.

Cowboys drank milk, of course, mostly the condensed variety that came in little cans. Once in a while, a householder might offer a passing cowpuncher a glass of buttermilk. Sometimes a ranch cook would keep a "milch cow" around. Otherwise, fresh milk was as rare as cheese and creamery butter, both of which commanded premium prices in town.

Even stranger than seeing a man milk a wild range cow was

how he was doing it. Most men would stay as far away as the length of their arms would allow, reaching in to do the squeezing from a half-crouch so they could jump away from slashing hooves. But the blond gent hunkered with his head against the cow's flank and seemed to be petting it with one hand as he milked with the other. When he had finished, he actually stroked and caressed the cow's neck while removing the lasso. Gabe had seen small girls do this with the family milch cow, many times, just as he had seen housewives pat their favorite cows and talk to them like members of the family, but those were tame brutes with big gentle brown eyes. Not range cows.

The blond man remounted his horse and rode away with his bucket on the saddle before him. Gabe followed at a careful distance, and before long the river and a shanty came into view. It wasn't much of a shanty. In fact, it looked like something that might have come drifting down the river until somebody dragged it out and decided to live in it. Behind it was a corral of sorts, scarcely large enough for the three miserable-looking horses it contained. When the blond man unsaddled his mount and opened the corral gate, the three scabs looked up with their sad horse faces as if to ask why they had to share their already crowded area. Gabe could not see the front of the shack, but he could see a pair of boots sticking out over the edge of what he assumed was a small porch facing the river. Probably somebody relaxing after a hard day's robbery.

So, there were four horses and three men, one of whom milked range cows. It didn't look much like a prosperous outfit, no matter what the Scot had said about their great success as brigands and highwaymen. If anything, it looked as though the herd of stolen cattle was their only tangible asset.

Gabe retreated quietly.

Sticking to the cover of trees, he made a thorough survey of the cattle and the terrain before trotting back to the camp among the cottonwoods. When he had seen to his horse, Eben brought him bread and cold meat. Dobé joined them, the lady preferring to stay by herself, seated on her bedroll and scribbling in her journal.

"I think there's three of them, like the Scotchmen said," Gabe reported. "And there's close to fifty cows grazing just past the shoulder of the hill. There's a shack down on the river, and a small corral where four horses are busy holding each other up."

Gabe picked up a stick and cleared a little patch of dirt.

"I'll show you the brands on the cattle," he said.

Dobé pointed to the inverted T Gate.

"That's Lady Surrey's brand," he said. "But these three outlaws. Can you handle them by yourself?"

Gabe grinned. "I have a few ideas about that," he said. "I believe I know a way for you and Eben to sneak the buggy and your lady across the river. I might stay a bit and join up with you later, farther along the trail."

"What're you goin' to do?" Eben asked.

"Well, that lady of yours, she doesn't approve of back-shooting and murder. She seems to take exception to 'malice and envy, contending against men,' as Plato put it. But what if you got yourselves ready to cross that river—staying out of sight, naturally—and then what if I was to stampede their herd of cattle off in the opposite direction? I'm betting all three of those gents would go after their cows and leave the river unguarded."

"A diversion," Eben said. "Might work! Especially since they don't know there's anybody around to worry about. Meaning us. But then what? You chase the cattle and we get across the river, then you circle around somehow and get back with us?"

"That's the plan," Gabe said. "In a general sort of way. Once I see what kind of gents they are, I might stay and have a chat with them. All about cattle brands and such like. A Keystone rider doesn't let rustlers get off scot-free, you know."

"When do you want to do it?" asked Dobé.

"Fairly early in the morning. I'm thinking of starting the stampede just about milking time."

The next morning dawned fair and clear of clouds. The air was cold enough that a fire would have been welcome, along with a cup of hot coffee. It was the kind of cool, dry morning when a man liked to walk away from camp with a tin cup of steaming coffee held between his gloves and watch the eastern horizon become lighter and lighter until the rim of the sun popped up. Here, however, they didn't want to risk a fire. And they needed to put their plan into operation.

"Go on down the track a ways," Gabe said while they were packing up to leave. "Find a good place to cache yourselves as soon as you figure you're near enough to the river. When you hear gunshots, make your run for the river crossing. Move quick, and don't look back."

Gabe rode off around the other side of the hill to where the cattle were grazing. The morning was so new that the sun had not yet appeared in the tops of the cottonwoods, and a chilly darkness lurked back in the groves. While some of the cattle were on their feet cropping grass, the majority were content to go on lying on the warm spots where they had slept. They looked at Gabe and his horse with indifference.

Getting a stampede started is going to pose a challenge, Gabe thought. *They've got good grass, plenty of water, no dust storms or lightning to make them edgy, no reason at all to start running.*

He studied the situation. If he rode down there shooting his gun, he'd probably get only a few of the brutes to move. And if he did that, Dobé and Eben might take it as a signal and start for the crossing before the three rustlers were gone from the shack. He could set fire to the grass, except it was green and damp. Maybe he could use his rope end to whip some of the cows into a run. But it didn't seem likely. And then he spotted his solution: it was standing right there at the high end of the pasture not more than fifty yards from him. It was a bull calf, still clean and slick, staring at its new world with wide eyes. It was no more than a day or two old.

Gabe figured its mother to be the cow grazing a few yards away.

Worth a try, Gabe thought.

He spurred up his horse and rode into bunches of cattle, whipping them with his lasso end and stirring them up, getting their attention and getting the lazy ones to their feet. He charged into the mother cow and bumped her to one side, then swerved toward her bull calf. Leaning out of the saddle, he scooped him up and tossed him across the saddle like a bag of grain. Gabe circled back through the herd as fast as he could go, still lashing out with his lasso end. Cattle began to bellow and complain, running from him with clumsy steps.

When Gabe finally took off for the ridgeline, things went as he had hoped they would. The calf resented the bouncing and jolts and began to put up such a bawling and bleating that all the cows looked to see whose baby had been carried off. True to the code of the bovine sisterhood, a half-dozen mothers began bawling as they started after the horse, running in that rolling, awkward way of heifers.

Gabe had seen this trick many times. It was a standard way trail drivers had of forcing cattle across a makeshift bridge or into a brush pen. Take a calf or two, and the mothers follow the bawling. Most mother cows would swim a flooding river if their calf was on the other side.

He made sure to bounce the calf enough to keep it calling to its dame, who in turn bellowed to the other females for help until the entire collection, steers, cows, calves, and all, were trailing up the hill after Gabe's horse. In another minute, he'd have them going over the ridgeline and out of sight of the river altogether.

Suddenly over the bawling of the cattle and the pounding of hoofs he heard a voice yelling.

"Halt! Halt! He! Sie! Haltstop!"

The milker was trotting toward them with his bucket banging from the saddle horn, following the wake of the cattle and calling to them. Gabe dropped the calf to the ground and rode back to confront the bareheaded blond man, who managed to yell, *"Hal—"* at the cattle once more, then, *"vas ischt . . ."* before he saw the muzzle of Gabe's Colt .44 pointed between his eyes. The blond man saw that the cowboy holding the revolver was also holding a finger to his lips in a universal gesture that may be translated—in any language—as "shut up if you don't want your head ventilated."

The milker shut his mouth and raised his hands. He was unarmed.

Gabe didn't have much time before the other two would come along to investigate the racket. He hurried his captive's horse under the nearest cottonwood, where he used his pigging string to tie the man's hands. He next tossed the end of his lasso over a branch and settled the loop around the man's neck. Gabe tied the end off to a branch. All that remained was to hold the fellow's horse from bolting while firing two shots into the air.

Blam! Blam!

On the far side of the hill, Eben heard the signal. He started his horse and the packhorse out of the thicket in which they had hidden, while Dobé slapped the lines and put the buggy team into a trot.

Still in nightshirts, the other two rustlers rushed from their shack, pulling on their pants and clutching their gun belts. One of them threw down the rails of the horse pen and tried to get himself aboard one of the horses while the other ran toward the cattle herd on foot. Both arrived at the pasture to find their brother trussed up with a noose around his neck, sitting on his horse under the tree. A tall, grinning cowboy was pointing a carbine in their direction. He signaled that they should drop their gun belts and come forward.

"Keystone Ranch," he said, speaking in a loud voice, in case they didn't understand English. "Some of these beeves belong to the Keystone Ranch. You savvy?"

The one on foot seemed to be the oldest. He held up both hands, palms outward to show he was unarmed, and came forward.

"I am understanding your English," he said. "Our brother *Jakob* you have already to hang, he only the Schweizerdeutsch speaks."

"*Grüezi,*" croaked Jakob to his brother, meaning something akin to "nice morning, how is your day going so far?"

"*Grüezi, Jäkli,*" his brother replied. Then, to Gabe, "how many of you are there here?"

"Altogether, I'd say seven or eight," Gabe replied, not bothering to mention he was counting the horse he was sitting on, a midget and his horse, a surly woman, a buggy team, and a pack animal. But he wouldn't need any extra help. These three looked like they belonged on a farm somewhere, not here in outlaw territory. The Scotchmen had exaggerated their ferocity. Hard to believe that a Scotchman would exaggerate, but there it was.

"You gentlemen don't look much like desperados," he said.

"*Nein,* we are Swiss," the man replied.

"Thieves. Outlaws, is what I meant," Gabe said.

"*Ach.* We only take some cows is all. We do not kill anyone. Some men, they give for crossing over here. Others we find and bring here."

"It's still called stealing," Gabe said. "Men hang for it."

"And if we do not keep these cows we find, if we do not ask to be paid for to let people make the river crossing, where should we get our living?"

"You speak fairly good English," Gabe said. "Can't you get a job somewhere?"

"Ach. I the *Schulbub,* not my brothers. Our mother and father send me to *Schüle* for English to learn, then come the hard times. My brothers do not learn. Then we are married and go away from home, and now we are the ones on hard times. Our wives we leave in Minnesota to be looking for gold and land in the west, *ja.* Hard it is, we tell them, but after a while it will be better and we send for them to come. But *ach!* God so cursed this land!"

"Times are certainly tough," Gabe agreed. He kept the Winchester pointed at the Switzer. "But rustling cattle is a sure way to make it worse for yourselves."

"What are we to do? Between us we have nothing. Even brother Peter there," he said, indicating the man in the nightshirt who still sat on his horse bareback, "he has no bullets for his gun. Nothing can we grow here to eat, only beef, beef, beef. All winter we freeze here. It is the cursed land. How can we live in such a place? You let the brother go and your cows, you take them. What brand is yours?"

Gabe touched the muzzle of the carbine to the *concho* on his saddle. The Swiss peered at it closely.

"Was sagt es?" said the one he called Peter. "What does it say?"

"Das 'K' im en Schlussstein." A letter K in a keystone.

"I'm afraid it's not so simple as just taking Keystone stock and leaving," Gabe explained. "For one thing, I'm pointed in the other direction. And for another thing, I need to figure out what to do with you three desperados."

"We are not bad men," the Swiss said. "If we could, we would work. Work hard. Our women wait for us to send for them too long, to come to this promised land. We thought to have jobs, at least. Or bags of gold from a mine claim. Something. My fault it is, this *Dummheit.*"

Gabe recognized that word. Foolishness. Stupid thing to do. *Dummheit.* One of the men he worked for during his long journey north had used it pretty often. The memory of that man now caused the germ of an idea to begin fermenting. Seeing that the three "outlaws" were in reality nothing more than three immigrants down on their luck in a very big and very foreign land, he relaxed his guard. He slipped the Winchester back into the saddle scabbard, being sure the men noticed that he was also packing a Colt at his hip. He untied the lasso to free the brother called Jakob. Or Jack. Or whatever. Jakob and the other one dismounted to stand next to their brother, the "scholar" who spoke English. All three looked solemn and discouraged.

"Is it our blame that we starve here?" the older brother repeated. He looked up at the Keystone rider with frustration. A look of strong-willed determination also showed in his pale blue eyes.

"A man of the old country, *ein Schweizer* like us, he wrote he would meet us in the place called Dakota and show us to find a gold mine. But all we find, he is also gone to California. You should know we ask everywhere for jobs. We try to fish this river and come here where the crossing is good. We look, we find cows to bring here. Men with many cows to cross the river make us a trade, two of theirs made too tired from long walk for one fresh one. It is not good. Too long we have been, too long."

"So your plan," Gabe said, "is to keep on stealing cows until you can sell them and send for your wives?"

"*Ach, nein!* We will not do that. Too long it takes. Others have come, bad men, they take everything too. One day in the small river Jakob finds one. Dead. This is not for us, this business. You will give us to the law now. There is nothing else to happen. If you let us go, we could not even go home on those horses. Without money."

"I got an idea you might like," Gabe said. "Let's go in the cabin and talk."

The man said something to his brothers. One nodded; the other seemed to ask a question.

"He wants to know about the cows gone over the hill."

"They'll come back," Gabe said. "Too much grass and water for them not to."

"Got something I can draw on?" Gabe asked, looking around the shack for a bit of paper. Rudolf, the one who spoke English, groped around under his bunk and brought forth a square of thick, coarse paper on which someone had attempted a sketch. Gabe turned it over. It would do.

"I need one more thing," he said, going out to where his horse was tied.

Gabe returned with the map he had made during his long ride toward the Keystone. After studying it a minute, he took the pencil stub from his chaps pocket and began to make a copy.

"Now this is the Keystone Ranch here," he said, drawing the brand to show where the ranch was. "Over here, this is your place. That line is the river. Here's the mountain range farther west. See?"

The brothers talked among themselves and nodded. Gabe next drew a line from the Keystone Ranch south and east, putting in the rivers he had crossed and the towns he had seen.

Finally, toward the bottom of the paper, he made a big circle and drew a picture of a cow's head in it. It looked more like something a little kid would draw, but you could tell it was supposed to be a cow.

"Now," he said, "here's my offer. You boys are rustlers. I could shoot you and take back the Keystone livestock. Or I could turn you over to those Scotch trappers and let them deal with you. Or I could take you to the nearest lawman, or bring a marshal here to see all these cattle you've 'collected.' "

"*Ja,*" Rudolf said. Sadly, with resignation, he translated for his brothers.

"Or," Gabe said, "together we could put things to rights. My boss, Mr. Pendragon, he always likes to put things to rights. Two of you could take all those Surrey brand cattle, the pale ones with the upside-down T and gate on them, and herd them over the mountain ridge and down the other slope until they're back on the Surrey range again. Take about a week. From what the lady tells me."

"Lady?" Rudolf looked puzzled. He hadn't seen any lady with the cowboy.

"Let's say she's the owner. Anyways, you get those T-Gate cattle back to their home range."

"*Ja,*" Rudolf said. "This we could do."

"Next. The three of you gather the Keystone steers and drive them back where they belong, like you can see on the map there. You'll need to take provisions. Jerk some meat, things like that. I'll give you a note and you give it to the first Keystone riders you run into, men with that silver *concho* on the saddle. They'll take you to Mr. Pendragon. He'll see you get some food and rest."

"*Ja,*" Rudolf said, brightening up. "Is good. *Gut.*"

He translated. Jakob was the next one to smile. "*Ja, da bin ich auch mit dabei!*"

"What?"

"Jakob says he agrees. We then work for this Mr. Pendragon of yours, *ja.*"

"No," Gabe said. "*Nein.* There's no jobs at the Keystone. Hard times. But look here at the map. You next head south. You come to more towns. The country's more settled. Railroads, folks moving in. After y' find this town, Waynesburg, you come to a dairy farm. That man there, he's a Swiss."

"*Ja?* Yes? A Schweizer? With dairy?"

"I worked for him a while back," Gabe said. "He's got nobody who wants to spend their life milking cows and shoveling manure. But he does a pretty good business in cheese and milk. He's lonely to talk to somebody who speaks his language. The way I see it, he needs you boys, and you boys need a place like his. You could settle in down there. Maybe start your own place, eventually."

"Tell about the cows," Rudolf said. "What kind?"

"Kind?" Gabe said. "Hell, I don't know. He's got a lot of them, though. They're not Guernseys. I know Guernseys. No, these are kind of pale-colored. Color of cream maybe. Big eyes, long eyelashes. Real big eyes."

Rudolf translated and the brothers began to jabber in high excitement, slapping each other on the shoulder. Jakob tipped his head back and laughed with delight.

"What's going on?" Gabe asked.

"Oh, they are happy!"

"I got that part," Gabe said.

"These cows. For sure they are Swiss cows! Tell me, the bells? What sort?"

"Bells. Oh, you mean on their neck. Bells as big as your hat. They make a big 'dong dong dong' sound."

"Dong dong dong dong" went Peter, laughing and slapping Jakob's shoulder. "Dong dong!"

"These are Swiss bells!" Rudolf said. "Swiss cows, Swiss bells! We go! We now do as you say, we take cows over mountain, to your place we take cows, your Keystone place, then we make journey to this man, this *Schweizer*! Is wonderful!"

Gabe had seen women cry over the loss of a pet, and once he saw a tough *vaquero* weeping over the charred corpse of a *compañero* who died in a grassland fire. But he'd never witnessed anything like these big strong blond men letting their eyes get all moisty at the mention of some milk cows.

Gabe got his little pocket ledger from his saddlebag and wrote the brothers a note to give to Art Pendragon. Then he was back in the saddle and back on the trail, splashing across the river to catch up with the buggy.

The light mist of morning had evaporated under the warmth of the April sun. The air was so clear that the hills and valleys seemed to go on forever.

Chapter Seven
JOSHUA GRUMM

One sure sign of spring in the Wyoming Territory is the way the late afternoon daylight begins to hang on. The light stays in the western skies after the supper hour, as if the sun is in no hurry to plunge down behind the mountains. No longer did the Keystone riders hurry from the warmth of the cookshack to the warmth of the bunkhouse to beguile the long darkening hours with busy work and games of cards by lamplight; now they gathered near the corrals, built a campfire, sat gazing into the flames, and told stories.

If Charlie Russell had been there, he could not have resisted opening his sketch book. A dozen men in well-worn boots and battered hats. Some had their pocket knives open and were whittling at chunks of wood. Others were smoking cigarettes or pipes. All of them were lounging in that picturesque manner unique to the lean western cattleman. The fire crackled and popped in the center of the conversation circle. White woodsmoke rose into the sky, a sky the color of April forget-me-nots.

Two strangers sharing the evening with the Keystone riders were surprised when the men ceased talking and rose respectfully to their feet.

"Sit down, boys."

It was Art Pendragon paying a visit to the fire circle to hear the strangers recount the story of their run-in with Gabriel Hugh Allen. Art had summoned one of his foremen shortly before supper.

"Build a campfire tonight, Bob," he said. "We'll gather 'round. I want to hear what these Rebs have to say. They said they have news about Gabe. They don't look like they'd be comfortable sittin' on the sofa at the big house. You get a fire going, and I'll be there directly after supper."

Lou Barlow hurried from his kitchen carrying a chair for the Keystone boss, which Art accepted. The ranch hands and riders resumed their Russellian poses around the fire and with the eastern sky just beginning to darken into deep purple shades, the strangers began their tale.

"Well seh," said the one with the bushy beard, "thet fella yon-dah is named Todd. Ah'm Karl. You already seen our buckles and buttons. So you know we took the Southern side of things in the war, more because of where we were born than any sort of politics. After Appomattox with nothin' much more than our horses and uniforms and guns, we headed out west hyah, thin-kin' to get into some sort of farmin' or livestock business."

"It's a familiar ol' story," the one named Todd added. "Y' probably heard it from half the men y' run into out hyah. We was three years gettin' a place."

The cowboys nodded in agreement. It was, indeed, common to meet Civil War veterans of both sides who had "gone west" in search of a new start.

"So," Todd said, taking up the telling, "One fine day we found ourselves with our little bit o' money an' stock all gone. We were flat and out of luck. Had t' hit the trail again. We got 'way down there along the *Rio Mimbrera*—what y'all would call Willow Creek—where we ran into a fellow southern veteran goin' by the name of Colonel Joshua Grumm. He omitted to mention th' name of his army unit, but somewheres along the way we came to the notion it was the Georgia volunteers. At any rate, hyah's how it happened. One fine day we was ridin' along hungry when we come into a broad valley. Acres of grass and trees. And signs hyah and there, warnin' travelers t' keep on travellin'. A ways futha into this little paradise we commenced t' notice banners hangin' in trees, banners of the Confederacy. Directly, we rode under a giant cottonwood, and one of its branches was sportin' a big Confederate flag."

"My partner's likely t' drag this story on all night long," the shorter man interrupted. He cleared his throat and stroked his beard.

"The long and short of it is, Colonel Grumm give refuge to a half-dozen Rebs jus' like us and formed hisself up a kind of private cavalry. We both signed the articles, too, seein' it as a way t' eat regular. He supplied us with uniforms and weapons. The colonel insisted we carry sabers and short-barrel shotguns on our saddles, just like support cavalry. It was a strange sight, I assure y'all, seein' us herdin' cattle with sabers clankin' at our knees."

"I didn't notice any sabers when you two rode in," Bob said.

"No, seh. That part of the story has t' do with your man Gabriel, which I'll get to directly."

"Go ahead," Art said.

"Colonel Grumm was mightily impressed how we'd both risen to the rank o' corporal back during the troubles between the states, and so we two come t' be his personal bodyguard when he rode out to look for trespassers. Mostly, we knew it was play-actin', but we went along with it. Food was good, and we had us a genuine log buildin' t' sleep in. No more leaky tents or brush huts. So we'd take our turns watchin' the livestock and cuttin' firewood and such like that, and now and again we'd put on the gray shirts and ride behind Colonel Grumm."

"And," added Todd, "it felt right strange, playin' soldier after all those years gone by.

"It was getting' late inta thawin' time. We were out on 'patrol' one evenin' when along comes a buggy wagon an' team. There's a man on the seat handlin' the lines, and next to him is a uppity-spoken woman. She was just a little bit too young t' be so prideful of herself. Then behind the buggy is a little midget of a youngster on a big horse, leadin' a packhorse along. Yuh need t' know the colonel was in the habit of 'foraging' for necessities, which meant he sent men t' steal from anyone they found, whether settlers or travelers. This lady Townsend, now, she was a fair hellion and wasted little time remindin' our colonel of his obligations as officer and gentleman. Before the day was out, she was installed in his best room, and two Confederate troopers were cookin' up a meal for her and her 'retinue.'

"Everthin' seemed right cordial and civil-like, y' understand. Hyeh's this fine lady orderin' her driver and the midget to act peaceful, and hyeh's the colonel in his best frock coat and brass buttons struttin' and posin' for her and givin' her all sort of assurances she was under his personal protection. However, Karl and me were more than a little worried he might take the notion t' offer the dwarf-boy or thet lady's driver the opportunity t' join him in his favorite 'sport.' "

"Sport?" Art asked. "What kind of sport?"

"Saber practice, seh," said the bearded Karl. "Y'see, the colonel liked t' invite strangers to join him on his 'field of banners' as he called it, and engage in a duel of sabers. In th' interest of fair play, he would tell 'em that he was givin' 'em a chance to ride away from our 'stronghold' unmolested. If they won, that is. All they had t' do was to best him in six passes, horses and sabers. T' my knowledge, no man lived through it. Todd and me, we buried four travelers who took him up on it."

"What if they didn't?" Bob asked.

"The colonel would hang them as cowards, seh. So later on your man Gabriel rode in. He saw two of them hangin' in separate trees, just about mummified by that time, right nigh the grove that's all hung about with black and red banners. We marveled at your rider's boldness, I assure yuh. Hyah he come ridin' with a smile as big as he was tall, askin' as polite as y' please for the whereabouts of the lady and the buggy and the little peanut with the packhorse. A nicely spoken gent. Never a mention of th' corpses decoratin' the cottonwoods, nor the Reb flags and banners."

"Tell the strange part, though," urged his partner.

"That ain't strange enough? Well. We conducted him to our colonel, who invited him to light down an' take a meal, all real civil and gentlemanly about it as usual. We o'course knew he had his 'challenge' in mind all the while. It bein' near supper hour, we all went t' sit at table in a cabin the colonel called his 'mess hall.' "

"That's where the strange part comes in," Todd said. "Tell it, Karl."

"Ah'm gettin' to it, if y'd kindly hobble your lip. Colonel Grumm bows all gracious t' the lady an' asks won't she honor him by sittin' on his right hand, which she does. She seems mightily impressed at his high manners and polite behavior. However, when he offers the left hand stool t' the newcomer, your man Gabriel, why, that's when Miss Townsend rises in a flurry. She's aflutter like a hen with a stiff breeze up her feathers. Huffin'! I hope I never live t' hear a female huff at *me* that way! 'What do you mean, sir,' she snapped, 'putting this kitchen help across your table from me in this manner!' 'But ma'am,' says the colonel to her, 'here's a rider of the famous Keystone Ranch, a gentleman of the revolver and saddle come all this distance on your behalf. His saddle bears the insignia.' 'Huff!' she says, eyes flashing. 'An undeserved insignia! Stolen, no doubt. I tell you he is a *gentleman* of pots and ladles. I requested riders from Mr. Pendragon, and to be rid of me and to mock me, he sent this cook's boy to hound my tracks and annoy me. I ask you to send him away at once!' Your man smiled and moved down the table without a word. Our supper turned mighty quiet after that."

"Tell about afterward," Todd said. "About the colonel."

"What mah jabber-mouth partner means," Karl continued, "is the change we saw come over Colonel Grumm's face. We ate quiet, like I said, but I watched how he made up to the lady at his elbow. Passin' dishes to her, tellin' her his best stories and such like. It was more than clear how he was warmin' to the notion of havin' a lady t' share his command post and be there every day t' admire his dashin' figure in uniform.

"After supper, we troopers were outside with your man, figurin' to while away a few hours in talk and such-like, when hyar comes the colonel in his full parade get-up, long frock coat, brass buttons, sword at his side. Slouch hat, too, with the cockade pinnin' up one side. We all knew what it meant. He'd come t' make his challenge. 'Seh,' says he, 'the lady yonder desires y' to quit her company.' 'Well,' says your man Gabriel, 'I'm afraid I can't accommodate you, for I'm obliged to go with her and save her mistress lady from a rustlin' scoundrel by the name of Rothaus.' He looked right in the colonel's eye when he said it. 'In that event,' replies the colonel, 'yuh leave me no choice. Ah have given orders for your horses, supplies, and such to be impounded immediately. And your servant as well. In the mornin', you'll be escorted to our perimeter and set free. On foot. Unarmed. Ah would order y' to be hung, but the lady won't have it.'

"Well, seh, Colonel Grumm started t' walk off. But then he turned agin and I saw thet gleam in his eye. Y' ever look in the eye of someone crazy? 'Unless,' says he, 'y'd prefer t' join me on th' field of honor. The lady need know nothing of it. Ah offer y' a chance t' redeem your horse and your arms, y' understand.

You and I, with sabers, at a certain little place in the trees ah keep for just such a purpose. Should yuh emerge victorious, ya'll be free to ride away t' wherever it is y' please. And that small attendant of yours as well. We'll see if you're a Keystone rider or just a kitchen boy like the lady says.'

" 'I see,' says Gabriel. 'I never used a saber, but I reckon I can learn.'

" 'There won't be any time for yuh to learn,' the colonel said. "I propose we meet at the Field of Banners first thing in the mawnin'. Sergeant Todd will loan you his saber.'

" 'That soon!' Gabriel said. 'Well, my mother always did call me a quick study, especially when it came to mischief of any sort.' "

Lou Barlow asked for a cessation in the storytelling while he went for a pot of coffee and a tub of doughnuts. He had intended them to be a special treat at breakfast the next day, but the evening's entertainment seemed to call for refreshments. If the story ended with that smart-aleck kitchen boy getting his head lopped off by a maniac, so much the better.

The riders went to get their tin cups, the coffee was poured out, and the account of Gabe's adventure resumed.

"I loaned him mah saber and relieved him of his sidearm, as the colonel requested, and he asked for us t' give his saddle carbine to the little fella who took care of his horse and camp and such. He explained it was only fair, seein' as how Karl and me was actin' as seconds to th' colonel with our shotguns and all. He'd make certain his man would merely stand by, but he'd be ready to shoot at the first sign of foul play. Now, the colonel was already down by the creek among the cottonwoods, practic-in' slashing and thrustin' and all, so we couldn't consult with him. We gave Gabriel's saddle gun to the boy—Eben's his name—and warned him not to get too close to the colonel. We didn't want him t' do anythin' of a threatenin' sort, yuh understand.

"Yuh need t' know one thing hyah. We never did take to the colonel. None of the Rebs did. We needed leadership. But any of us could see he was crazy. Karl and me went with our shotguns, bein' his seconds like, but I doubt that we'd of ever shot your man.

"So, there we was under the cottonwoods, sun comin' up through the branches, banners and flags movin' a little in a small breeze. Air a bit on the cool side. Like I said, I gave my saber t' Gabriel and took his Colt. Karl and me went to the colonel. I saw Gabriel take a few practice swings and test the edge of m' sword by cuttin' a few willows. Maybe y'all aren't familiar with our Confederate swords? Mine was the long kind, the kind with the deeper curve t' the blade. Against regulations, I'd sharpened the edge as well as the point. Polished it till it shined like a mirror, too. Now, the colonel, he carried a officer's model, shorter and straighter. Not so much weight. A man can be quick with it.

"Gabriel, he calls out across the clearing, 'Six passes, you said?' and the colonel calls back 'Six!' Then Gabriel does somethin' unusual. He turns his horse so his back is to us and looks straight at where the sun is peekin' through the branches. Due east, I figure. He stays there a minute, like he's contemplatin' pretty heavy. Then he turns and slowly rides to the little stream and does the same, facin' south like a man in a dream. Then Ah'm damned if he doesn't ride to where we are and looks west. Ah don't need t' tell y'all what come next. Same thing, lookin' off t' the north. Directly, he rides back to us, looking all smilin' and easy about it, like a man about t' go t' a picnic. He's holdin' my saber across his saddle.

" 'If you don't mind,' says he to Colonel Grumm, 'I'd prefer to start from the west side.'

"The colonel laughed in that evil way o' his and galloped across the clearing. We followed, o' course. It seemed t' me the boy had disadvantaged himself some, facin' into the risin' sun, but ah figured he was stallin' for time. Then he shifted here and there, movin' his horse around like tryin' to find just the right spot. Colonel Grumm got uneasy about it, then became downright agitated. His horse—the colonel's, I mean—he sensed the colonel's impatience and commenced to hack his front hooves and jerk his head back and forth like a racehorse bein' held at th' starting line. Y'all ever have a horse like that, that can read your feelin's? Well finally, Grumm couldn't stand it anymore and all of a sudden he yells 'Charge!' and his mount rears and goes plungin' forward. Gabriel starts his horse, too, a nice steady gallop.

"The colonel charged straight ahead at full speed, presentin' his saber in 'first thrust position outside' pointed straight at your man's chest. In saber practice, y'd ordinarily meet that sorta thrust with what they call the 'hanging guard,' meaning yuh have your saber held downward across the body so as t' slash the enemy's sword upward. Gabriel, of course, didn't know anythin' about such matters. No, seh! He kept mah saber down along his leg right till the last second, then swerved his horse right direct into the colonel's while he swung the saber up and over, deflectin' the colonel's saber so it came down hard. The flat of the colonel's own blade delivered his own horse a hard knock next t' the neck.

"Well, seh, the colonel was mighty upset. He wheeled around quick and come chargin' back again to attack Gabriel with an inside cut, where yuh keep the saber level and use th' wrist t' slash forward. Yuh can't put much weight behind the stroke, but yuh might unhorse the enemy that way. Make him dodge, at least. Gabriel, though, he doesn't know to dodge. He sees the sun in the eyes of the colonel's horse—Karl and me saw it too, straightaway—and Ah'm a coon if he don't swerve again and makes 'em collide horses. He's holdin' mah saber straight upright so when the colonel's blade hits it, there's a shock that makes the colonel rear back in the saddle. By this time the colonel's horse is nervous as a cat in a hailstorm. An' wouldn't yuh be! Hyar comes another horse outa nowhere, yuh can't see him, he collides with yuh, your own rider's haulin' back and weavin' around . . . it's enough t' make yuh want to go back t' the barn."

Todd paused to savor the hot coffee and compliment Lou on the quality of the doughnuts. The Keystone men muttered among themselves, each telling another how *he* would have handled the situation Gabe found himself in.

"Where was I?" Todd said. "Oh, yeah. Ah neglected t' mention the yellin'. When Gabriel came abreast of the colonel the first time, he yells out *'one!'* just as loud as he can. Same with the second pass, he yells *'two!'* loud enough t' wake the dead, and it seems t' me he's yellin' right into the ears of the colonel's horse. 'Why,' says Karl to me kind of quiet-like, 'ah do believe thet young man's fightin' the horse rather than th' colonel!' There comes another pass, this time with the colonel feintin' an outside thrust toward th' chest and shiftin' at the last second into a outside cut, and it very nearly worked. Your man managed to duck just in time, but not far enough. Grumm's blade sliced into his hat and sent it a-flyin'. But even so, Gabriel yells *'three!'* hard into the horse's ear as he goes by.

"Number four was what set Colonel Grumm into a right pure rage. He set himself one more time, spurred the horse, came chargin' t' make his thrust again. Gabriel smiled. Didn't he smile, Karl? Yessir. Grinned out loud an' hauled back t' make his horse rear up, front hooves goin' like fury. The colonel's horse, he puts his neck down and tries t' swerve, and naturally the colonel tries to rein him, but in the whole process he ends up just ridin' past Gabriel at a kinda angle where he can't bring his saber to bear. That's when . . ."

"Thet's when your man went on the offensive, that's what!" Karl suddenly interjected. "Ah'm damned—beg pardon f'r the language—if he didn't wheel and commence usin' the flat of his blade t' smack that colonel's horse about the haunch and flanks! Well, seh, Todd and myself had t' laugh—isn't that right, Todd?—t' see this lanky youngster suddenly chasin' the colonel, smackin' that horse with the saber. How that horse jumped and danced! Eyes rolled back, tryin' t' see who's beatin' on him. Hah! And the boy keeps yellin *'four, four, four!'* Like that.

"Now, he wheeled off directly, and the colonel manages to turn and come after him. But Colonel Grumm, he's forgot all about his code of chivalry and honor of officers and gentlemen an' all that, because we see him lower his point and charge right at your man's back. He'd stick him right between the shoulder blades. Had that crazy look to his eye, too. We both yelled. It wasn't fair. I thought about firin' off a barrel just t' bring Colonel Grumm back to his senses, but I think he was too far gone with blood rage for anythin' t' stop him. It was lucky your man heard him comin' at him like that and got turned in time. Colonel slashed at his leg this time, but Gabriel managed a low parry. Clumsy, but it served t' protect his leg and flank anyways. Colonel, he turned short, haulin' that horse's head around somethin' cruel, but by this time Gabriel was already yellin' *'five!'* and the colonel's horse didn't want a thing t' do with him. Shied away. Colonel is off balance, yuh understand."

"All right!" Todd interrupted. "Now yuh've ruined my story, maybe yuh'd like t' shove another doughnut in your cake-hole an' let me finish!

"Colonel Grumm is off balance and his horse won't face Gabriel now, like m' partner told yuh. Then quick as anythin' yuh can imagine, Gabriel reaches out with the saber and uses the point of it t' push the colonel out of the saddle altogether. Plump onto the ground, *whump*! Like that. I look over and see that little Eben fella jus' leanin' on that saddle carbine and he's grinnin' as big as Gabriel.

"Gabriel dismounts. The colonel gets up off his butt, sort of dusts himself, then he assumes a kind o' swordplay pose. Saber held out, other arm kinda back for balance.

" 'I'm tired of your game, sir,' Gabriel says, walkin' straight toward him. 'I'll just give number six to you. I'll take my gear and ride on out with the lady. You did give your word on it.'

"Colonel Grumm, he's got blood in his eye. Unhorsed? Right in front of his troopers, not to mention a midget? An' made a fool of by some cowboy. He just flat went crazy. Called 'im all kind of names a man oughtn't repeat anywheres. But your man, he smiled that big smile. Grumm stopped for breath. Cowboy headed t' where we were. Carryin' my saber. Then here come the colonel chargin' t' stab 'im in the back. I was ready t' shoot Grumm myself. Might have, too, except cowboy turned. Kinda twisted like a man dodgin' a mad bull and put the saber right through Grumm. All the way through! Grumm looked surprised as I ever seen. He falls over. I figure he was dead 'fore his head hit the ground.

"Gabriel looks down at him. Kinda sad-like. He reaches down and takes Grumm's slouch hat. Plucks the cockade off and lays it on Grumm's body. Then puts the hat on his own head. 'Replacement,' he says, or somethin' like that."

Art looked at Link.

"Who the hell is this kid we sent out, anyway?"

"I told you," Link said. "That boy's deeper than he is tall. If I didn't know better, I'd think you sired him yourself."

Darkness descended over the group. More firewood was brought, and Art Pendragon called for more coffee to be made.

"This is one campfire story I've got to hear the end of," he said, "even if we need t' stay here all night."

Some of the men went to get sheepskins or a blanket. The night had a chill that crept right up a man's backbone.

Todd and Karl continued telling how the lady Townsend had come to find them and discovered Grumm skewered on a cavalry saber. She found her host's corporals being held hostage by a kitchen helper. Stunned by the outcome of the duel, they had lowered their guard and allowed Gabe time enough to grab his carbine and get the drop on them.

The lady was distraught.

"You mean to kill them all!" she screamed at him. "Have you no honor?"

"I'll spare these two," Gabe said with assumed seriousness, "but only if you'll ask me to. Politely. It's time you came down off your high horse."

Gabriel pointed the carbine at Todd and cocked the hammer.

"All right!" the lady cried. "All right! I beg you then. I beg you to let these men go! Is that what you wanted me to say? I *beg* it of you!"

"Fair enough."

He turned to his prisoners.

"Now, you two. Here's what I want. First, one of you Rebs go find me a good shirt. Your colonel's sword ripped mine. Next, you let th' other Johnny Rebs know it's all over. No more stealing, no more thieving from passersby. Then I want you two t' round up every Keystone animal. You deliver them personally to the Keystone Ranch. I'll write you a note to tell 'em you're working for me. We'll say you're bringin' back cattle somebody else stole.

"If you make it to the Keystone with cattle, we'll call it a sign of good faith. Means you deserve another chance. So here's what else you do after you deliver the bunch. You ask at the

Keystone for directions into town. In town you'll find a sickly
sort of man who runs the mercantile. Needs cheap help. So
does the livery stable. I figure you two owe society about a year
of working for nothing much more'n board and room. Mebbe a
trifle more for smokes and a beer now and then. A bargain?"

More than a bargain, it was a good bargain.

The closer they got to the Keystone Ranch with their herd of
"returned" cattle, the more the pair realized how lucky they had
been that Gabe showed up. Instead of an uncertain future as
highwaymen posing as corporals in a bogus Confederate unit,
they had a chance to be seen as honest cowpunchers doing a
good turn for a powerful rancher.

"We figure we're damn lucky your man Gabriel come along,"
Todd said to Art Pendragon.

"Does seem that way," Art mused. "I wonder how he's getting on since you saw him last."

"Last time we seen 'em," Karl said, "thet witchy woman, she
was goin' on agin about how he was goin' to get his come-
uppance once they got t' the spread where . . . what's his name?"

"Rothaus?" Todd said.

"Yeah, Rothaus. She was a-sayin' once they got t' his place
he'd find out what was what. She allowed as how Rothaus
wadn't about t' put up with kitchen help actin' like he was a
one-man vigilante posse. Your man, he just grinned thet grin of
his and rode on out ahead of the buggy, so's he wouldn' hafta
listen t' her no more."

"So what happened to your sabers, speaking of uniforms?"
Art asked. "You were goin' to tell us."

"Well suh, there ain't much t' it. Us six soldier veterans had
us a little ol' ceremony about the war bein' over. Once we'd
buried the colonel, we dug us a pit and made a bonfire in it
outa all them insignias, banners, flags, all of it. Even throwed
our sabers in, too. I reckon someday, some sodbuster'll be dig-

gin' around in that bottomland and plow up a stack of rusty ol' swords and wonder how they got there."

CHAPTER EIGHT
RED THE REBEL

Gabriel had met quiet men before. But Trooper Red could make a fence post seem loquacious. His low hat brim concealed a pair of dark and shifty eyes. The hunch and stoop of his shoulders made him look lonely, forlorn; his right hand was never far from his holster. Following the breakup of Colonel Grumm's "post," Trooper Red muttered that he would "ride along a ways" with the lady Townsend retinue. He figured he'd travel as far as the next valley where he would try to get hired on by one C. M. Smith, a frontier entrepreneur who had laid claim to a salt spring. The rumor was that he was shipping wagonloads of the stuff.

"How's the road between here and there?" Gabe asked. "Safe for the lady?"

"Former Grumm territory," Trooper Red mumbled. "Safe as kittens."

"And Mister Smith, he's hospitable? Not a threat, is he?"

"Mean. Runs a tight ship. But he's all right."

Nothing more did Red say; merely collected his blankets and belongings, rolled them, and tied them behind his saddle. He mounted up and sat waiting for them to get the buggy ready.

On the trail, Gabriel and Trooper Red plodded along side by side. Red would not respond to any of Gabe's cheerful remarks concerning the fine weather and the nice landscape. Gabe even went so far as to quote Plato, but whatever was said to Red appeared to enter under his broad slouch hat, find its way through the brim's shadow to his earholes, and vanish into his cranial cavity unacknowledged and unanswered. The small party made its way across clearings, following the dim tracks through groves of trees, up slopes of sage and down the other side, and into detours around long gulleys and arroyos. On the third afternoon they spotted a column of white smoke rising at a distance among the hills.

"Comin' from Smith's place," said Trooper Red. "Another fifteen miles or more t' go."

"Ah," said Gabriel. "Maybe we should make camp somewhere around here tonight. There's probably a stream on the far side of that next rise, don't you think?"

The stream bottom was fair land. It was green land, land with grass so damp and vigorous that the horses hardly left a track. The dense willow thickets showed shining green down in the flat bottom, while up on the south facing slope the junipers sported a duller, more grayish green. Groves of cottonwoods gave a tang to the air. Gabe tipped his hat back and rode grinning into the bright late afternoon sun, looking all around him as if he couldn't bear to miss catching a single shade of green or the chirp of a solitary bird.

The verdant valley made easy going for the buggy. Gabe didn't believe anyone could be in this place on a day like this and not feel happy and content; yet when he looked at Lady Townsend, he saw the grim look, the tight little upper lip, the squint to the eyes. He didn't know what it would take to make her happy, but he was pretty sure it would involve his own disappearance.

He was looking around for a good place to camp—although anywhere in this grassy little valley would be a good place—when his ears picked up a familiar sound. A calf in distress, bawling for its mother. Gabe didn't know how many times he'd heard it. Usually it meant some dumb youngster had toppled into a gulch or had tangled itself in a fence. Except there weren't any fences. The wailing came from the south side of the valley where there was a deep draw choked with tangles of old brush and fallen trees.

"Hear that?" he said. "Some dogie up that way. Scared or hurt, by the sound of it."

Trooper Red nodded slightly.

"I guess I'll look into it," Gabe said. "Can't just ride by."

A cowhand of Gabe's stamp couldn't ignore the distress cries of a calf any more than he could ignore a lady's need of assistance.

"I'll ride over that way and see what the ruckus is about. You and Eben and Dobé set up camp for the lady. It's early yet, but no sense passin' up a good spot like this. Maybe one of you could hunt up a rabbit or grouse for the pot."

Wordlessly, Trooper Red plodded on. Eben came riding past, followed by the packhorse and the buggy.

"Nice day, isn't it?" Gabe said brightly.

"Real nice," Dobé agreed. "Just about perfect."

"Yes," said the lady Townsend. "Quite a pleasant day."

For the briefest of seconds Gabe thought he saw the beginnings of a smile come to her face. Then again, it could have been a nervous tic.

"Been hearing that calf bawling its head off," he said. "Somewhere up that gulch over there. Hear it? I need to go take a look. We saw what looks like a good camp spot further on up the track. Near those cottonwoods. See 'em tops sticking up beyond that rise? You go ahead. I'll be along directly."

The gulch was easy going for a hundred yards. But then the jumble of downed trees began to look like a kid's game of pick-up sticks made by a giant. All the deadfall and gooseberry tangles made it impossible to take the horse any further.

"It's a pedestrian job, I reckon," Gabe said, dismounting and untying his lariat from the saddle. He tethered the horse to a tree branch and went ahead on foot, pushing his way through thorny gooseberry canes and prickly wild plum bushes. His leather chaps were clumsy for this kind of foot work, but he was glad to have them to ward off the spines.

"Shoulda brought that Rebel saber along with me," he muttered to himself. "Could've used it t' hack a trail."

The calf had stopped crying, then resumed as Gabe worked his way through the brush tangles and across the logs and rocks. He worked his way around the biggest of the fallen trees. He struggled up steep sandy places where the slick soles of his boots threatened to take him skidding down into the brambles. From above him and off to his left there came a long "moooooooooooo" and he looked up to see a worried cow staring down into the gulch. She closed her eyes, stretched her neck out full length, and aimed a "moooooooooo" at something up the gulch.

The calf bawled in reply and the cow mooed again.

"All right, I'm trying!" Gabe called up to her. "What's the matter? Did your baby get himself down in here where he can't climb out?"

It was worse than that. Much worse.

Gabe discovered the calf down on its front knees with its hind end sticking up. It had its head thrust into a scraggly willow bush and was whimpering and bawling.

"Come on outa there," Gabe said, grabbing the calf by the haunches and pulling it back. He nearly lost his balance on the slope, but managed to get the animal out where he could inspect it.

"Ah, dammit! Youngster, you sure did put your nose where it didn't belong! Painful lesson, isn't it? What did you do, run down into this gulch to hide?"

The calf's pain came from porcupine quills. Gabe had seen it before, even in New Mexico, where there were fewer of the varmints. A calf, sometimes even a full-grown cow, would notice old Mr. Porky ambling along through the woods or next to a creek minding his own business, and the dumb bovine would just have to put its big pink snout right down there and sniff to see what it was. You wouldn't be likely to mistake the waddling pile of hair and quills for a bunch of grass or anything else a cow might be interested in eating, but many a calf had gone to sniff at a porcupine and gotten itself slapped in the nose.

This porcupine had done it in spades. Long shiny quills protruded from the calf's lip, from the sides of its snout, and from the underside of its chin. There were quills up in its nostrils. He even had quills in his tongue, probably from trying to lick them off his nose.

Gabe held the calf with one hand while he patted his pockets with the other, seeing what he had with him. One Barlow clasp knife. One waterproof match holder. His pocket watch. A few coins. Pocket bandanna. A little coil of stovepipe wire he'd picked up on the trail. A couple of leather whangs. He looked down the gulch. It was a long way back to the horse, but that's where his fence pliers were, in the saddlebag. There was no way to get the horse and bring it up here. He figured he had just two options. Either he could tie up the calf and leave it here while he went for his pliers. Or he could take the calf to where the horse was.

The sun was on the verge of dropping behind the hill, and the gulch was already showing deep shadows.

"Damn," said Gabriel Hugh Allen.

Splicing the two leather whangs into a piggin' string, he hogtied the calf's feet in a bunch, then stooped and hoisted it over his neck and onto his back like a man carrying a rolled blanket over his shoulders.

"Ugh," said Gabriel. "You could do with less weight right now."

Down and down he struggled, sometimes slipping, sometimes sliding, dropping the calf more than once. The calf's mother followed along the ridge above, giving constant voice to her concern.

"Doing the best I can!" Gabe yelled at her.

The calf also did its share of yelling.

Gabe worked his way over the fallen logs, clambered over the rocks, and slid down the other side, wondering if he might be rubbing a hole in the seat of his pants.

"I should have put on my chaps the other side 'round," he said.

He reached the gooseberry thickets and plunged through them with less caution than he had used in going up the gulch. He was tired, it was after sundown, and a few more scratches just didn't seem to matter. Still lugging the calf, he untied the horse and led it down to a relatively flat spot that looked to be clear of thorny things. There he tied the horse again and tossed the calf down in the grass. He got out his fencing pliers and hoggin' string.

"This is going to hurt," he told the calf as he bound the feet more securely.

He tackled the longest quills first, the ones sticking out of the snout. One by one, the quills came out, followed by blood. Each time he pulled a quill the calf went "whuuuh!!" and blew blood and calf snot all over his arms and hands. The pliers got slippery with it. The calf tried to struggle free and Gabe had to hold him down with his knee so he could twist the head into position. Some of the quills ended up stuck in his own forearm.

"You're acting ungrateful," he told the calf, "but I see your point of view. Reminds me of goin' to a Mexican dentist to get a bad tooth pulled. I didn't blow snot, but I sure passed a few cuss words. Hold still! Just a few more of these stickers to go."

By the time Gabe released the calf to go crying after its mother, the darkness had almost done with the day. He was bone-weary, sweaty, and dirty. The idea of riding into camp in that condition didn't have any appeal for him at all. Might as well stay put. He had hardtack and jerky with him, and his good sheepskin. There was a little water trickling through the bottom of the gulch. After he cleaned off the blood and calf slobber he would get a fire going and have supper, then lie down. Eben might get concerned, a little, but he couldn't do anything about that. The dwarf would be all right.

Morning sun and a cloudless sky. Dewdrops on the grass sparkled like tiny diamonds. Gabe rose, washed his face, combed his hair, and saddled the horse. He rolled his blanket and tied it behind the cantle. Just over the hill, he told himself as he set off along the tracks the buggy had left in the grass. Just over the hill, and there'll be a hot cup of coffee and some bacon and biscuits.

Just over the hill, however, the tracks kept going. There was no camp in the cottonwoods. There wasn't a sign that anyone had stopped to make camp.

"Strange. Lady must have decided to keep on going awhile," Gabe said to the horse, there being no one else around to talk to. "Some say your cousins are stubborn, but that lady would put any mule to shame. She's just plain contrary."

The tracks led across the stream bottom and up the other side of the valley, but when he reached the top of the hill he still couldn't see hide nor hair of the buggy.

"They must have traveled all night," Gabe said.

Around noon he came to a well-used wagon track. Most of the trees near the track had been cut down. The biggest ponderosas remained, the ones too big and heavy for a freight wagon. Nothing else was left except stumps. Even the limbs had been hauled off. Gabe reasoned it had something to do with the column of smoke ahead of him, for the road led directly toward it.

The road showed fresh buggy tracks. The road would make for fast traveling, which probably explained why they had gone on all night instead of making camp. Maybe they met somebody who said if they went along the trail just a few more miles they would find this road and they could follow it by moonlight. Then Gabe remembered. That smoke came from the salt works, and somebody in the bunch wanted to get there. Trooper Red.

Gabe put his horse into a half trot. Crossing a low rise he saw the stone chimney rising into the air. He rode past a fenced pasture where several horses and a couple of goats grazed. Farther on were several one-room shacks facing the wagon track, then two larger cabins. Next was a building without windows, a storehouse or barn of some kind, then a bunkhouse and cookshack, and finally, he saw the salt works at the base of the chimney. It was a stone platform about twenty feet across and chest-high. Two men could be seen feeding wood into a firebox.

A man on top of the platform had a long wooden paddle with which he stirred the evaporating tubs. It looked a whole lot like another salt works Gabe had seen down along the Brazos, where the heat from the fire went through tunnels underneath big iron tubs. Water from a salt spring was poured into the tubs where it evaporated and left the salt crusted around the inside.

It crusted more than the tubs. The open-sided shed over the tubs was white with salt. The lower half of the chimney was white. The side of the storehouse was white. Even the ground was white, as was the freight wagon used to haul firewood. Just a short distance off he saw another open shed where an ox hitched to a long sweep pole walked around and around in a circle. Water dribbled from a wooden pipe into a storage basin. Gabe figured the ox was hitched up to some kind of primitive water pump, probably a long screw or maybe one of those bucket-and-chain contraptions. A small Mexican boy with a buggy whip kept the ox moving.

"Hola, Conejo!" Gabe called to him. *"Donde es el Patron?"*

The boy, who was no doubt daydreaming of other places, glanced up with wide eyes and open mouth. Mutely, he pointed toward a low, one-story building that looked like a house and office combined.

"Gracias," Gabe said.

He tied up at the hitching rail and went in through the door marked OFFICE.

"Now here's the thing," C. M. Smith continued, leaning back in his chair so he could hitch his belt up under his ample paunch. "Trooper Red is known to me as an honest man. I am inclined, therefore, to believe his account of your fight with Colonel Grumm, whose hat you have in your hand even as we speak. However justified your actions, it is difficult to see how you are to be let go without penalty. Even out here in the wild frontier we need to keep law and order."

Gabe stood there, his ingratiating grin on his face. He looked around the room at the lady Townsend, the pale Dobé, and little Eben.

"Moreover," C. M. Smith continued, "there is the matter of trespass. These three admit to entering my property without permission, and the slender gentleman admits to shooting at my game."

"I took a shot at a wild turkey," Dobé explained, turning to Gabe. "Some fresh turkey would've tasted awful good."

"Aha! The buggy driver has hit upon my very problem.

Indeed he has. Young man," Smith said, addressing Gabe, "as it is generally agreed by these parties present that you are in charge of this expedition, I wish you and I could come to an arrangement about this matter of murder and trespass. Justice must be done, and all that, you know."

"Well," Gabe replied, "old Plato said justice is not good for much. But in my opinion he was just saying it as a way to agitate his friend Polemarchus. Say your piece."

"My 'piece' is this. Inasmuch as Colonel Grumm and his cavalry post provided me with trade—he would exchange beef in return for salt—and as my own company has been trespassed upon and upset by your group, I feel you owe our little society some kind of repayment. Having learned that you hail from the Keystone Ranch, and hoping one day to extend my distribution of salt into that area of the territory, I am rather inclined to let you off easily."

"That's a awfully wordy piece," Gabe said. "You seem to have an idea in mind. Care to share it?"

"Indeed," said C. M. Smith. "My crew and myself have run out of beef of late. We were hoping to be resupplied by Colonel Grumm. The men, and myself especially, grow exceedingly weary of venison. Also, we have grown tired of our own attempts at cooking. I like to eat. I like to eat well. But fried venison and stale Indian bread is not my idea of eating well."

"You've got my sympathy." Gabe grinned, looking at the man's girth. "But I don't see how we figure into your problem."

"The lady," C. M. Smith said. "She has narrated her sad tale, and I believe I have found a solution pleasant to all concerned. She apparently has no fondness for traveling with you, is that correct?"

Smith looked at Gabe, who only smiled, and then at the lady, who only sniffed.

"And I imagine the feeling is reciprocal," Smith continued.

"It may not have occurred to you, but from this point onward you could easily find your way to the lands held by Mr. Rothaus. Or the buggy driver could serve as your guide. You and Miss Townsend here need no longer travel together."

"You know," Gabe said, opening his clasp knife to dig at a broken point of porcupine quill that was starting to fester in his palm, "I like a good round dance as much as the next man, but the way you waltz around with words is gettin' tiresome."

"Very well. Here is the arrangement, then. You and these two fellows will take your horses and proceed on your way toward your rendezvous with Mr. Rothaus. You are foolish for wanting to confront Rothaus, but that is none of my affair whatsoever. Meanwhile, the lady will remain here and do the cooking for myself and the crew until she has worked off your penalty for murder and trespass. I think a mere two weeks of good meals should be sufficient. I will leave you to discuss it."

"Two weeks?" Gabe said.

"Anything more would seem like kidnapping," C. M. Smith said. "Besides, I anticipate Mr. Rothaus will kill you within that space of time, which leaves our lady with few options except to remain here. She might as well cook for us as become a servant for Rothaus."

With that, Smith heaved himself out of his chair and waddled from the room. Seeing that their "host" was out of earshot, Gabe turned to Dobé.

"Turkey?" Gabe asked.

"There was a bunch of them in that swale a ways back, where the willows are," Dobé replied. "I don't know why they're eating venison when there are so many turkeys."

"Turkeys!" the lady Townsend screeched. "Turkeys! Why are you two talking about turkeys! I am *not* going to remain in this awful place! The man must be mad to think he can keep me prisoner here. To do the *cooking*, indeed! The moment I saw an opportunity, I would run away into the wilderness rather than be subject to this. The only woman among all these ruffians! Indeed!"

"You wouldn't be the only woman," Gabe smiled. "I caught a glimpse of a black-haired *señora* peeking out from behind one of the shacks out there. But the question is, can you sling a fry pan?"

"What?"

"You don't strike me as the sort who would do much cooking of her own. Of course, my own opinion is that this Smith *hombre* would be crazy to keep you here anyway."

She looked at him. He saw in her face a mixture of desperation and pleading. There was no mistaking it: for the first time since their departure from the Keystone, the lady was looking to him for help. He grinned and she sniffed, but his grin had a tiny grain of sympathy in it, and her sniff seemed lacking in sincerity.

"All right," he said. "You all stay here while I go and find Mr. Smith."

Smith was not a hard man to find. Gabe saw him over at the spring, watching the ox plod around and around the pump. Smith blotted out a considerable amount of sunlight.

"You are leaving, then?" Smith inquired.

"No. It's my turn to talk. Now, we could sit us down here and argue about definitions of 'justice,' like old Socrates and Glaucon, but I doubt whether it would get us anywhere. So, let me tell you where I think we stand in this little game of yours. I'm thinking the Keystone brand on my saddle bothers you some. And you'd be right. You got a salt operation up and runnin', and it seems like things could go either way on you. With the Keystone behind you, you'd stand a chance of doing well for yourself. After a year or two. That's one thing. Second thing is, I don't think you'd give a penny plug of chaw for Colonel

Grumm, alive or dead. I think you're happy he's dead. Now, I can see where you and your people are in need of a little boost from all that deer meat. Plus, now that you went ahead and 'caught' us, you can't just let us go. You need to show your crew you're the man in charge. You need to get somethin' out of us. But for the sake of your future you'd rather let us go."

"You have summarized the situation admirably," C. M. Smith said softly.

"Well, here's my admirable way out, then," Gabe said. "First, Trooper Red bothers me. He's got a burr under his saddle. I'm afraid if he remains here much longer he's likely to get all sulky and shoot somebody. He's the kind of man who can get other men all stirred up, too."

"What do we do with him?" Smith said.

"Hire him. But not to work here. What you do is pack up some samples of your best salt. Have Red take it to those little towns south of here, or over into the gold fever country, see if he can't line up buyers. Like one of those advance agents who work for cattle drives. He'll get happier once he's out of this area, and he might actually stir up customers for you. Give him supplies, a little salary. Tell 'im he'll get a commission for each contract he gets."

"Seems a sound idea." Smith said. "Next?"

"Next, you let the lady and Dobé take the buggy and keep movin' toward home. Tell your crew she paid money for a fine or something like that. But she leaves."

"Or?"

Gabe put his hand to his Colt. Smith saw the grin fade and there was no trace of amusement in Keystone man's eyes.

"Or," Gabe said, "you could pull that pea shooter you got hidden in your boot and we'll burn some gunpowder. How many of your 'crew' do you reckon will stand with you in a gunfight?"

"You are once more correct," said Smith. "They work for wages, which are meager. I doubt whether any of them has so much as fired a gun in the last six months. Except to kill deer. So. I will allow the lady and her driver to take their leave unmolested. I do protest, however, that I expected some kind of consideration—however small—from a Keystone representative."

"I didn't say I was going. Eben and me, we'll work off our trespassing 'fine' with a feast. Cook you the best turkey dinner you ever put a tooth to. It'll raise the spirits of your men better than a visit from Santa Claus."

"What did you say?" the lady Townsend asked.

"I said you and Mr. Dobé better get going. Don't look back. Y' try to stay out of trouble another day or two, and we'll catch up with you. Or you can stay here. I'll leave it up to you. It could be dangerous out there, and it could be risky to stay."

The lady was puzzled.

"You're always telling people I'm a kitchen boy," he said. "Potboiler, ladle wrangler, biscuit shooter, and all that. So I'll stay here t' cook for them until I can get away. Better me than you. Right?"

So it was decided, and it was Gabriel Hugh Allen who made the decision. The young grub rider. The one who was so determined to rise from the ashes and assume the mantle of a Keystone rider. To help a woman he hardly knew, he was ready to resume his indenture to pots and pans. It would be poetic justice if she had to stay and fend for herself, to rustle meals for a bunch of rough laborers and wash their dirty dishes until her hands were raw from boiling water and lye soap.

Eben helped the lady get settled in the buggy.

"Why is he doing this?" she whispered to the dwarf.

"Doing what?"

"All this. Helping those Scotchmen. Those brothers with the cows. Risking his life, then sending men to find work at Mr. Pendragon's ranch. Trying to help this Smith person."

"Because of who he is," Eben said. "You're thinking he's trying to get into good with Mr. Pendragon? But that ain't it. It's who he is. He can't do otherwise. Tell you one thing."

"What?"

"Gabe Allen ain't his real name."

Chapter Nine

JUAN GREGORIO DE GALVEZ, CABALLERO

"Eben!"

Gabe was calling him.

"Let's go get us some birds."

Having seen the buggy carrying Dobé and the lady Townsend on its way, Gabe and Eben mounted up and rode back toward the swale where Dobé had seen the turkeys. The flock was just where he said, more than two dozen plump black gobblers browsing in the grass for pine nuts and bugs. A few looked up as the men approached them on foot, but neither flew off nor raised an alarm. A half-hearted trill came from a sentry on the other side of the bunch, but the warning went unheeded. The two-legged animals were neither mountain lion nor coyote, so the turkeys ignored them and went on eating.

"Good lookin' critters," Gabe observed.

He was right. The turkeys strutted in shiny, healthy plumage like New York bankers leaving a big lunch. The rosy wattles swinging beneath their beaks looked like fat jowls.

Lacking a shotgun, the question became one of method. Here were the birds, but how to get them? Gabe's first impulse was to simply shoot them with his carbine, although the first shot would likely scatter them. Eben's idea was to weave a snare of some kind, or find some light cord or twine and make a catch-pole contrivance. The longer they stood there among the wild birds discussing various alternatives for assassination, the more they realized that the birds were ignoring them. Eben went to the chokecherry thicket and returned with a thick, long cudgel. The dwarf was able to club two of the wild turkeys before the others became suspicious. Then the flock moved away as he approached, gobbling and chirking amongst each other.

"Better give it up," Gabe said. "If y' chase 'em much further, they're gonna fly away on us. I'll try the carbine."

He circled the flock looking for the best angle, trying to figure out which way they would fly. If he could get them to fly into the trees, they might come to roost where he could get a shot at them. Eben smiled at the sight: Gabe walked stooped over, as if by making himself only four and a half feet high the birds wouldn't notice he was there.

Finally, he was in the right position.

The Winchester barked three times in quick succession— *"blam! blam! blam!"*—and the flock took to their awkward wings and headed for the protection of the trees. Three of their comrades remained in the grass, never to fly again. Gabe spotted one escapee sitting on a high branch, making it a total of six. Six fat, juicy turkeys to sling over their horses and take back to the salt works.

They took the turkeys a little way up the hill near the shed where the ox was walking around and around at the end of the pump sweep. While Eben unloaded the horses, Gabe struck up a conversation with the little boy who kept the ox moving.

"You're a good bullwhacker," he told him, using a mixture of Spanish and English.

"*Sí*," said the boy proudly.

"Got a momma hereabouts?"

The boy pointed to a small hut up the hill.

"How would you like to help us cook some turkeys? Maybe your momma would help?"

They made a good team, Gabe, Eben, the dark-haired *señora*, and the small boy. Gabe called the boy *"Conejo"* because he was small and quick like a rabbit. Eben and the *señora* started plucking and gutting the turkeys.

"All right, *amigo*," Gabe said to the boy, "now we need some cooking stuff. And if you're like most kids, you'll know where to look. Right?"

Conejo smiled up at the tall cowboy.

"Cutting board," Gabe said, illustrating with hand gestures. *"Un cuchillo, largo.* A long knife. And *platos hondos."* Gabe drew a big circle in the air to show how deep the mixing bowls needed to be.

As Gabe had expected, the little rabbit dove into the cook-shack cupboards like a ferret after a rat. Before long he had everything piled on the table—long knives, big bowls, and an ancient cracked dough board.

"See any cans anywhere?" Gabe asked him. Gabe was searching a dark closet where the previous cook had apparently thrown anything he had no use for, such as tins of mustard powder and cans of beans with badly swollen sides.

As soon as *Conejo* understood what Gabe wanted, he set a wooden crate on a kitchen chair and climbed up to retrieve a big skeleton key from the top of the doorframe. He jumped down and beckoned for Gabe to follow him.

Out in back of the buildings he opened the low door of a spring house where several generations of cooks had stored everything from fresh meat and poultry to dried grasses. There was a basket of potatoes, most of them still edible. From the dark corners of dusty shelves the boy pulled large cans and jars that proved to contain stewed tomatoes—standard saddlebag fare—and preserved grapes. The gunnysack hanging from the ceiling contained some pretty fresh bacon.

Conejo held up another discovery, a pot so large he had to strain with both hands to lift it. It was full of candles.

"Don't need candles," Gabe said, "but we can use the pot for the potatoes." Leaving Eben to finish plucking the last two turkeys, Gabe gathered up a couple of pails and flour sacks and took the *señora* and her *Conejo* on a little hunting expedition among the thickets and logged-over clearings. They found tiny wild onions growing where the soil had been disturbed by logging. They picked a gallon of dried-up chokecherries and rose hips left on the bushes from the previous autumn. They brought back handfuls of soft tips of wild sage, together with pine nuts stolen from the midden hoards of squirrels.

Back at the cookshack, *Conejo* was put to work pounding the chokecherries and rose hips together with bacon grease into a kind of oily pemmican. His mother went to her *casa* and returned with dry Indian bread, which she crumbled into a bowl with the chopped wild onions and bits of sage. Pine nuts followed and *Conejo*'s concoction of chokecherry and rose hip was added to the mix.

Satisfied with the progress being made on the stuffing, Gabe sent the boy to find a couple of shovels. Together they began to dig a fire pit near the salt boiler where there was plenty of hot coals and firewood.

Two feet down, they came to a layer of yellowish adobe clay, which Gabe carefully piled to one side. When the hole was big enough, Eben brought wood and coals and made a deep bed of glowing hot embers. Gabe stirred water into his clay pile until it was yellow mud.

Into the wild turkeys went the stuffing mixture of bread, bacon, wild fruit, sage, and wild pine nuts. Heavy jackets of sticky adobe clay were slathered onto the birds until they resembled huge eggs. Then into the fiery pit they went. Gabe buried them under layers of moist green pine branches and dirt.

Where the pit had been there was now a mound of earth giving off steam and smoke.

"*Bueno*," Gabe told his crew. "All we need to do now is sit back and wait until tomorrow. That turkey meat ought to fall right off the bones."

Conejo's young mother entered into these culinary proceedings with curiosity and enthusiasm. When Gabe said they needed bread for the feast she mounted one of the horses and rode away back into the hills, returning in a couple of hours with a gunnysack full of fresh Indian loaves. She took *Conejo* scavenging into the dark depths of the cold cellar where they found dusty bags of pinto beans. She sent the boy home for a *ristra* of red *chiles*. She would need the big pot; perhaps the potatoes could be boiled in one of the salt kettles, if the *vaquero* would persuade *el jefe* to fill one with fresh water.

She smiled at Gabe, her dark eyes betraying her pride. There would be potatoes and hot *chile* with beans to go with the turkey. And fresh bread! With nothing to do while the birds baked, Gabe hunkered against a wall in the afternoon sunshine. The *señora* scurried here and there, coming up with ideas for ingredients.

"All it takes sometimes," he said to Eben, "is finding a way to get somebody interested. Our friend Smith, he didn't even know he had a *primo* cook waiting to be asked to get to work."

"Yes," Eben said. "But keep an eye on her. I don't like the way she's been eyeing that billy goat over there."

"You ever taste shredded goat meat stewed in red *chile*?" Gabe grinned. "Beats Texas beefsteak any day."

"Blacksmith will be pleased," Eben said. "When he hears what you have done."

"Seemed like it oughta be done," Gabe said.

After three days at the salt works, they were back on the

road, riding toward the Surrey Ranch.

"You did well, rider," the dwarf said.

"Not bad. Even if I say it myself," Gabe grinned. "But that young *Señora* Castillo, she was born to cook. See the way she took over the cookshack, once she got over being timid? Can't blame her for hanging back before, nor little *Conejo* being scared as a rabbit. Having her husband die, leavin' 'em in a company cabin with no way to leave . . . that's a tough row to hoe. And didn't we have a fine feast, though! I do believe I could stay another couple of days and cook up a bunch more turkey."

"Maybe on the way back," Eben suggested. "Now, where did Mr. Smith say our lady Townsend would be headed for next? We should be getting fairly close to her place, I'd think."

Gabe took a folded scrap of paper from his shirt pocket and studied it.

"According to Smith's map, we ought to cross a creek this afternoon. Then we'll see a pass through the hills. We look for a stone tower. A *torreón*. Marks the east edge of *Señor* Galvez's *hacienda*. Smith said we'd come over a rise and see it."

Gabe and Eben topped a hill just after noon, and there was no sign of the Galvez *torreón*. But the landscape was memorable all the same. They were on a rising of land where a man could tell that summer had truly arrived. Chubby pine trees spread resin incense on the light breeze. Blue jays warbled and yodeled; chickadees sent out cheerful trills and pine squirrels chittered. The long slope welcomed them with wildflowers, purple and yellow, while new grass and fresh rabbit brush and mountain mahogany showed a dozen shades of green.

Gabe was remarking that it was an excellent fine day—an observation he had made more than once—when he was interrupted by two gunshots.

One shot was a sharp crack, like that of a rifle. The other was a deeper *whump* like a black powder pistol might make.

"Trouble?" Eben asked.

"Might be. Or somebody hunting supper," Gabe said.

They turned to ride toward the gunshots, remaining watchful and staying among the pines wherever possible. They heard another rifle shot and saw the puff of smoke. When they came to an opening in the trees they saw the shooter. Or shooters. One man was clearly visible behind a stump, aiming across the open ground at a derelict log cabin. Gabe glimpsed another man moving down a shallow gully.

"Another one," Eben whispered, pointing.

The third one was behind a dead cottonwood not far from the first man.

A shot came from the cabin, announcing itself with a puff of white smoke and the dull *whump* sound.

"Somebody in that cabin seems to have gotten himself into a pickle," Gabe whispered. "Let's hide these horses and work our way in a little closer. Got your gun?"

Eben twisted around to get his revolver from his saddlebag. It was only a small caliber Smith and Wesson. But at least it was a gun. Gabe dismounted and filled his chaps pocket with extra shells for the carbine. He checked his Colt. They made an unlikely looking pair, the dwarfish Eben and the lanky cowboy, sneaking from tree to tree and rock to bush until they came to where they had a better view of the cabin. In its heyday it had been a stronghold. Thick log walls, small windows like gun ports, and the fireproof sod roof showed that it was built to hold off Indian attacks. The builders had also cleared all the trees for fifty yards around. To the rear of the little log building was a log corral.

"Look at that," Gabe said, pointing.

The lady Townsend's buggy was parked next to the corral. One wheel was broken. Over the log wall, Gabe could see the ears of several horses.

A rifle shot from behind the dead cottonwood was answered by a *whump* from the cabin.

"Somebody's in there, for sure," Eben said. "Probably the lady. What you gonna do?"

"Fix things, I guess. You take my Colt. Scout yourself a half-dozen hiding places to shoot from. Savvy? Like that old log over there. When you see my signal, take a shot from there. Then skip real quick behind that stump over there. Got the idea?"

Eben nodded. "What's your signal gonna be?"

"Not sure yet," Gabe said. "Smoke from the chimney, maybe. Just stay hidden. You'll know when. Then you shoot and move and make 'em think there's a bunch of you."

Eben slid the heavy .44 into his belt. Gabe gave him the shells from his gun belt.

"Looks like I can slip from tree to tree until the trees give out," Gabe said. "Then I'll get down on all fours and try t' work closer. After that I reckon there's about fifty yards of open ground to cover."

Eben got ready to cover Gabe's run. When Gabe came to the edge of the woods he got into a crouch and went slithering through the brush like a fox sneaking up to a henhouse. Then the sage gave out, and he faced open ground between himself and the cabin.

"Well," Gabe said to himself, drawing a deep breath, "as old Plato remarked, it's better to begin sooner instead of later."

Without waiting for gunfire to cover his movement, Gabe made his dash for the cabin. Weaving, ducking, legs pumping up and down like a man being chased by a mad bull, he heard a couple of shots fired and thought maybe he felt something go through his sleeve. He finished his wild run with a belly slide that brought him up against the log wall. He scrambled into the angle between the horse pen and cabin, where the shooters couldn't see him. He hoped.

"Made it," he panted. "For now, anyway."

"Who is there?" came a Spanish male voice from within. *"Quién es?"*

"Un amigo," Gabe wheezed. "Who's in there?"

He looked up and saw the small window. There was silence, then another voice, one with a familiar ring to it.

"Mr. Gabriel?"

It was Dobé.

"Hiya, Dobé," Gabe said. "I saw your buggy out here. Havin' any trouble?"

"You had better get yourself inside," said a sharp female voice. "I will *not* be responsible for your getting shot out there."

"Yes, ma'am." Gabe grinned.

The next rifle slug smacked into the logs just under his boot-eel as he bellied in over the windowsill and tumbled ungracefully to the earthen floor. When his eyes got accustomed to the gloom, he saw the lady Townsend sitting on a bench against the wall. Dobé was standing next to one of the windows with his shotgun. At the next window stood a stranger whose flat-brimmed hat and embroidered short jacket were those of a *vaquero*. In his hands he held a formidable lever action Henry rifle.

There was another man in the cabin with them, one who also wore a large Mexican *sombrero*, not as wide as that of the *vaquero*. And embroidered. He sported a short jacket, also embroidered, and tight riding trousers tucked into elaborate boots. A Mexican *charro*. He was not a *vaquero:* he was a *don*. His weapon, which he held almost carelessly pointed in Gabe's general direction, was a big cap and ball revolver.

Gabe made a very slight bow toward the gentleman.

"I am Gabriel Hugh Allen from the Keystone Ranch," he said, using the formal speech one was expected to use when addressing a Spanish person of importance.

"Juan Gregorio de Galvez," said the other. He did not introduce his *vaquero;* it would be bad manners to assume that a stranger would be interested in such mundane matters as the name of a man's employee.

"I am here to see if I can help," Gabriel said.

He heard the sniff even before he saw the lady stand up.

"Help?" she said. "If you had 'helped,' perhaps we would not be hostages to those ruffians outside. Ugh! You still smell of roasted bird flesh. You just *had* to play at being a kitchen helper again, didn't you? If you had scouted our trail, perhaps we would not have been set upon by bandits. Perhaps Dobé would not have driven over the rock that broke the wheel. As it is, we have only the good offices of *Señor* Galvez to thank for our very lives. Our very lives! Kitchen boy! Hmmpf!"

Two shots came from the trees, and a bullet smacked into the wall opposite the window where the *vaquero* stood.

"I hate to correct you, ma'am," Gabe grinned, "but I believe the proper term is *'Don'* Galvez, not *'Señor'* Galvez. Right? *Es verdad?*"

"*Sí,*" said the gentleman. "But . . . kitchen help? What is this?"

"Long story," Gabe grinned. "Very long story."

"If you wished to help," the lady said, "why didn't you begin shooting when you saw we were in this difficulty? Instead, you plunge in and place yourself in the middle."

The *vaquero* leaned out the window and took a shot at the ambushers.

"I wasn't sure who was in here," Gabe grinned. "I didn't want to shoot up a legal posse trying to smoke out some outlaws, for instance. A man shouldn't take a chance of shooting innocent people."

"Commendable," said *Don* Galvez. "Most commendable."

"Maybe we'd better get to work on this problem of yours.

Excuse me for sayin' so, but I don't believe this cabin is your usual dwelling. I've seen *casas* a lot fancier than this."

Don Galvez chuckled.

"You are not subtle. But you are polite. I like that. No, you are quite correct, *Señor* Gabriel. Unfortunately, my *casa* lies some distance away from here. Worse than that, my employees do not expect me to return any time soon, so there is little chance of anyone searching for us."

More shots came from the trees. Bullets whacked into the logs. The *don* continued his narrative as if he had not noticed.

"The manner of it is this," he said. "With my *vaquero* here, I was making inspection of the more distant corners of my *hacienda* when—like you, I suspect—I heard the sounds of gunfire. What I discovered was a lady and her driver. They suffered a broken wheel while fleeing from three or four brigands. Or renegades, perhaps they are. Lady and driver had taken refuge in this old outbuilding. These outlaws prevent us doing anything toward repairing the wheel or sending for assistance. And so here we are. *Ratónes* in a trap, no?"

"Well," Gabe smiled, "like Plato said, there's rats and then there's rats."

"Plato?"

"Never mind. Got any sort of plan?"

"Nothing, *nada*. Perhaps when night comes one of us might go for help. My *vaquero* is willing to attempt it."

"Mind if we try my idea first?" Gabe said.

"Be my guest," said *Don* Galvez.

"Good," Gabe said. "What've we got that'll burn? Any kindling, old cloth, such stuff as that? We need t' send a thick smoke up the chimney. For a signal."

The *vaquero* brought some rags from a corner. He opened a trapdoor in the back wall, an opening into the horse pen barely large enough for him to crawl through. He came back with a clump of dry rabbit brush and a handful of brown juniper twigs.

"That'll do," Gabe said. "I'm glad to know about that trapdoor, too. Here's what we do. I'll get a smoke coming out the chimney. That'll tell my partner up in the woods yonder t' start shooting. He'll use two guns and he'll keep moving around. Leastways I hope he does. So with any luck, those *hombres* out there will think there's more than one of him. If he gets 'em distracted I'm going to slip outside with my carbine and surprise them. I'd rather fight in the open than all cooped up in here."

"So your plan is to crawl out the trapdoor and around the building," the *don* said.

"No. Not at all. My plan is for the lady and Dobé to crawl out there if this scheme starts to go south. Their last chance might be to climb aboard those horses and light a shuck toward your place."

"Go south? Light a shuck?"

"Never mind. My point is, I'm going out the front door standing up. The idea of crawling and shooting from ambush doesn't appeal to me."

"My compliments, *Señor*," *Don* Galvez said. "Spoken like a gentleman. I will, of course, be at your side."

Dobé and the *vaquero* got ready at the windows flanking either side of the door. Gabe put a match to the pile of cloth and brush. In less than a minute Eben saw the signal and took a carefully aimed shot at the hiding place of the man nearest him. Firing twice, he thought he had nicked the ambusher but didn't stay to find out. Quick as a mouse he scurried to the next place, threw himself down, and hauled out the .44 Colt.

"Wham!"

A second outlaw looked up from his concealment, amazed that someone was behind him. He saw the gun smoke and snapped off a shot toward it, but by that time Eben was on his way to the next stump.

"Bang! Bang!" went the Smith and Wesson. One of the attackers stood up and looked in all directions to see where the shots were coming from. Wisps of gun smoke hung over a rock here and next to a tree there. Another heavy "Wham!" of a .44 came from some bushes almost out of pistol range. He yelled to one of his confederates, who also stood up to look for the source of the shots. In a moment four outlaws were on their feet swinging their guns here and there, pointing into the woods. It took them a minute to remember the cabin.

They saw two men walking toward them as calmly as if strolling out to look at some cattle or get a drink. One was tall and wore Levi's and had a cowboy hat. The other was less tall and was dressed like a Mexican grandee with his big *sombrero*. The cowboy held a carbine. The Mexican held a revolver.

"Who the hell . . . ?" said one of the outlaws.

"Get 'em!" suggested another outlaw. "Get 'em!"

Gabe and *Don* Galvez presented a picture of perfect calm as they waited for their opponents to declare their intentions. The outlaw who had yelled "get 'em!" took a shot, but he was walking backward at the time and the bullet went several yards to the right of the two quiet men. *Don* Galvez turned sideways and raised his weapon in the classic offhand stance for shooting targets.

"Con permiso," he said to Gabe. "If you will allow me."

"Of course," Gabe said.

Don Galvez cocked the hammer, sighted down the long barrel—ignoring the fact that the outlaw was steadying himself for a second shot—and squeezed the trigger. The bullet did not go squarely into the man's heart, which was where *Don* Galvez had aimed, but sufficiently close to render that particular organ permanently inoperable. The outlaw dropped like a ruptured sack of grain.

"Señor," said the *don,* pointing to a second man who had just

fired at them.

The single word, *"señor,"* meant that the *caballero* was offering his guest the next shot. "If you please," it meant. Or, "This man who is now discharging his weapon in our direction, I would be honored if you would deal with him."

Gabe took the shot from the hip. The Winchester went "carrr-ang!" and the outlaw was looking down at a bloodstain spreading across his shirt. He sat down abruptly, his neck bowed as if he needed to get a better look at the damage, and he moved no more.

A third outlaw came charging toward them in a fury, shooting his revolver as he ran. Gabe saw a puff of smoke from behind the man, which was Eben trying to help, but Eben's slug either missed or had no effect. The man kept coming like a frenzied dog with rabies. And *Don* Galvez dealt with him as he would deal with a foaming-mouth mad canine, namely by assuming the sideward stance, arm extended. He sighted along the barrel and calmly dispatched the brute with a fifty-grain ball placed precisely between the eyes.

The fourth man came out of concealment holding his rifle above his head as if intending to surrender. But when he got within twenty yards of Gabe and *Don* Galvez he changed his mind. He snapped his gun down and fired it; however, he was in such a hurry to kill one of them that he jerked the trigger before the barrel had come down far enough. His bullet sailed high over the cabin and wounded a pine branch somewhere back in the woods. Gabe and *Don* Galvez looked at one another as if wordlessly coming to an agreement over who had the honor of replying to this display of treachery. With the apologetic look of a man about to take the last strawberry, *Don* Galvez cocked his gun and fired from the hip. For the *bandito* it settled forever the question of whether he wanted to try another shot.

★ ★ ★ ★ ★

"My *casa* lies there," *Don* Galvez said to Gabe, pointing into the distance. "You are seeing the *torreón* now, the stone tower from which a sentry watches for my return. I will ride back and tell the lady, if you will excuse me."

Gabe and Eben rode on, admiring the pastures and the fields, the good road and fences. Behind them, Dobé drove the lady Townsend in her buggy. *Don* Galvez's *vaquero* had repaired the wheel well enough to get them to the ranch.

"*Señora,*" said the *don*, wheeling his horse to ride beside the buggy, "it is my *casa*. Please make it home for yourself, your driver, and your riders for as long as you wish."

"Those two are *not* my 'riders,' " the lady huffed. "I have mentioned to you before. He—the tall one—comes from the kitchen of the Keystone Ranch. His employer sent him as a joke, an insult. He is not a Keystone rider. Merely a sort of servant, a low one at that."

"Ah, *Señora,*" said *Don* Galvez. "I would not presume to make you a lecture upon this point, nor would a *caballero* ever accuse a lady of being in error. You understand? However, it is as a gentleman that I must come to the defense of this *hombre* who rides before us. Have you perhaps heard of the difference between what my people call a *vaquero* and a *caballero*?"

"One and the same, I would think," the lady Townsend replied.

"There is some difference. You see, the *vaquero*, such as my brave *hombre* who now follows behind to assure we are not attacked again, means 'a man of cattle,' a skilled rider and a man also skilled in the ways of cattle. He takes his title from *vaca*, the cow, and carries it with pride. The *caballero*, on the other hand, is a horseman. In English, perhaps, there is the word 'cavalier'? Also from *cabal*, the horse. The code of *el caballero* is that of honor in all things. Chivalry? You know this word, I think? This Gabriel, surely he is *caballero*. He would not crawl from a hole and kill from ambush. He stands facing his enemy and fights with honor. With courtesy. This is an unusual *hombre*, *Señora*, an unusual *hombre* indeed. I would not be surprised if one day he becomes one of the most renowned riders of the famed Keystone Ranch. With pride I welcome him to my table and to my home. I stood with him in battle, one of the best times of my life. But come! I see the sentry waving to us from the *torreón*! The entire *casa* will be coming out to greet us."

CHAPTER TEN
LEON SNATH, FOREMAN

Being a student of chivalry and practitioner of hospitality, *Don* Gregorio de Galvez ate two suppers each night. The lady made it clear that she regarded the *don*'s other guest, Gabriel Hugh Allen, to be a lowly pretender to the title of Keystone Rider, a mere *peon* from the Keystone Ranch *cocina* who hoped to become a hero by attempting a rescue of her mistress. The only way she would tolerate having him at the same table as herself was if he sat at the far end among the *vaqueros* and household staff.

But to this demand *Don* Galvez could not accede.

"Surely at the table of *Don* Pendragon our young man has a seat of respect," he told her.

"No," she said. "No. I saw him serving and clearing away dirty dishes. I tell you, Mr. Pendragon sent him with me as a joke. I will not eat with him."

"I cannot believe it. The small one, Eben, he is in the service of the blacksmith. You have not encountered the blacksmith? Trust me, if this Eben rides with Gabriel, it means he is no ordinary man."

"He certainly tries to convey that impression," she said with a sniff. "At every opportunity. You may think he is someone special, but I do not. He will sit at the end of the table, or else I will eat alone."

Don Galvez had an instinct for these things. The young man was no ordinary *vaquero;* it would be an insult to seat him below the salt. Therefore in the name of graciousness *Don* Galvez ate twice. Taking early supper with the lady, he gave her the respect she was due. Later in the evening, when she had retired to her rooms, he ordered that the dining table be prepared again. Now *Señor* Gabriel sat at the *don's* right hand.

At both meals the richly oiled oak of the long table reflected the light of candles ensconced in silver candelabras. A mute servant saw to it that the silver wine chalices were always filled and that neither the *don* nor any of his guests had to reach for a serving dish or ask for a condiment. One had merely to glance at the salt dish or the bread plate and it was set in front of them. The *don* noticed that Gabriel accepted such service with polite graciousness. The young man was neither surprised nor seemed embarrassed when the servant held his chair for him, another sign to *Don* Galvez that he had the natural deportment of a true *caballero*.

They were joined at supper by the *don's* most valuable rider, the *vaquero* who had been at the battle of the log cabin.

"If you don't mind my saying so," Gabe said, "you gentlemen seem to be a long ways north. We don't see many Mexicans living this far from the southwest."

"Ah," *Don* Galvez smiled, "you are correct. Please understand I do not say this as any kind of—censure?—of your *region*, but yes, we would prefer to live in Mexico where the winters are not so long. I am, you see, in exile. My brothers resented my claim upon the family fortune. With a few dozen faithful *vaqueros*, I made the long trip north in the hope of discovering gold with which to redeem my inheritance. We found no gold. However, we found a wealth of cattle. The raising of *primo* cattle is in my blood. I know nothing about digging for gold or silver. As you know, it takes years to build a purebred herd. There are many risks and dangers. But we have—is 'persevered' the word?—and soon we are on our way back to the land of *llanos* and *mesas* with a magnificent herd of fine livestock."

"And so, *Señor* Gabriel, you have ridden to the Keystone from Kansas Territory, you say?" the *vaquero* asked.

"In a way, yes," Gabe replied. "I took the long road around gettin' there from Kansas. But us westerners like to be on the move. It's the way of my family. Lost our father in Kansas. Then my three older brothers lit out for the cattle trails and gold country. Mother moved herself, me, and my sister down to Cimarron country. That's where I grew up on *chiles* and *frijoles refritos.* She's an educated lady. Could have been a schoolteacher. She met a farmer near *los Robles,* and before we knew it they got married and moved us back to Kansas to raise crops. Call it co-incidence or irony, but I had a brother who left before I was born and rode for the Keystone Ranch awhile. Then he traveled south and married into a big *hacienda* near the *Río Purgatorio.* You see? I went where he'd been, and he ended up where I'd been! And we still haven't met one another."

The *vaquero* cut and stabbed another piece of meat. It was halfway to his mouth when his fork halted in midair. He stared at Gabe as if seeing him for the first time.

"Ah! *Señor!*" the *vaquero* said. "Forgive me for speaking of it, but I know who you are! It was your *madre,* I think, who was of help to my brother Lupe and me as we were making the journey from Durango. As you say, a strong woman of books and learn-ing! On the Cimarron!"

Turning to *Don* Galvez, the *vaquero* spoke with careful respect. But his speech was tinged with enthusiasm, for he had made the realization that he was seated at the table with not one but *two* great gentlemen.

"The lady of whom I speak," he continued, "she had another name. Not 'Allen.' But the boy I remember. *Banditos,* vigilantes, someone fired upon Lupe and me from ambush. The lady and young boy hurried with guns, drove these bad *hombres* away.

She—what is the word—saw to our wounds, gave us food, a place to sleep. We spoke together, many times. She told us of this son who lives below the *Rio Purgatorio*. She is—if I may say it, *Señor?*"

"Sure," Gabe replied. "Don't imagine the *don* would tell anybody. Go ahead."

"*Gracias, Señor. Don* Galvez, if I may be permitted, you have the honor of having as your guest *el hijo del*—the son of—*la hermana de Don* Pendragon. *El hermano de Don* Godinez."

"*Verdad!*" *Don* Galvez exclaimed. Not only was *Señor* Pendragon of the Keystone a renowned figure, but a recently married *caballero* who had inherited the Godinez *hacienda* south of the Purgatory River and was now making a name for himself as a leader of men.

"Then your brother, it is he who married the young *Señora* Godinez and took her family name to honor her father. A much respected man in that region. But the lady," *Don* Galvez continued. "*Señora* Townsend. You do not wish her to know who you are? That you are the nephew of the famed *Don* Arthur Pendragon?"

"No, sir," Gabe grinned. "Not for a while yet. Seems to make her happy to keep treatin' me like a kitchen boy. Let's just let her go on doing it awhile. Besides, I want to figure her out a little more. There's something that just doesn't ring right about that lady."

"It is—you will excuse my saying it—a difficult thing for you, putting up with her harsh words when you do not have to."

"Plato said a man's of little worth who can't bear with a woman."

True to his word, *Don* Galvez kept Gabe's secret. Nonetheless, during their final supper together, he took the opportunity to remind the *señora* that he felt the highest respect for the young man. Few men, he said, would risk themselves as he had when he came to their rescue.

"It is a rare thing, a man who would walk out the door into the guns, preferring to die on his feet than to strike from hiding like a serpent. No," the *don* said, "this is the conduct of a man of high bearing, a man born to chivalry."

The lady looked at him with her chin high. Tomorrow she would continue on with her journey. She would not be surprised to find the grub rider, the kitchen helper, tagging along behind. As for her opinion of Mr. Pendragon and his Keystone Ranch . . . it was better not to ask.

On the morning of their departure Dobé and Eben were loading luggage into the buggy. Gabe was tying his bedroll behind his saddle. *Don* Galvez came riding out in full costume. His pale dun horse was resplendent with silver mounted saddle and bridle, the leather carved and embossed all the way from the top of the flat saddle horn down to the sharp points of his *tapaderos. Must be a pretty sturdy horse,* Gabe thought. The leather and silver looked like it weighed as much as the rider.

The man himself wore the short black jacket, all embroidered, the tight trousers with silver *conchos* running from hip to cuff, high heeled boots, and big embroidered sombrero, which he solemnly removed to bow to the *señora* in the buggy.

"If the *señora* will permit," he said graciously, "my *vaqueros* and I will escort her to the edge of my lands."

He raised his left hand slightly.

The six mounted Mexicans took up positions on either side of the buggy. They were armed with short-barreled rifles and revolvers in addition to the big knives they carried on their belts. *Don* Galvez rode ahead of the buggy. Gabriel joined him.

"My regrets. I cannot accompany you to your destination," *Don* Galvez said as they rode along.

"It is an understanding I have with *Señor* Karl Rothaus whom you seek. A truce. At the edge of my land is a trail across badlands. A dry *llano* of cactus and sage. Water is very scarce. After eight or nine leagues there is a river. Neither of us, by agreement, will cross into the territory of the other."

"What kind of man is he?" Gabriel asked.

"Twice I send messages to *Señor* Rothaus. Both *vaqueros* beseeched me never to send them again. They are brave men, but what they saw . . ."

"Rothaus is that bad?" Gabe asked.

"Oh, *sí*! But the place, you understand. My men have a term for the entrance. *El Paso de Peligro.*"

"The Dangerous Pass. Don't care much for the sound of it."

"Prepare, *amigo*. The lady in the buggy, she knows what lies ahead there, even though she took a northern route to reach Keystone Ranch. She has seen skeletons hanging in trees. The field, the bones of horses, saddles rotting away. It is said that he has killed forty men. It is also said he has the big *rancor*. The grudge. Against the Keystone. He wishes—as I understand it—to have the bravest men of Pendragon come and fight with him. The *hombre* who told me this told me that *Señor* Rothaus becomes enraged with drink. He fires his guns into the wall, shouting for the *caballeros* called Link and Pasque and Kyle Owen and Garth to try to defeat him. It is his passion."

"Sounds like a heck of a grudge, that's for sure."

"Word came to me: he holds a lady in thrall in order to make Keystone riders come for him. Vengeance? A grudge, who knows? It is said he wanders his place by night, unable to sleep for the hate in his heart."

"No rest from evil, huh?"

"Pardon?" said *Don* Galvez.

"Plato again." Gabe smiled sadly. "Plato said some people—like some nations—never have any rest from evil."

★ ★ ★ ★ ★

In the afternoon they crossed the last of the spring-fed creeks and rode onto a plain where the grass was drab and sparse. They looked out on a seemingly endless expanse of short, angry cactus, greasewood, and yucca. The brush seemed locked in a struggle with the arid wind. A light breeze rose up, sighing as if in mourning. It parched the lips and grated the eyes and filled the ears with a never-changing note of loneliness. A faint two-wheel track led out into the emptiness. In the far distance, under the shimmering heat waves, Gabe saw the track take long bending turns, dipping down into arroyos only to reappear again.

"If Moses saw this," Gabe smiled, "his people'd still be working for the Pharaoh."

"An hour past sunset," *Don* Galvez said, "you will arrive at water, a few trees. After that, it is a long day to come to the place of *Señor* Rothaus. Perhaps you will need to make a camp and divide your journey."

The good *caballero* made his formal farewell speech to the lady, and then gripped the hand of Gabe with affectionate respect. He was caught in a dilemma, wishing on the one side to linger with them and make further talk, to indulge in more advice and cautions, while knowing they needed to be on their way if they were to reach water before dark. He assured Gabe of his friendship, offered him his *casa* as his home whenever needed. Almost overcome with the emotion, he made his ultimate pledge.

"You will convey to *Don* Pendragon," he said, "this message from *Don* Gregorio de Galvez. If he is ever in need, whatever the danger, he is to send word to me. Wherever I am. Even from old Mexico I will come with a score of *vaqueros* at my back to fight alongside his Keystone Riders."

"I will tell him, *Señor. Muchas gracias, y adios.*"
"*Con dios.*"

They reached the far edge of the barrens at noon of the third day. The sun had been blazing down for hours. Heat rose in transparent undulating waves, making sage, saltbrush, and yucca spikes appear to be weaving and dancing like plants underwater. Only there was no water. The sun had sapped the moisture from everything, from the plants and the earth itself, leaving only husks and stalks sticking out of the dead brown crust. The very dirt was nothing but lifeless powder. From the buggy wheels it rose in feeble, dispirited puffs only to fall over upon itself and sink into the ground again, too hot even to form dust clouds.

Gabriel and Eben rode across the top of the last featureless, grassless hill of cactus-infested sage land and saw a greener swale off in the distance. There were dark dots against the green, which could be cattle grazing, and some puffs of shadowed green, which were probably groves of trees.

"Probably find us a spring down there," Gabriel said.

Eben pointed down the hill at a crooked line of tilted posts. Each post had a weathered scrap of board nailed to it.

Without waiting for the buggy, they put heels to their tired horses and rode down to investigate. They were on land claimed by the notorious Rothaus. His signs were crudely lettered things, nothing more than box ends and bits of lumber upon which someone had painted warnings against trespass. They were intended for the Mexican "neighbor" whose property abutted the far side of the long reach of badlands. In bad Spanish they proclaimed "NO ENTRADA PERMISO" and "ENTRA PRO-HIBITAR" and "NO TANGA PERMISSIO."

The message of most effect was the signboard on which the

painter had given up trying to use Spanish and had simply drawn skull and crossbones in black paint.

At the sluggish creek they waited for the buggy. They let the horses drink and filled the canteens before moving on. The cart track led through tangles of wild plum and willow where shadows seemed to spy on them. Dobé glanced back with nervous apprehension lest there be silent dark riders appearing behind them. He held the lines in one hand and kept his other hand on the shotgun in his lap. At each unexpected noise, even a rabbit in dry leaves, Eben reached for his .38 revolver.

The track twisted one way and then another, sometimes crossing wet places of floating slime and duckweed. Sometimes the trail emerged on a rise of ground where they could see a little distance ahead, but it always led down again into the shade.

Gabe was wishing *Don* Galvez and his *vaqueros* had come along when he remembered the mirage he'd seen the morning on the hill, plucking chickens when phantom riders rode down out of the sky. And instantly he was no longer alone. He didn't know what that mirage meant. But remembering it, he recognized that he wasn't feeling alone.

The track began to climb upward. Toward the top of the hill the willows and thickets pulled back and the sun found them again. Now they could see grazing land punctuated by rocky knobs with pine trees. Far in the distance a horseman seemed to pause and regard them; he continued on his way, vanishing around one of the tree-covered hillocks.

They followed the wagon track into creek bottoms and up long grassy hills. They opened a gate through one fence and then another, and just as they caught a scent of woodsmoke they saw five horsemen riding toward them.

When the riders drew near, Gabe heard the lady Townsend's loud "harrumph!" The strangers were something to sniff at. Two of them wore shirts that had been white, but now were a vile shade of gray over-streaked with yellow, as if the wearers had used them to wipe up some vomit. Another wore a calico shirt under a ragged vest, both bleached by sun and stained in sweat. Their broad hats slouched and drooped as if the wearers were sitting in a downpour of rain. Like their hats, the men slouched in their saddles. They stared at the intruders with insolent, bloodshot eyes.

The man who rode forward was the ugliest of the lot. He gave the lady Townsend a facial expression he probably thought was a smile, one side of his mouth arching below the tattered end of an unkempt mustache. Anything but ingratiating, it revealed two broken teeth and two intact teeth, all four of which were the color of rotten egg yolk.

"Boys," he said, turning back to the other riders, "we got us some visitors. Dick, you ride and tell Rothaus."

"Why me?" whined the one in calico and rags. "I wouldn't even git there till dark. Send Scabby."

The smiling foreman drew his weapon, a formidable Navy conversion of Remington manufacture, cocked it, and calmly sent lead blasting through the floppy sleeve of Dick's shirt. The smoking, smoldering bullet hole did little to improve the appearance of the garment.

"You ride for Rothaus, damn you. Or I'll bury you right here."

Deciding that obedience was the better part of valor, Dick rode.

The foreman made a display of twirling the Remington on his forefinger before dropping it into the holster with a flourish. He now bestowed his mustache-driven, yellow-toothed smile upon Gabe.

"Snath," he announced, as if anyone of worldly experience would instantly recognize the name.

"Pardon?" said Gabe.

"Snath," the other repeated. "I'm Leon Snath."

The way he pronounced the name seemed to convey the idea that in all the Christian world it was a name synonymous with death, mayhem, and general fear, a name men whispered behind their hands while casting baleful glances about them lest they be overheard.

Gabe chuckled, just a little. But he grinned a lot.

"Afraid you have the jump on me, partner," he said engagingly. "Don't know as I've ever heard of you."

Snath was visibly annoyed at this. Not so much at not being heard of, but at the other man's effrontery in saying so.

"Search that buggy," Snath ordered his men. "Let's see what we got us here."

A tableau of frozen attitudes ensued.

Dobé sat with his shotgun halfway raised; Eben had his hand on the butt of his .38 in its shoulder holster; the four horsemen remained stiffly posed like men who intended to ride forward to the buggy but who had gone petrified. Their eyes were on Gabe, and they were motionless because his Colt's revolver had appeared in his hand.

"No," Gabe explained. "We're not goin' to do that."

The three subordinates drew back. The one called Snath glared and put his hand on the grip of his own gun. Gabe raised his Colt to eye level and aimed along the barrel like a marksman sighting on a target.

"And we're not goin' to do that, either," he said. "Why don't you fellows just turn around real peaceful and follow after your *compadre?* You all go tell this Rothaus gentleman we've arrived. I imagine he knows who we are . . . or at least who this lady is. We've got business with him."

Snath threw a shifty glance at his henchmen and began to sidle his horse off to the side, real casual, like he was getting out of the way of the buggy. Gabe kept his eye on Snath while making certain he could see any movement the others might make. He kept the Colt aimed.

"Ain't intendin' to harm the lady," Snath said apologetically, raising his hands in resignation. "But we ain't gonna let just anybody ride in carryin' anything they want, neither. We got orders t' get her to Rothaus *un*-molested. You, you're another story. Rothaus never said nothin' about not hurtin' you. Matter of fact, we got word you killed some friends of ours a while back."

"Heard about that, did you?" Gabe said. "I suppose that Johnny Reb told you."

Snath sidled a few feet farther. Gabe would have to turn his horse if he wanted to keep facing him. Now there were three back-shooters behind him where he couldn't see what they were up to. If he turned to bring his gun to bear on them, he'd never make the distance. It would take too long to swing the barrel around. Seemed like a standoff. If he shot Snath, the three guns behind him would bring him down. If he turned to deal with the three, either they would get him or Snath would draw and fire as soon as he turned.

"So," he said to himself, "I guess the thing is not to turn."

They were expecting him to make some kind of move. He relaxed his arm, letting the Colt drop until it rested on the saddle horn. He caressed the horse with his heels to urge it forward. The tired mount plodded gently toward Snath's horse like it was some long-lost herd companion he had just recognized. Gabe put on his guileless grin. When his horse's head was nose to nose with Snath's horse, Gabe spoke again.

"See the problem?" he said. "Your men shoot me in the back and they're pretty certain to hit you, too. So. Maybe instead of takin' that risk, why don't you show them how big you can smile? And hand me that cannon you're carryin'. Maybe we can all live to talk t' Mr. Rothaus."

Leon Snath, however, had not become Rothaus's head hench-man without acquiring certain useful skills in the art of human relations, the most notable being guile, duplicity, and cunning. He recognized the cleverness of this lanky stranger's tactic of riding so close to him. Now he figured to use it against him.

"Yeah," he said. "That's if they'd stayed put. I figger you can't take a chance. Turnin' around t' look, y'd see my men comin' up on your back. I'd say you got about ten seconds before they're so close as not t' miss."

Gabe studied the other man's eyes. They were not focused on anyone immediately behind him, but were looking off at some distance instead. Could be another trick, but he didn't think so. Gabe lazily raised the muzzle of Mister Colt's .44 so it was aimed between the top two buttons of Snath's grimy shirt.

"What would you say are the odds that I'll miss?" Gabe asked.

He thumbed back the hammer.

CHAPTER ELEVEN

FRANCIS BACON AND A GREASY SHIRT

Gabriel Hugh Allen had the upper hand. His problem was what to do about it. What would a real Keystone rider do? The lady would be watching. So would the blacksmith's helper. What did they expect of a man who rode for Art Pendragon?

Link Lochlin was Pendragon's top hand. What would Link do with Leon Snath and his unwashed confederates? Probably use his Colt to knock Snath unconscious, then deal with the other three.

Sudden, deliberate action. That was Link's way. Quick, precise force.

Gabe preferred cunning.

Among his mother's books there had been one that was his particular favorite, after the story of Plato. He first noticed this book because it had the word "Bacon" on the spine. Little Gabe was fond of bacon. The book had nothing to do with bacon, of course. But he worked his way through the words, asking his mother to read to him and tell him what the words meant. Mr. Bacon's name wasn't the only funny thing about him; he wrote funny, old-fashioned words. Sometimes even Gabe's mother couldn't understand what the book said.

One evening he lay on the floor reading in the light of the fireplace. Mr. Bacon was talking about "cunning." Gabe's mother explained cunning. She used vivid examples drawn from life and her imagination.

Gabe was a hunter. Once he got the idea what "cunning"

meant he started to see it in coyotes he stalked, and in prairie chickens that pretended to be injured so as to lead him away from their nests. Cunning, his mother told him, is what keeps the fox alive. And probably Mr. Deuters, the horse trader. Gabe saw the connection.

So it was cunning that made Gabe unexpectedly turn his back on Leon Snath.

He ignored the yellow-toothed leader altogether and rode back to the three unpleasant horsemen clumped near the buggy. Snath remained in the clearing, bewildered. As Gabe approached, the three henchmen put their hands to their guns; Gabe grinned at them. The muzzle of his .44 drooped carelessly toward the ground. A gesture of peace.

"Gentlemen," he greeted them.

They said nothing. Their narrowed eyes looked like those of snakes watching a wagon wheel coming.

"Gentlemen," he repeated. "Your *Segundo* and I have reached an impasse. It concerns who is going to shoot whom. As this lady probably told you, I'm only a kitchen helper from the Keystone. Don't really have a stake in the matter. On the other hand, it would do my career and my reputation a whole world of good if I could be the one."

"The one what?" the short one asked.

"The one to finish off Rothaus. Seems he's been in a decline lately."

"Decline?" growled the one with the unshaven upper lip. "What you talkin' about, 'decline'?"

"Hmmm?" Gabe said. He acted as if he had surprised himself by mentioning it.

"Oh. Nearing his end, you mean? Well, it's just that Mr. Snath probably heard the talk that's going around. Rothaus is just about finished. Rothaus has come to the attention of various agencies. Regulators, vigilantes, the territorial militia. Believe me, his day is about over. Snath's probably been thinking where he might look for his next job. Getting himself shot dead would put a crimp in his plans. You see?"

"Wait a minnit. Y' sayin' that's why he ain't shot you yet?"

"I believe so. Hard to tell. At any rate, I rode over to see if you gents were going to interfere with us. If Snath and I had a gentlemanly duel, I mean."

"Why not?" the first one growled. "We're just doin' what Rothaus tells us."

"Of course," Gabe said. "Of course you are. Is Rothaus as insane as people say he is? Never mind. You have to do what he tells you. Right up to the end."

Gabe's voice dropped to a conspiratorial whisper.

"I might point out that Snath allowed me to come riding up to you three with my gun drawn. Didn't make a move to stop me. To keep you from being shot."

There was a long silence. One might call it a thoughtful silence. Or a confused silence.

"He's right," the unshaved lip finally muttered. "What the hell's the matter with Snath, anyway?"

"Shut up," said the greasy shirt.

"All right," said the third one, who had no distinguishing features other than being short and as greasy and unshaven as the other two. "All right. You an' Snath do your so-called 'duel' and kill each other, but we still gotta take the woman to Rothaus."

"Fine," Gabe smiled. "Just one thing. Mr. Snath is guilty of several murders?"

"Hell, yeah!" the third one boasted. "He gunned down maybe six, eight men this past year. Got a couple skeletons of his own hangin' up toward th' house."

"I see," Gabe said. "Another thing. Mister Snath didn't mention which of you was to take over. In the event of his death. I suppose he forgot."

"That'd be me," said the one in the greasy shirt, jabbing a filthy finger at his own chest.

Keeping with Mr. Francis Bacon's seventh (or perhaps it was the eighth) "pointe of cunnyng," Gabe put on a very thoughtful face. He studied the man as though seeing qualities of leadership. He turned and looked at Snath, who had grown tired of waiting and was coming toward them.

Gabe's expression of concern and decision caused Greasy Shirt to see himself as a possible foreman. He didn't know why he hadn't thought of it. After all, Snath was a sneaky, back-shooting slippery sidewinder.

"I reckon Snath wouldn't want no help shootin' you," he said. "He never asked us for none."

"Good decision." Gabe smiled. "A natural leader."

Gabe backed his horse away and turned and rode toward Snath. Without further preliminaries, Gabe raised his .44 and took careful aim.

"Shoot him, you bastards!"

Snath wheeled his horse and made a break for the trees.

"Shoot him!"

Snath's accomplices preferred to be spectators. Gabe had planted the idea that Rothaus's days were numbered. Why risk getting shot? All they had to do was wait for the outcome. Then they could take the buggy lady and the Keystone man to the main house and see what happened next.

Gabe trotted after Snath until he was within pistol range again. Then he reined left and went trotting away. Looking back over his shoulder, Snath saw Gabe turn away. He'd planned on reaching the trees, taking cover, and shooting his pursuer from ambush. Now it seemed the lanky kid had the same idea and was heading for cover himself. Snath needed to stop him. Right now. If he got away he'd start all kinds of trouble. Snath turned, aimed awkwardly over his horse's haunch, and snapped off two quick shots.

Both of them missed.

Gabe turned his horse and rode back along his own tracks like a mechanical target in a shooting gallery. Snath fired again. This time, Gabe was not as lucky. The bullet creased the leg of his chaps and went into the horse's shoulder. The horse shied and stumbled. Seizing opportunity, Snath spurred his horse and came racing toward Gabe; he crouched down along his horse's neck, his pistol aimed, his eyes intent on the kill. And whether deliberately or accidentally, his next bullet went deep in the neck of Gabe's horse. The head went up and the front hooves left the ground together as he made his last leap and fell off to the side. He crashed to earth, pinning Gabe's leg beneath him. Worse yet, the jolt sent Gabe's Colt flying out of reach.

Snath rode up and aimed deliberately.

But there was no shot to echo across the clearing. Nothing was heard but two men breathing heavily, Snath's horse blowing blasts of air, and Gabe's horse in its final sigh as life left it. The only other sound was a soft, almost apologetic little "click" as the hammer dropped on a brass cartridge that was already empty. Like many owners of that particular firearm, he had learned it was prudent to keep an expended round under the hammer while carrying the gun in a holster.

Prudent, that is, until you needed that sixth bullet.

Snath saw Gabe struggling to reach the Winchester carbine in the saddle scabbard. He reined around and trotted away, fumbling the spent cartridges out of his revolver as he bounced along. Gabe used his free foot to push against the saddle, gained a few inches, sat up with his back in great pain, got finger and thumb on the carbine's stock, drew it out of the leather, and levered a shell into the chamber. When he got himself twisted around he saw Snath trotting back with his revolver reloaded.

Gabe would take no more chances. He squeezed the trigger. Mr. Winchester issued a DuPont summons, and the accused murderer went to appear before the Supreme Judge.

Gabe worked his leg free and got back on his feet. Limping, he managed to catch Snath's horse and get his saddle off the dead one. No one bothered him and no one helped. He rode back to the group waiting at the buggy.

"Guess we oughta go ahead to Rothaus's place," Gabe said. "I dunno. Wonder what we ought to do?"

Francis Bacon's tenth point of "cunnyng": make the *other* person suggest the action you intend, and they will be filled with the certainty that it was their own idea.

"Reckon we'd oughta git this here lady to Rothaus," said Greasy Shirt. "Then I reckon I'll git a couple of men t' come back and bury poor ol' Snath."

"Good plan," Gabe said. "No wonder you're the choice for foreman."

Now it was Gabe and Eben who rode on either side of the buggy. The three unkempt associates of the late Mr. Snath rode at the head of the procession. The track wound in and out of thickets and among scraggly stands of trees and finally into an open expanse of thin grass bordered with tall old cottonwoods, aspens, and lofty ponderosas. A few shacks huddled against the trees, some with lean-to cowsheds and patches of earth where gardens were being attempted. The gardens looked as discouraged as the shacks. A rough mountain cliff made a western wall. Sitting on a rise of ground was a house bigger than the Pendragons' back at the Keystone. It was clearly intended to dominate everything around it.

Lady Townsend looked up at Gabe.

"Don't you see your foolishness?" she asked. "You have had very good luck, but now the danger is too great. Take yourself back to your kitchen while you still can. Get away from these filthy men. You must do it now. Make your escape. Send real Keystone riders to free us. Turn and ride now before it's too late."

"I guess not," Gabe grinned. "Goin' back to kitchen work sounds pretty dull. I suppose I'll go ahead and see this Rothaus and find out what he wants."

Dark clouds gathered cold and gray, chilling the air. The lady Townsend drew a fringed shawl from her valise and pulled it tightly around her shoulders. Dobé hunched into his jacket and glumly gripped the lines. Eben experienced an involuntary shudder and looked to see if Gabriel had noticed. Gabe was listening to a low moan coming from the trees.

Somebody mourning, out in the shadows? Or a breeze blowing across a hollow stump?

The first hanged man was a stone's throw from the road.

A weathered rope ran from the high branch to the neck. The corpse was lashed to the trunk of the tree. Rotting clothes and mummified skin kept the bones from falling. The lady Townsend buried her face in her shawl.

Once past the gruesome sight she looked up only to see another skeleton, this one wearing only boots and a broad hat, lashed securely to the trunk of a tree. Gabe looked out into the grass flats and saw the bones of two dead horses, saddles still in place.

The wind in the trees found another hollow stump on which to play its dirge. Out of the gray overcast a chilling mist began to fall. The next victim of Rothaus's madness was a skeleton sitting in a saddle, the saddle cinched to a cottonwood limb ten feet off the ground. Someone had taken care to tilt the spine forward to make it look as though the bony rider was going hell-bent for leather.

The breeze whined in the skeleton's ribs.

A horse's bones were stacked like firewood under the tree with the grinning horse skull perched on top as a welcome to visitors. Nearby was a skeleton swinging gently from a hangman's noose. The bones were wired together with stovepipe wire; this dead man would hang there until the wire rusted or the rope became dust.

They passed another mummifying corpse tied to a tree, then another skeleton and still another.

"Notice anything?" Gabe said to Eben.

"What?" Eben replied.

"Bullet holes. Probably tied up and shot. But none of 'em in the head. Not a single bullet hole in a skull."

"What do y' guess?"

"I guess Mr. Rothaus isn't a very good shot. Or his eyes aren't so good. He goes for the body, even if his target is already tied to a tree."

"That's supposed to make me feel better?" Eben asked.

"Nope. I'm just saying it, that's all. Look at that poor devil over there, upside down with his boots on."

"Stop it!" cried the lady. "Stop talking as if these poor wretches are some sort of sideshow! Both of you just turn around and ride! Fast! Maybe you can still get away. Go! Go back to your pots and pans, *please!*"

Hearing this, Rothaus's men shifted in their saddles and gripped their revolvers.

"And you'll go on alone, is that it?" Gabe asked. "I got an awful strong feeling you know something. I'll make you a bargain. You tell us the whole story, and I'll consider turning back. If there's time. Looks like we'll be at that house pretty soon now. What's the real truth?"

It was Francis Bacon's last point of "cunnyng': "practice the use of the sudden, bold, and unexpected question," Bacon wrote. And it worked.

156

"Very well! But promise you'll ride away if I tell you!"

"No, I'll promise to consider it, once I know the facts. Best I can offer. What's going on with Rothaus?"

She cast an apprehensive eye at the house in the distance and motioned to Dobé to slow the buggy. She spoke to Gabe in a whisper so the henchmen might not hear her.

"All right. I'll tell you, but you must get away. I am not exactly who I said I was. I *am* Mrs. Lynette Townsend and I am widowed."

"Not 'exactly'?"

"Catherine Surrey is not my employer."

"Oh?"

"She is my sister. Rothaus has her and he is certainly insane. He and his father and younger brother came to claim this whole region. They took up as much homestead land as the law allowed, then preempted all the grazing and water rights for miles around, including our Surrey range."

"I'm with you so far," Gabe said.

"The winter our father passed away from pneumonia, my sister knew she had to do something. We knew we'd lose the entire ranch to the Rothauses. Catherine hired cowboys with quick guns and sudden tempers, terrible men who couldn't get jobs anywhere else. She began the rumor they were Keystone riders. She told everyone we were under the protection of the Keystone Ranch. In truth, we only knew of Mr. Pendragon by reputation. She let it be known that she would hire cowboys who could shoot, to assist these 'Keystone men' in 'cleaning up the territory.' "

"I see," Gabe said. "A young fellow with a gun would find it hard to resist. Most men want to ride with the Keystone."

"Yes," she whispered. "Rothaus's father and brother came riding against the hired guns. Both were killed in a fight that lasted two days. Rothaus was delirious with fever, so he was not there. He recovered, but seemed insane. He challenged our gunmen all alone. He sought them out one by one or even in pairs. He bludgeoned and stabbed them and hung them in trees. As a way of getting 'justice' for the deaths of his brother and father. He rampaged, beating and killing every man who showed up. When he learned—I don't know how—that the riders we had hired were *not* from the Keystone Ranch, he came with a mob of his men. He surrounded our house and took away my sister. He keeps her prisoner in the upper floor of that ugly house."

"Let's hope she's all right," Gabe said. "So you went to get Keystone help? Because he told you to?"

Her eyes moistened and Gabe saw her lip quiver. She sat up straight and clutched her shawl. He glanced past her and saw another skeleton lashed to a tree stump.

"Mr. Rothaus intends to rule this territory. To be the power, as Mr. Pendragon is in his territory. Killing Keystone men will give him the reputation he wants. He is obsessed with the idea. He actually sent me—and poor faithful Dobé—to bring him someone such as Link, someone famous for gun-fighting skill. Or perhaps the one they call Pasque, or Kyle Owen. Then would he release my sister."

"I'm starting to see the picture," Gabe said. "Problem is, you're comin' back with a lowly pot wrangler. What happens when he finds out? We all get killed?"

"No!" she cried, again attracting the attention of the three rough men riding out ahead of them.

"No!" Her voice dropped to a whisper. "We can't let that happen. There has been enough blood spilled because of Catherine and me. I'm going to tell him what happened. I will tell him the truth. That you are a kitchen boy, nothing more. Nothing about those men you dealt with. Nothing about that. With luck, he'll make you a hostage in hopes of bringing the real Keystone riders here. He is a monstrous man, much too big for you to challenge. Don't even think of it. I'll promise to return to the Keystone and bring one of the riders. Perhaps Mr. Pendragon would come."

"You don't learn real fast, do you?" Gabe asked. "Even if you could do that, it's certain to start a full-scale war. Art wouldn't come alone. You'd be looking at a couple of armies facing off. But look: somebody comin'."

"Ride!" she said. "Ride away now! You said you would!"

"Don't think there's time enough," Gabe replied.

Three more riders came at a gallop and stopped alongside Greasy Shirt and his two confederates. Dobé halted the buggy. Gabe couldn't hear what they were saying to each other, but he could guess. Greasy Shirt was gesturing with both hands, describing what happened to Snath.

Without so much as a nod, the new arrivals went around behind the buggy. The other three went ahead. They were on their way to the house, and nobody would be turning back.

They passed through a gap in the pole fence. Gabe saw more mummified corpses, two on one side of the gap and one on the other, both lashed to the fence. They had been arranged to stare up at a second floor window of the old gray house. He saw another dead man, this one lying on its side straddling a saddle, empty eye sockets turned up toward the window.

Gabe heard the lady Townsend's sharp gasp. She, too, was looking up at the second floor window. Looking back at them was one of the prettiest faces he'd ever seen in his life.

"My sister," the lady Townsend whispered. "Still alive!"

"That's where he keeps her?"

"Yes."

Gabe grasped the horror of it. If that was the only window the captive had, she couldn't look outside without seeing those

159

leering skeletons peering up at her. The only *living* beings she could see would be the dirty half-animals who rode in and out of the compound to do Rothaus's work.

Their escort led them down a narrow alley between the looming house and a high barn. The horse's hooves echoed hollowly. The buggy wheels in the dry rocky dirt made a grinding sound. The clouds had come ever lower now, making things so dark that there were no shadows.

"Rothaus won't come out now," the lady Townsend whispered. "Only in daylight. You'll be safe from him until morning. Find a way to escape!"

They emerged from the long alley into a yard surrounded by stables and granaries. Greasy Shirt ordered them to "sit tight." Dismounting and handing his reins to the one with the broken teeth, he disappeared into a black slot in the wall. Gabe looked up and saw another figure standing behind a window. It was a giant of a man with a massive head. His skin was pale, like an albino, and he had yellow hair falling across huge shoulders. He was wearing smoked spectacles with round black lenses that made his white face look like a skull with empty eye sockets. He turned as someone came into the room. After a few minutes he came back to the window and resumed staring down at them through those black, round spectacles.

Greasy Shirt came back.

"You," he said, pointing to the lady. "You know where's yore room. You an' yore driver git your things and git to it now."

He pointed to Gabe.

"My boys'll show you where you're sleepin'," he snarled. "You git there and stay there. The boys'll take care of th' horses. That little dwarf comes with me."

"What?" Gabe said, putting his hand on his Colt.

"Rothaus wants him. Y' don't want t' argue, neither. Y' don't know how many guns might be on y' right now."

Gabe glanced around. Greasy Shirt was right. There were dozens of gloomy windows and not a few dark doorways. Could be shooters in any or all of them.

"What's he want with my friend?" Gabe asked.

"Well, I guess I just plumb fergot t' ask," Greasy replied. "Or ain't my business. Maybe he's gonna eat 'im for dinner."

Eben dismounted and handed Gabe his reins.

"Don't worry," the dwarf said. "Rothaus knows who I am. The blacksmith's the last person he wants trouble with."

Gabe was led away to a small room in a low building facing the dirt yard. It was furnished with cot and washstand. There he would await the morning and a challenge from the giant man in the dark spectacles. He had ridden into a valley of death. Up to this point he had tried to do everything the way a Keystone rider would be expected to do. But now it seemed he would either have to turn coward or turn killer. If Link Lochlin were here, what would he do?

"Maybe too much cunning can get a man into trouble," he muttered as he poured water to wash his face. "I wonder if Mr. Francis Bacon ever thought of that?"

Chapter Twelve
LADY CATHERINE SURREY

Food was brought to his room, salt pork and a boiled potato with a jug of buttermilk. The sullen woman who brought it came back later to retrieve the plate and leave a fresh ewer of water and towel. Apparently he had the free run of the place, but his host didn't want him as a dinner guest.

No matter.

Like in that book Plato wrote. They weren't there to eat together. They were there to settle a difference of opinion. In this case, the difference of opinion was clear: Rothaus had a high opinion of himself and Gabe differed with him.

Gabe slicked down his hair, dusted off his pants, and went walking out into the evening air. A Keystone rider would size up the place, get to know the terrain so to speak. He worried about Eben, but there was nothing he could do except trust that Rothaus would do nothing to harm him.

Eben had said Rothaus knew who the blacksmith was? Gabe had a strange feeling that Evan Thompson was around, somewhere. Just a feeling. Anyway, despite Eben's assurances that he'd be all right, Gabe thought he might just go on a stroll around the big grim house. Maybe he'd find out something. He wanted another look at one window in particular.

If she were a character in one of his mother's storybooks the beautiful woman would be at the window hoping for a glimpse of him. The sun would be dropping in the west, its dazzling beams of light through the panes turning her auburn hair into a glowing frame for her perfect face. But that was storybook stuff. The corrals and barns and outbuildings of Rothaus's place lay under the deep gloom of dark clouds. Barely audible and distant, somebody was playing a harmonica.

Gabe walked along the alleyway and past the corner of the old house. He kept on until he came to the field beyond the corrals, where he nearly tripped over another of Rothaus's macabre displays. This skeleton was lying on the grass looking up at the sky, arms and legs spread-eagle, wearing nothing but boots and hat. It wasn't hard to see the damage; an arm and collar bone were busted as if the waddy had been holding up his arm to defend himself against a club. The skull was caved in, just above the jaw. Most of the ribs were broken. How long the body had lain there he couldn't tell, but from her window the lady would have seen it decaying a little more each day, with birds and God knows what kinds of varmints pulling off strips of skin and flesh. Gabe had an eerie impulse to take his Colt and shoot the skeleton through the head to end its pain and humiliation.

"What kind of hell is this?" he asked himself.

He turned around and tried to look casual as he glanced up toward the window. At first he saw nothing but a dark rectangle in the wall. Then he saw the sharp flare of a match and the rising brightness of an oil lamp.

The woman stood in the window.

Catherine Surrey's face and upper body were illuminated by the lamplight, like the woman in an old picture his mother had hanging on the wall when he was a boy. She knew he was standing down there, dark and gloomy as it was.

"Like t' know what she's thinking," Gabe whispered to the deaf, dead air.

Was she frightened? Did she see him as just another victim of Rothaus's madness, another rider to get turned into an arrangement of moldering bones? Could she stand to witness it again? Seeing one more murder might drive her as mad as Rothaus. If she was anything like her sister, she probably had no hope that he was going to rescue her.

Gabe expected her to turn away, indifferent like her sister. Maybe just numb from seeing all this.

He had underestimated her. Over the beauty of her face, framed in softly falling auburn hair, there came the most gentle, welcoming smile he had seen in his life. It was the sweet smile of a schoolmistress receiving a wildflower bouquet from an eight-year-old, or a woman opening a Valentine's card from a "secret admirer" whose name she knows. Gabe raised his hand in a greeting. She bowed her head gracefully and then raised her own hand to him. There they stood, she in lamplight at a window, he in early evening gloom in the courtyard of a murderous madman, holding their hands up to one another. Gabe felt his chest swelling. His heart was hammering. He had never known this sudden feeling before, yet he knew what the feeling was. He was afraid to pronounce the word for fear the feeling would vanish.

She acknowledged him. She was not frightened for him. It was as if she had been waiting for the right man and she knew he was the one. Gabe couldn't help the big grin that began on the left side of his mouth and spread all the way to the other side, uncovering his teeth as it went.

She was beautiful.

She needed him.

There was something Gabe did not know. Eben had been granted an audience with the Lady Surrey. The dwarf had told her all about Gabe's cleverness and resourcefulness, his strength and prowess with weapons. Eben had hinted that he was sent by Thompson himself, the mysterious blacksmith. When she smiled down from her window, it was a smile of hope and appreciation. But it didn't matter where the smile came from. He had seen the face and the smile, and he was caught.

Gabe found the sullen old woman waiting for him when he got back to his room. She had a message.

"He'll see you in morning," she grumbled. "Go in at the red door, there."

She pointed a crooked finger toward the big dark house. Gabe couldn't tell if the gloomy recessed door was red or yellow.

In the morning he would find the red door and come face to face with Rothaus. For now he would lie on his bunk looking at the ceiling, lost in the remembrance of the face he had seen at the window. The face with lamplight falling across it. As long as he lived, he would never forget the little dip of her shoulders as she bowed, nor the graceful hand lifted in greeting and how the sight made him stop breathing.

The red door led into a hallway smelling of dust and rats. This hall turned abruptly to the right, then to the left, then opened into a room twice the size of Art Pendragon's dining hall back at the Keystone. Unlike the Keystone dining room, however, one end of Rothaus's looked like it was under construction.

Or destruction by somebody in a mighty rage.

A wall was torn open. Boards and broken furniture lay scattered about as if someone had started to demolish the room and had walked away. A heavy chair had been thrown at the wall; the remains lay among busted bits of wall planking.

The table in the center of the room was the size of a railroad flatcar. The chairs were high and wide, as if made for a race of huge people. A sideboard against the wall was twice ordinary size; next to it was an oversized couch. A wall was decorated with crude artwork and battle trophies. One was a drawing of a cowboy, a drawing such as a child might create. A nail held it to the wall; from that same nail hung a single spur. On another wall panel was a cross made of saddle *conchos* tacked to the wood. Farther on a crude, childlike crayon drawing showed a big man stabbing another man in the chest. Red crayon streaks represented the blood spurting out.

A screeching, grating sound come from the back wall and echoed in the room.

A section of paneling drew back to show a doorway next to an oversized carved chair. The giant Rothaus emerged and sat down in this throne without saying a word. He wore a brilliant red tunic, open to show a red shirt beneath. His leather belt was two hands wide. His trousers were a velvet material, deep maroon. His high-button boots were such as a little boy might wear to Sunday school.

He held a thick cudgel with a heavy knob on the end.

His pale and watery eyes studied Gabe. Contempt was written all over his pockmarked face. After several minutes, he spoke.

"Are you two men, you?"

"No," Gabe said. "Just the one of me."

"Two men," Rothaus repeated it like a riddle. "The tiny squire told Lady Surrey you are great hero, fighting man with few peers. But Lady Townsend swears you are kitchen boy, far beneath me. She says not waste time with you. Not a Keystone rider."

"Where is Eben?" Gabe asked.

"With lady. He amuses her. And he harmless. You puzzle me."

"You puzzle me, too," Gabe said.

"Tell me."

"Your story spread all the way to the Keystone Ranch. How a man named Rothaus keeps Miss Surrey a prisoner. How he trespasses on her land. What puzzles me is how you call this prisoner your 'lady.' Your lady?"

"Because my lady. She will be wife, too, after I kill one called Link from Keystone Ranch. Many men I fight. For her, many men. Some come to claim her and wife her. Some to kill me because I kill their friend. All men, I fight for her. So my lady."

"And you figure Link Lochlin is going to come riding in here one fine day? So you can kill him, too?"

"Listen me, kitchen boy. It is known. It is the story. The strong rider comes, the best rider, the best shooter of all, best fighter. He comes. It is known. I fight him for my lady."

"Why?" Gabe said.

" 'Why'?"

"Don't like to be nosy, but what does she have against Link? Why does she want to see him killed?"

Rothaus laughed. "She? Nothing against anyone! Hah! I am the one! *Me!* You talk too much."

"So I've been told. But if I'm to rescue the lady from Rothaus—which I assume is you—I need to know some things. For instance I don't see she's any too friendly toward you."

Rothaus's rolling laughter bounced from wall to wall until it seemed like the pictures might fall down.

"You rescue her!" he guffawed. "You rescue her! Hah!"

"That's the idea."

"Kitchen boy, you saw how I plant my garden. Out there. You saw bones. Many men. Bigger than you. Hah! You need beware making me angry, beware by dead men hanging in my trees. Make your knees shake!"

"Rothaus, you ought to be ashamed."

"What!" the giant man roared with laughter again.

"Ashamed. You ever hear of anything like this at the Keystone? Decent men, decent cowboys never would do anything so evil. Not like you've done. It's insane. Anybody'd say so. No self-respecting woman should have anything to do with a man who tortures men. Or puts bodies to rot where she has to look at them. Sooner somebody deals with you the better. I reckon that somebody is me."

Rothaus stared at a distant wall, not listening. A kind of trance came over his huge features, an almost peaceful expression. Then he roused himself, shaking his head like a buffalo bull. He looked at Gabe again.

"What do you reckon?" Gabe asked.

"Who are you?" Rothaus roared. "Kitchen boy! I decide. You live here. You work in my kitchen. If you strong enough. Look skinny, too weak to carry wood, kettles of water. Too skinny. But you work anyway."

The giant smiled generously.

"Better'n being one of your trophies, eh?" Gabe said. "I guess not."

"If not kitchen help, you are great hero. The dwarf says. So you die. You die today."

"I guess not," Gabe repeated.

"See this?" said Rothaus, brandishing the knobbed cudgel. "I play fair. Lady would like it, play fair. You go. Find your stick like mine. Anywhere, I don't care. We do not fight today. Tomorrow, in the morning, you meet me. Outside. Get a good stick, kitchen boy. Good stick and we fight. Tomorrow."

Rothaus took out a pair of smoked spectacles. He made a dramatic show of putting them on his face and adjusting them, then leaned forward and looked hard into Gabe's face.

"I will look like this, so you will know me. Outside. By garden of heroes' bones where we fight. Sticks. And knives. Don't forget knives. Fair play like the Keystone."

"Tomorrow it is. Now I want to see Eben."

Rothaus yawned with indifference. He rose from his throne.

"Maybe I send him," he said.

★ ★ ★ ★ ★

An hour went by before Eben came to the cavernous dining hall. Gabriel was examining the rest of the childish drawings tacked to the walls. A few he recognized, like the skeleton sitting on a saddle wired to a tree branch. Then there was the damaged wall. It looked like Rothaus threw a tantrum and attacked the paneling with a sledgehammer after trying to throw the chair through it.

Eben came into the room.

"So he let you come," Gabe said.

"Here I am," said the small man. "But I'm not allowed to leave the building. He's afraid we'd run away."

"And there'd go his entertainment," Gabe said. "What about the ladies?"

"They're all right," Eben said. "Nobody bothers them. They've got the run of the second floor. Even their own kitchen and cook. Just can't leave, that's all."

"What do you think of our host?" Gabe asked.

"Rabid dog crazy," Eben said. "You notice his eyes? He doesn't seem to see real good. Miss Surrey says he carries a shotgun when he goes outdoors, a short-barreled one with the trigger guard sawed off. Probably 'cause he's got such fat fingers. And a knife and club all the time, carries them, too. Easy to see why his men are afraid of him and scared to leave. I don't think he pays them too good, either."

"I think you're right. The ones we ran into sure don't look like they've got money for clothes. Or soap. Well, that's encouraging!" Gabe smiled. "When I kill him, maybe they'll be grateful and let us go."

"It won't be easy," Eben said. "The lady told me he cut down three or four men with his shotgun. Others he beat to death with that club. According to her, he enjoys breaking a man's legs and arms, then slicing at him until he's dead."

"He mentioned knives. Warned me to get a good, stout stick for our little social encounter in the morning," Gabe said. "Maybe I better get out there and hunt one up. You sure you'll be all right?"

"I'm sure. Good luck to you, grub rider."

Gabe smiled. "Good luck to all of us."

He saw several men working around the place, but none offered to stop him from going wherever he pleased. He got his long Bowie knife out of his saddlebag, thinking he would use it to cut himself a stick. But then it occurred to him that an axe would be better. With an axe he could cut a really thick green wood club. He found a cluttered tack room back of a stable. There was an axe. And a heavy longhorn pick.

"Don't need the pick," he said to himself, "but that pick handle could be useful."

So saying, he stood the pick on end, knocked the head down with the axe, and took the pick handle with him. He was still going to look for a club, but the heavy oak handle would do for a backup.

Making his way among old wagons and plows he found a stout singletree and took it, along with an old-fashioned plow staff. He hid the plow staff inside a dark doorway that didn't look like it had been opened in years.

Gabe walked to the field where the "duel" was supposed to take place and looked around until he located a big varmint hole behind a low rock.

"Mr. Groundhog won't mind if I hide my pick handle in his front room awhile," Gabe said. He slid the handle down the hole until just the end was showing. The singletree he hid by hanging it from one of its hooks in the branches of a scraggly tree at the edge of the field.

When he began to look around in the patch of woods, Gabe

realized how smart he'd been to hide extra weapons. Among the bushes and fallen branches he found a half-dozen broken clubs, crudely trimmed and with hand grips whittled into them. Each one was broken. Gabe pictured in his mind the giant man swinging his club, a cowboy defending himself with another club until it snapped in half from a blow, then Rothaus tossing the broken club out into the woods after using his knife to kill his victim.

Behind a tree, half-hidden by vines, he found one club still intact. It was well seasoned and nicely tapered and smoothed. It was also twice the size he could handle. It would take a giant arm to swing it.

So!

He wasn't the only one who had thought of hiding extras. Rothaus did the same.

"Might turn things around," Gabe said.

He stood the club on its thick end and used the axe to split the handle a third of the way down. If Rothaus hit anything with it his hands would get a damned nasty pinch.

When he found Rothaus's second hidden club he chopped it in half. A third one he chopped and threw so far into a thicket that it would lie there until hell froze over. For his own weapon, Gabe found a young spruce tree, about the thickness of his arm. He hacked the ground around it until he could tear it out of the ground with its roots still attached. He used the axe to whittle it into a club a yard long with a heavy root knob at the thick end.

Gabe figured Rothaus would probably try to keep the sun at his back if he had any sense at all. He'd probably show up in the shadows down in the east end. Maybe he'd be on horseback and challenge Gabe to come across the field to him so he'd be looking into the morning sun. The only place to retreat would be into the woods or back toward the house and ranch buildings. Either way, it would be a long way to run. But what if Gabe was carrying a gun? Surely Rothaus would have thought about that. He was probably counting on the "chivalry" of a Keystone rider, who wouldn't draw on an unarmed man.

Or maybe Rothaus would send somebody like the crone who brought the food to sneak into the room while Gabe was sleeping and disable his weapon. A man might go to shoot and find somebody had drawn his bullets or bent the hammer pin or even plugged the barrel.

Gabe drew his Colt and checked it. Still operational.

If worse came to worse, it'd be good to have another ace up his sleeve. Take this stump, now, the one he was sitting on. A man might just wrap his bandanna around his Colt to keep the dirt out and hide it between the old roots. He'd have to do it real careful in case he was being watched from the house.

The afternoon passed slowly. Gabe checked on the horse, made sure his saddle and bridle were still hanging under the shed next to the corral, sat and whittled awhile, and sharpened his Bowie knife with a whetstone from the tool shed. He even napped a little. He wandered into the kitchen and found nobody there, so he took a pitcher and helped himself to hot water from the tank on the back of the range. Might as well go to his room and have himself a shave.

"A man ought to die looking good," he said to the reflection in the broken mirror while he scraped away at his whiskers.

The hag brought his food and he ate. Afterward, in the dim dusk of late evening, he saw Rothaus emerge from the house. He wasn't supposed to see him; in fact, if Gabe had not been sitting in the outhouse, and if the outhouse had not had cracks between the boards, Rothaus would not have been observed at all. But Gabe heard a door groan and looked through the crack in the outhouse wall to see his giant host sneaking out the back door. The giant was carrying a shotgun.

Gabe pulled up his Levi's and quietly, slowly, opened the outhouse door. There was just enough light for him to see Rothaus heading for the dueling field. Gabe followed. Rothaus went to a tree not far from the rock and hole where Gabe had hidden his pick handle. When he turned to go back to the house, he was no longer carrying the shotgun.

Takin' out a little insurance, I guess, Gabe thought. *What kind of sneaky rascal would hide a gun? Same kind who'd bend a shotgun's firing pins or plug its barrels, I guess.*

As soon as Rothaus was back inside, Gabe took another walk to the battleground. It struck him as funny, how he and Rothaus thought alike. "Maybe I'd better watch what I think," he said to himself as he unscrewed the shotgun's firing pins. "In fact, I'd better make it a policy to think otherwise."

He slept lightly that night. His mind kept conjuring up images of Catherine Surrey. In his half-dreams she ran through green meadows, sometimes toward him, sometimes beside him. He imagined a horse for her, a high-neck, high-stepping horse. A black one to set off her auburn hair and fair skin. He gave his vision a soft voice and it wafted through his mind's pictures like music. The hours passed until in the darkest part of the night someone came into his room. He opened his eyes slightly and saw the dull yellow of a shrouded candle. He lay still. When the person had gone again, Gabe fell into a deep sleep that lasted until morning returned. Heavy clouds. Another thick gray day.

It was the raucous cawing of ravens that woke him. They were insistent, as though the birds had not been fed and needed a nice fresh corpse. The gloom and dark birds made him think about Rothaus in his black spectacles.

Puts me in mind of a drawing in mother's books, he thought. *That giant in* Jack and the Beanstalk.

He looked toward the cracked mirror propped up on the

washstand. Mirrors and dark spectacles, he thought. Spectacles and mirrors.

He swung his legs over and got off the cot, pulled on his pants, and went outside where there was a crude bench. He sat down to pull on his boots. Across the dirty yard came the grouchy old woman, bringing a pot of coffee and a plate of biscuits and cheese.

"Last meal for the condemned?" he joked.

She glared at him and carried his breakfast into his room. She took her time coming back out, so Gabe knew she'd been told to look for his gun. She was probably the one who came during the night to look for it.

Sorry, mamacita, *he thought. I seem to have left my Colt over at the playground.* Perdòn.

"Pardon me, ma'am," he said with his most engaging grin. "I was wonderin' if I might get a lantern of some sort. That room's as dark as the inside of a cow. I'd like to clean up a bit before . . . well, you know. Before I go to my meeting with your boss."

She grunted something and hobbled back toward the house.

He retrieved his breakfast from the little room to eat outside on the bench with his back against the building. Most mornings he preferred to do it that way, when he could, letting early morning sunshine flood over him while sipping strong, hot coffee. The hag's coffee was passable, but there was no sunshine. Only gloomy low clouds and deep shadows everywhere.

He heard the sound of a window latch being pulled back and the squeak of hinges. He looked up to see someone holding a candle. It was her. Catherine was there just as she had been at the other window. Was she smiling down at him? It was too dark and too far away to tell. He could see only a little gleam of autumn-maple hair and a glow of creamy skin. He thought he saw her lift her hand to him and he raised his hand to her.

The final meal. A final salute from a lady. This was shaping up to be a pretty interesting day, except for all the finality involved.

The old woman returned with an oil lamp. Gabe guessed that she had been ordered to give him whatever he asked for as a way of getting him to feel more confident, to let down his guard a little. As soon as she was gone, he removed the lamp chimney and dumped a handful of fine dirt into it, swirling and shaking the glass until the grit had scoured off the soot and left a network of tiny scratches. He took down the mirror and did the same, scouring it with dirt. He checked the lamp wick and trimmed it and made sure the lamp would light. Finally he set the mirror to face the door, put the lamp in front of it and set the glass chimney next to it along with his Lucifer matches. As an afterthought he went out and found a smooth stone to put by the matches.

"I bet y' don't know it," he said to the stone, "but David killed Goliath with a little rock probably no bigger than you."

CHAPTER THIRTEEN
DAVID AND GOLIATH

Eben and Gabe rode onto the field, Gabe carrying the spruce club across his saddle. His sheathed Bowie knife hung from his cartridge belt.

"There he is," Eben said.

"Damn, but he looks big."

"Sittin' with his back t' the sun, just like you said he would be."

"Close t' the shadows, too," Gabe said. "Plans to make me come to him, I guess. Well, we'll see about that. Going to be an interesting game. Think it'd be fair if I checked and then raised?"

"There's poker tables where a man could get shot if he checked and raised."

"I could get myself shot right here," Gabe smiled.

"So, what do you want me to do?" Eben asked. "I still got my sidearm."

"None of that," Gabe warned him. "Keep your .38 out of sight. I'm pretty sure Rothaus has shooters watching us. You or me, we pull a gun, they're likely to cut us down quick as a rattlesnake. You just hang back. Stay inconspicuous. Unless you happen to end up anywhere near one of Rothaus's men. Then you might see if you can't get them into conversation. Try and find out—real casual, you know—what they'd do if I killed him. I've got a hunch they'd want to light out for sunnier territory. Maybe, some of them would want to move to the Surrey ranch and work for the ladies."

"All right," Eben said. "I'll see what I can find out. Don't forget I got my gun if you need it. You just holler, and I'll be there."

Gabe thought about the small revolver in Eben's shoulder holster and tried not to smile. It would do very little damage to a man the size of Rothaus. More than likely it would merely irritate him. And Gabe had already thought of plenty of other ways to irritate Rothaus.

"I think we've got him out-horsed, at least," Gabe observed.

"What?"

"Look how big his horse is. Back at the Keystone they pull hay wagons with smaller horses than that. Ever see a horse that heavy? Hell, even this nag of Snath's could run circles around that big ol' plodder. Horse like that, it's probably too gentle for this kind of action. You couldn't even get it to chase cows, probably."

"Maybe," Eben said. "Take my advice and stay outa his reach. I wish you had your Colt . . . where *is* your .44, anyway? Back at the bunkhouse?"

"I know where it is, in case I need it. But don't worry: a man like Rothaus, he's not going to shoot an unarmed man if he can club him to death instead. With his poor eyesight, he's going to have a hard time hittin' me."

"Don't trust him, that's all. If you can get to your gun and get a chance to shoot him, do it."

"Don't worry," Gabe repeated. "Get on back toward the buildings. And if I do get myself killed . . ."

"You want me to rescue the ladies?"

"No. They'll be all right. No worse off than when we got here, anyway. If he gets me, you ride like hell out of here, and don't stop for anything. I'd hate to think of you ending up like his other trophies. Tell your blacksmith he'll have to send somebody else."

★ ★ ★ ★ ★

Rothaus did not like the way cowboy was acting. Despite repeated challenges, his lanky opponent wouldn't come any closer. He only sat there grinning at him. It made him angry. He would make kitchen boy die very slowly of many blows.

"Why don't you come out here instead?" Gabe called to him.

"In hurry to die, kitchen boy?"

"No! It's not a very good day for it!" Gabe replied. "Don't you ever see the sun in this place? At all?"

"Come closer!" Rothaus yelled.

"Maybe in a minute," Gabe called. "Need to size you up! Never fought with a man as big as you before."

Gabe did let his horse take a few steps forward, but just to annoy Rothaus a little more. He wanted to see how angry and impatient he would get. With those spectacles and their round black lenses, it was hard to read the expression on his face. But that wouldn't matter. Maybe.

"Nice horse you got there!" Gabe shouted. "What is it, a cross between an elephant and a buffalo?"

Rothaus growled and fidgeted with his club.

"Better not fall off!" Gabe continued, gripping his own club. "A man could kill himself falling from that height. Like in that story. Remember Jack and the giant with the beanstalk? I'll tell you. When Jack cut that beanstalk in half, that ol' giant fell so hard it buried him in the ground. The giant I mean, not Jack. Jack was all right. Jack got the beautiful maiden and the harp and treasure and all."

"Shut up!" Rothaus yelled. "Come fight me!"

"Over in those shadows?" Gabe said. "I guess not. You come here."

Rothaus fidgeted, but made no movement toward Gabe.

"That pretty long hair of yours!" Gabe shouted. "Reminds me of another giant story, but I can't recall the names. Maybe it was Gogmagog. I read about him a long time ago. He had long hair like that so it would hide his ears. He had the ears of an ass. Big, furry ears. Funny, huh?"

Rothaus lunged forward but checked his horse at the edge of the shadows.

Almost got him that time, Gabe thought.

"Let's see, how did ol' Gog get killed? Oh, yeah. He got tossed into the sea and drowned. There was other big giants, ones Hercules took care of. He shot 'em all up with arrows. Maybe I should've brought along a bow and some arrows!"

"Fight!" Rothaus called. "Time to fight! Shut up!"

Gabe went on grinning.

"In a minute! Tryin' to enjoy my last few minutes on earth here. Remembering stories and all that. Say, you know that Shoshone giant legend, the one about Badger and the Giant? Giant went bad and nobody could stop him. Nobody until wily ol' Badger got on the job. He tricked the giant into a hole in the ground, then stopped up the hole with a big rock."

"No hole big enough for me!" Rothaus challenged.

"Or that elephant horse of yours either," Gabe agreed. "Then there's always Goliath, of course. David's little ol' slingshot took care of that. Ever see a slingshot, Rothaus? I used to be pretty good with one, when I was a boy like David. Easy to make, too. All it takes is a couple of whangs and a scrap of leather for a pouch. I might have one hid in the pocket of my Levi's right now, in fact. A few pebbles in my front pocket, why say! I might pop you right between the eyes!"

"Hah!" Rothaus laughed. "A Keystone rider, throw rocks! No!"

"Hey, now," Gabe said. "You gotta make your mind up. Kitchen help or a Keystone rider? Which is it?"

Kinda be nice to know the answer myself, Gabe thought. *If I'm gonna die, I'd like to die knowing.*

Rothaus rode forward another ten yards and brandished his club.

"No matter," he said angrily. "I beat whichever one you be. Pound you a hundred blows, dead."

"Yeah? And I might take your pretty long hair, scalp you like a Pawnee. Like what happened to ol' Samson when that pretty little Delilah got through with him. Afterward, I think I'll burn down your house and take Delilah home with me."

That did it.

Rothaus roared and kicked his oversized draft horse until it began to run. He came charging with his club waving around his head like a roper twirling a lasso. Gabe spurred his own horse and it shied off, causing Rothaus's ferocious blow to miss him completely. By the time Rothaus had recovered his balance, Gabe had trotted around behind him. *Draft horses,* he was thinking. *What's their weakness?*

Rothaus turned and was looking into the morning sun. He kicked the draft horse into a lumbering gallop again, swung and missed again. Gabe wheeled quickly and kept close behind the draft horse, the safest place to be.

Big and gentle beasts, those. Very careful where they place their feet. More than once Gabe had seen a big Percheron or Belgian accidentally step over the traces and stop perfectly still while it figured out how to lift its huge hoof and put it down where it belonged. Plus, draft horses can stop awful quick.

He rode around in front of Rothaus and turned to face him. Rothaus raised his club high over his head and once more kicked his huge horse into a lumbering charge. This time, however, Gabe did not dodge or ride away. He merely took off his hat—the wide gray Stetson formerly worn by Colonel Grumm—and calculated the distance. When the draft horse was close enough, Gabe sailed the hat through the air to land just in front of him. Just as he had figured it would, the horse planted its feet and stopped dead to look down so it wouldn't step on this strange thing. Rothaus lost his balance, pitching forward with the weight and momentum of his club pulling him down against the horse's neck. Gabe spurred his horse and plunged forward. He used his own club to knock Rothaus on the knuckles. Rothaus dropped the bludgeon. Gabe followed up with a fierce thrust in the ribs as he went by.

The result was better than Gabe had hoped for.

Hundreds of pounds of flesh met the dirt in a satisfying "whump!"

Gabe turned his horse and grinned at Rothaus sitting on the ground.

"Mind handing me my hat, as long as you're down there?" he said.

Gabe cantered away; Rothaus got to his feet with his club and was running after him, swinging wildly. His horse had seen enough hitting and shouting and was headed for the barns, being careful not to step on its dragging reins.

Gabe trotted off a safe distance and taunted Rothaus again.

"Don't think you'll get a job at the Keystone," he yelled. "You don't ride so good! Too clumsy to work in the kitchen, too!"

Rothaus roared and came running, swinging his club so madly that Gabe was afraid he'd end up breaking the horse's legs. He trotted off again, the huge man still coming and hacking at the air and the ground.

"We're wearing him down," Gabe told the horse. "Let's lead him over to that bush and rock yonder. Then you can get yourself out of harm's way."

"Fight!" Rothaus yelled. "Or my men will kill you! Fight!"

"I think he means it," Gabe told the horse. "Wouldn't put it past him to have sharpshooters out in those woods, would you? If he gets discouraged, he might just give the order. Time you and me parted company."

So saying, he swung a leg over the saddle and dropped to the grass, giving the horse a good slap on the rump to send it away.

Seeing his victim afoot gave Rothaus renewed encouragement. He came lumbering on, his thick boots making the ground shake. Gabe stood his ground. He saw the sneer of victory growing on the hulk's wide face under the smoked eyeglasses. But Rothaus was tired and out of wind. And a little too sure of himself.

Gabe remembered what Rothaus had said about killing him with a hundred blows, a slow and painful death. Would Rothaus go for a leg, to cripple him? Or an arm, to leave him with only one to fight with?

It turned out to be a chopping stroke coming from high overhead and slashing downward, aiming to cripple Gabe's shoulder. He ducked and spun around, but not quite fast enough. At least he took it on the back, and it hadn't broken his arm or collarbone. Rothaus pivoted, looking for him, and brought the long club down again in a ferocious diagonal slash, which Gabe once more dodged too late. This time, it caught his heel.

Gabe limped out of range and turned to face Rothaus again.

"Is that one of your hundred strokes?" he taunted. "I'd say y' pretty much wasted two of them."

"Fight!" Rothaus screamed. He tried to turn as Gabe made a quick feint. In the time it took Rothaus to plant his feet and get his balance Gabe was able to swing his own club against the back of Rothaus's left leg, directly behind the knee. Rothaus saved himself with his club, using it like a cane to keep himself from falling. Gabe swung again, this time aiming at the club, and moved away the instant he felt wood smacking into wood. Once again he heard the "whump" of flesh against earth. The giant was down.

But still dangerous.

Gabe kept his distance.

Rothaus used both hands to rub his knee. *Looks like he's gonna cry,* Gabe thought. *Puts me in mind of a schoolyard bully findin' his nose drippin' blood.* Gabe picked up a rock and threw it at him.

"You just gonna sit there?" he said.

Rothaus said nothing, but hoisted himself to his feet and began walking away, heading toward the edge of the woods. He dragged his club behind him and carelessly let it drop as he neared the trees. He was crippled and unarmed.

Same trick I might use, Gabe thought. *Pretend to lose interest. Make it look like you're goin' off into the bushes and sulk. Drop your weapon like you don't want to fight anymore. Get to the woods and grab up something to hit with. Like that big club he's got hid in there.*

Gabe moved after Rothaus, but went carefully, warily watching every movement of the massive frame. He lost sight of him when he went behind a cottonwood tree in a chokecherry thicket. Gabe stopped. He watched and waited.

"HeeeeYahhhhhh!"

Rothaus busted out of the bushes like a silvertip grizzly rising on hind legs and slashing with long claws. He was yelling and swinging a club bigger than the one he had dropped. It was the one Gabe had sabotaged. Rothaus screamed and thrashed chokecherry branches out of his way, taking long strides toward Gabe.

One hard hit, Gabe thought. *C'mon, you human griz. Take one hard swing at me.*

Rothaus would oblige.

Raising his thick club with both hands, reaching his arms as high as they would go, he clenched his teeth in an evil smile.

The little round lenses of the dark glasses caught the reflection of the slender cowboy caught in front of him.

Gabe hesitated a second, then twisted around and threw himself full-length away from the killing blow of the club. It thudded down next to Gabe's boot and hit so heavily that it shook the ground. The split handle caught both of Rothaus's palms like a vise.

"Ow!" came the anguished yell. "Ow! Ow! *Ow!*"

Gabe rolled to his feet and scampered out of range. When he looked back he saw Rothaus cradling both hands in front of his face, shaking them and blowing on his palms. He made pitiful attempts to rub them together.

He should've checked his equipment, Gabe thought. Gabe had tried to use a split maul handle once, and had caught both hands in it. Blood blisters for two weeks after. Damn, that hurt.

Gabe retreated, picking up Rothaus's first club. He backed across the uneven ground out into the open again. He didn't need to hurry. The huge man was still standing there looking like a hurt little boy blowing on his injured palms. There was an instant in which Gabe almost felt sympathy for him.

Then Gabe hefted Rothaus's heavy club and remembered the skeletons lashed to trees. All sympathy vanished.

Rothaus seemed to have forgotten all about Gabe. He walked toward his house, kicking stones and clumps of grass as he went. He limped a little and held one hand in the other. Gabe gripped the club and whirled around twice before releasing it to fly out into the bushes. He followed Rothaus at a distance, expecting him to suddenly turn and attack. But he didn't. A few times, he stopped in his tracks as if he had no interest in going on, but each time he stopped, he only lifted his thick shoulders and dropped them again and resumed his slow way home.

Gabe moved cautiously. He caught his horse and took it back to the corral next to the stable. He wished he had his Colt.

Maybe better leave it hidden where it was.

All that afternoon and into the evening, Gabe saw no more of Rothaus. From time to time, he heard hammering and crashing coming from the house. But there was no other sign of Rothaus. Gabe avoided his bed and slept under straw out behind the stable. At dawn he went back in the room. Eben brought his breakfast to him.

"What's goin' on?" Gabe asked.

"I dunno. I checked on the ladies. They're all right. There's nobody else in the house except him and that old woman. I can wander around all I want. The ladies are worried, but they're safe."

"What about him?"

"It's like he's all of a sudden gone deaf and dumb or something. Wanders around, maybe just sits down and stares at a wall. Couple of times he went 'way back in the house somewhere. I heard him hammering like he was tearing something down. I opened the door a crack this morning and saw him just sitting on that big chair staring out into empty air."

Gabe ate his cold porridge and drank the harsh coffee. That done, he went around to the stables to saddle Snath's horse. He took his time brushing the horse, straightening the saddle blanket, tossing the saddle into place, methodically fastening the girth and checking the stirrups . . . and realized another of Rothaus's weaknesses.

"I think I know why he gets all mad and gets in a sulk," Gabe told the horse as he led it toward the open field.

"I figure he goes about these 'duels' the same way every time. He gets a couple of his men to box in the other man, then he comes in and corners him with that ol' plow horse of his. Then he commences to beat on him. It's the only way he's ever done it, the only way he knows to do it. When it's over he ties the corpse to a tree, or else props it up where he can see it. It's like he's making sure the man won't ever get up again."

Only this time, the giant seemed to be making it a one-on-one fight. Was Rothaus overconfident? Maybe it's how the giant would act if he thought he was a real Keystone rider.

The horse was listening, although without as much interest as Gabe might have hoped. He went on talking as they walked.

"Ever see a grizzly burying a kill?" he said. "Maybe not. But your average griz, he'll drag his kill to where he wants to bury it, then he'll put it down where he can keep an eye on it while he tears up the ground and makes a kind of hole. I'm thinkin' our unfriendly giant's the same way. Hammers a man to death, then needs to deal with the body. Like tying the body to a tree. Then loses interest. Calms down."

The horse flicked its ears toward the house, toward the shadowy edge of the woods. Somebody was coming.

"Thing is," said Gabe, noticing, but not looking around, "when the fight doesn't go according to expectations, he gets confused. Gets all in a fury. Takes it out on walls and furniture. Like a little kid whose mommy sends him to a room by himself."

By this time the horse had stopped listening altogether and was watching the shadows where the big, bulky figure once again sat on his oversized horse. Gabe stepped up into the saddle and rode to the center of the clearing.

Rothaus looked to be rocking from side to side in the saddle, mumbling to himself like a man working himself into a mood. *Probably another part of his routine,* Gabe thought. *Better break into that mood again.*

"Good mornin', Mr. Rothaus!" Gabe called cheerfully. "What'll we do today? Clubs again? How's your hands feeling? Sore, I'll bet!"

Rothaus kicked his horse and plunged forward into the sunlight, raising a club. *So far, so good,* Gabe thought.

"I'll have to admit it!" he called out, "my back's pretty sore where you hit it yesterday! Probably got a big ol' bruise there. You didn't do my foot much good, either!"

Rothaus hesitated as if unsure what to do with a man who would just sit there trying to have a conversation with him. Then, apparently having made up his mind to kill him rather than talk to him, Rothaus resumed his attack.

Snath's horse was not only far quicker than Rothaus's, it was enough of a cowpony to recognize a charging animal when it saw one. With a shake of its head it galloped out of range. Gabe was thinking about Rothaus's horse.

One thing about a draft horse, he thought, *they're not overly fond of turning in circles. They're bred to plod along in straight lines, they are. Hauling wagons, pulling plows and so on. And so . . .*

He reined the cowpony to circle Mr. Rothaus at a safe distance and far out of reach of his club. Rothaus turned the draft horse. Gabe kept circling. Rothaus reined around again. After three or four such maneuvers the big beast decided it no longer wanted to perform pirouettes and stopped in its tracks. Rothaus kicked and threatened, but his horse remained rooted in place.

"Stop it!" Rothaus yelled at Gabe as he circled again. "Stop and fight me! Coward! Kitchen boy! Not a Keystone man! Stop!"

Coming abreast of the giant's shoulder, Gabe turned and dashed behind him, smacking the draft horse on the haunch as he went by. His aim was true, but Rothaus was quicker than Gabe had figured; he swung around with his own club and knocked Gabe's club flying into the dry grass.

Now the race was on.

Rothaus came at a heavy gallop, closing the distance while Gabe got his balance and looked around. Needed to figure where to go. The rock with its scrubby bit of brush hiding the varmint hole was in sight, but to get to it he'd have to make a wide detour around Rothaus. Rothaus seemed to read his intentions and rode to cut him off. The massive club came down again with a whoosh of air. It glanced off Gabe's thigh and raked the horse's flank.

Gabe swerved, gained a few yards, changed direction again, then made his run for the rock. He gripped the saddle horn and prayed the cinch would hold, then leaned out and down, down almost to the ground. His fingers closed around the end of the pick handle. Another blow came from Rothaus, catching Gabe's horse on the rump. Gabe came up swinging, smacking the pick handle into the giant's left shoulder. Rothaus was startled and broke off his charge.

Once again Gabe had a little breathing room.

His leg burned where the club had caught it. The horse was gimping. Upsetting Rothaus's deadly routine didn't seem to be much of an advantage.

"So," Gabe said to the horse. "What'll we try now?"

What would most men try next? Gabe thought. *I guess most men would charge ahead. Looks like he's sitting there waiting for it. A man's been hit and scared wants it over with. Last resort, charge straight at him. Best way to handle a bully, charge in and let him have it.*

And get his own brains scrambled for his trouble.

"Hah!" Rothaus roared. "Hah! Hah! Little man afraid now!! Come fight!"

I'm better off when he comes at me, 'stead of the other way around, Gabe thought.

"All right," he whispered to the horse. "Let's change tactic. Might get hit again, but if it works, y' can head back to the stable."

Snath's horse cocked his ears but said nothing.

Gabe held the pick handle straight up, like a horseman carrying the flag in a parade. He galloped toward Rothaus, just like Rothaus wanted him to do. The giant started forward.

They were no more than ten feet from each other when Gabe whirled the pick handle and let it fly straight at Rothaus. His aim was true: the heavy oak handle connected with a thud. Reining around and racing off, Gabe saw Rothaus rubbing his chest. And now the killer was in a perfect fury. Sensing an advantage, he came galloping after Gabe.

And Gabe made a beeline for a certain scraggly tree at the edge of the clearing.

He ducked under the branches and pulled the horse around tight in order to reach up and get hold of the singletree he had hung there two days earlier. It was a good piece of wood, solid oak and more than three feet long with an iron hook on each end. Rothaus slowed down at the edge of the trees. He could see the other horse in the shadows.

The kitchen boy was trying to hide.

The kitchen boy, however, was fixing up a surprise. The giant's club couldn't bend around trees to get to him. The branches were too thick for Rothaus to get a good swing at him.

Doing the unexpected again, Gabe urged the horse through the branches and back toward the open ground. But he stopped at the very edge of the trees. When Rothaus came lumbering out behind him, he saw Gabe out of the corner of his eye but it was too late for him to turn or stop. The iron hook grabbed his collar. Down he went, whumping into the ground. Gabe jerked the singletree loose and sent a blow to Rothaus's head. The black spectacles flew into the dirt, smashed and bent.

"Ow!" the giant yelled, struggling to his knees. He held one hand to his head and groped around for his club. "Ow! Kill you! Kill you! You dead, dead!"

Gabriel, however, felt disinclined to stay around and be killed.

189

"I guess we'll go now," Gabe told the horse.

He put heels to Snath's cowpony and went at a gimpy trot back toward the house. When he was almost clear of the field he heard a shrill whistle, a warning from Eben.

"Watch him!" Eben yelled. "Over there!"

Greasy Shirt was sneaking along the edge of the trees, carrying the short-barreled shotgun.

"Drop it!" Gabe called. "Drop it now!"

Greasy Shirt ran, trying to head Gabe off before he could reach the house. Gabe galloped for the big stump. Greasy was lifting the shotgun when Gabe hurled himself out of the saddle. He collided with the stump; ignoring the pain in his side and shoulder, he pulled his Colt from hiding and ripped the bandanna away. He twisted around half sitting.

He fired.

Greasy Shirt lowered the shotgun. He looked down as if wondering what he was doing with it. He dropped to his knees and fell over sideways. Gabe heard Rothaus roaring and turned to see the draft horse coming across the field. Rothaus was squinting into the sun, shielding his naked eyes with one arm, blindly charging as fast as his horse could go.

Gabe ran.

He headed for the narrow alleyway between the buildings, where Rothaus's draft horse would have to slow down. Going past the disused doorway he grabbed up the plow staff he had hidden.

Once inside his room, there was nothing he could do except wait like a cockroach caught in a corner. He had one trick left. He had his Colt, of course, but that was a last resort. Every instinct went against shooting an unarmed man in the dark. He could only do that in order to save a life. In this case, his.

The lumbering monster dismounted and came searching for his victim. He peered here and there into dark stables, shadowy storage rooms, and behind piles of moldering old hay. He was like a boy playing at hide and seek, a boy carrying a frighteningly big club and a long knife.

He finally came to the doorway of the dark room where the kitchen whelp had slept.

Gabe set down the plow staff where he could grab it. He flattened himself against the wall, one sulfur match held in his hand and another in his teeth. With his other hand he picked up the smooth stone.

He waited.

The big ugly head peered in, trying to see in the dark. Rothaus's bulk shut out what little light there was from the doorway. He poked his club ahead of him like a blind man waving a cane. Gabe had to wait, and wait, until Rothaus was far enough in. And finally he was: Gabe dragged the sulfur match against the stone. The match snapped and hissed to life. He applied it to the wick of the oil lamp. The lamp flared up and Gabe quickly set the chimney in place. The mirror behind the lamp caught the sudden glare, the hundreds of scratches acting like prisms.

Rothaus cried out. He dropped his club, covering his face with his hand and slashing in all directions with the knife. Gabe stepped behind him and applied the solid oak plow staff to the thin part of the skull just behind the ear. Rothaus pitched forward on his face and lay there, peaceful as a sleeping baby.

CHAPTER FOURTEEN
THE BLACKSMITH'S HELPER

"That's a nice job of wrapping," Eben observed.

The small man was looking at Rothaus lying on the dirt floor. He was whimpering and complaining like a bullied ten-year-old. The hulk was indeed well-wrapped, tightly hogtied with a good manila lariat. He whined that his head was sore. He said he couldn't breathe for the dust. He roared threats and called for someone to come help him, until Gabe stopped his mouth with a gag torn from a dirty blanket.

"Down home we'd hogtie mustangs and range bulls to castrate them," Gabe told Eben. "You take a wild bull that's been ruling the roost, havin' his own way, and you cut him. It's a marvel how quick he settles down. Just another peaceful steer."

Gabe's tone was neither teasing nor taunting, just matter-of-fact.

Rothaus's eyes went wide. He made frantic efforts to free himself. But the rope got tighter the more he struggled.

"Question is, what to do with him now?" Gabe said. "He's too heavy to hang. He's even too heavy to load into a wagon. Much as I'd like to, I can't just shoot him. Or maybe I can. He'd of shot me, given the chance. Haven't made up my mind on that one. Yet."

"There's a forge out back of the wagon shed," Eben said. "Why don't you guard our host and I'll go fire it up?"

"Doesn't seem like a time to do blacksmithing," Gabe said. "But go ahead."

Gabe relaxed on the bench outside the building, holding the Winchester. Just in case somebody took it into their head to try and rescue Rothaus. His vigilance, however, was unnecessary. Two of Rothaus's riders appeared but passed on by, leading a packhorse. Another rider trotted past the entrance to the alleyway, a thick bedroll tied behind his saddle. The rider looked neither right nor left, just straight ahead.

Gabe got up and ventured to the corner to look up at the big house. The only face he saw at the window was that of the old hag who had brought him his meals. She looked as though she were afraid to come down. Gabe wanted to see Catherine Surrey, but that would have to wait.

Why wasn't she at the window? Maybe she couldn't stand the thought of seeing him get his head smashed in. Not enough confidence, that was the problem with Catherine Surrey.

He liked repeating her name to himself.

"Catherine Surrey. Catherine Surrey."

After a time, a gray column began to rise from behind the sheds. Gabe smelled coal smoke. Then he heard the rhythmic banging of hammer on anvil. He couldn't imagine what little Eben was up to, but the steady rhythm of "bang ding a ding *bang* ding a ding" sounded like the dwarf knew what he was doing. Gabe rubbed his sore shoulder and walked up and down to work the limp out of his injured hip. He lost count of the number of times he went out of the alleyway to look up at that one certain window, the window where he might see her. He had never known love at first sight, didn't know whether he believed in it. But he knew something had hold of him.

The more he tried to concentrate on what to do with Rothaus, the more he found himself distracted by the image of Catherine Surrey.

Gabe heard a horse trotting away and caught a glimpse of yet another rider leaving in a hurry. He saw the old hag woman scurrying out of the house and into the maze of outbuildings. Then came a slight sound of footsteps, slow and cautious footsteps, moving toward him down the alleyway. He held the Winchester at the ready, finger on the trigger and thumb on the hammer.

There was a whisper.

"Mr. Gabriel?"

It was Dobé.

He showed his head around the corner, his eyes wide with caution and apprehension.

"Hello, Dobé," Gabe said.

"Thank God," said Dobé. "Is it all over? Has he gone?"

"If you mean our host, no. Hasn't gone anywhere. He's inside. Hogtied to a fare-thee-well. We're figuring what to do with him. The ladies all right? Any guards left in the house at all?"

"Thank God," Dobé repeated. "What a horrible person! I knew you'd be the man to do it. I knew you were. I said so!"

"The ladies?"

"Oh," Dobé said, "they're fine, just fine. Rothaus had two men stationed in the house, but another man came and told them something and they all left. I saw them riding away. Even the old woman has vanished somewhere. She's awfully afraid of you. Where's Eben?"

"Had a sudden urge to do some blacksmithing," Gabe grinned. "So the lady Surrey and her sister, they're coming down?"

"Well, they don't know what's happened. Maybe you should come up and tell them how things stand."

"I can't, not just now," Gabe smiled. "I need to watch over our friend Mr. Rothaus awhile longer. Why don't I put you in charge of gettin' the ladies to pack up their things? Maybe you could round up a wagon for their belongings. You could get the buggy ready, too. Tomorrow morning all of you could head back to the Surrey ranch. They're probably anxious to be home."

"Oh, they will be delighted to leave!" Dobé exclaimed. "They have an excellent foreman back at their ranch and several loyal men. They'll be overjoyed to see them again. No more visits from Rothaus's men to collect 'rent' from them! Wonderful! I'll go and tell the ladies at once. At once! But . . . what about Rothaus? What will become of him? Will you be coming home with us?"

"I'm not sure what's going to happen," Gabe said. "But Rothaus won't be a threat when we get through, that's all I can tell you. Eben and I will stay on another couple of days, I imagine. You take the ladies home. And if Rothaus has any men left, you can tell them they need to clear out. Tell 'em not to let me find them."

"Yessir! Thank you. A thousand times thank you! I'll tell the ladies right now!"

Gabe watched Dobé hurrying away and wished he could deliver the message himself. There was nothing he would rather do. He wanted to meet Catherine face to face, to hear her voice and touch her hand. But it could not yet be, not until he was finished with Rothaus. Even then he would have to be patient. She must ride away from this place, as soon as she could; whatever he was going to do to Rothaus, he did not want Catherine Surrey to be around to see it.

He'd be patient, but the waiting would not come easy.

Gabe looked in on his captive and found him almost asleep. Or comatose. It was hard to tell. At any rate, he was peaceful. Gabe went exploring further down the alleyway until he came to an unusually heavy door. He lifted the thick timber that held it shut and pushed. When his eyes became accustomed to the dimness, he saw that it was a food cellar. The walls were quarried stone.

"Built like a dungeon," he observed.

He checked on Rothaus again, who was still lying as he had left him, and went to snoop around some more. He discovered another cellar door and stone steps leading down into a black hole beneath the big building. Only this hole was different. Rothaus had not used this cellar to store food. Gabe shuddered and hurried back to the light.

"Looking for a place to keep him?"

Eben was standing there when Gabe came out of the cellar.

"You're back," Gabe observed. "Take a look down there."

Eben went down into the cellar and came back with a grim face.

"Jeremy Biscuits!" he said. "Was he planning . . . ?"

"What else? He said he was waiting for a Keystone gunman to come and fight him. And if he lost, I bet he was going to head for this cellar—"

"And light the fuse. There's enough blasting powder to bring the whole place down around himself."

"It more or less answers one question, anyway," Gabe said.

"Question?"

"Of whether he knew all this killing was wrong. That he'd have to pay for it if he was caught. He knew they might come with enough men to catch him. So, he'd blow himself to kingdom come before going to jail. That's what I figure he was thinking. He had a plan to blow up the house and everybody in it. I think he would have been too afraid."

"Afraid to do it?"

"Yeah. It's one thing to pile up kegs of powder and twist fuses together and get everything ready like that. But putting the match to it, that's a whole other proposition."

Both of them stood a moment looking into the dark cellar hole and imagining the destruction.

"Anyway," Gabe said, recovering himself, "what have you

been up to? Been building a steel cage for him?"

Eben led the way back to the room where Rothaus lay bound and gagged. Beside the door lay a pile of newly forged metal bands and chain. Eben picked up one of the bands and handed it to Gabe.

"Fetters!" Gabe exclaimed. "Just what we need! You made us some gyves, too! Excellent. Do they work?"

Eben demonstrated. The thick bracelets for Rothaus's wrists were connected by a short chain. But the gyves for his ankles were connected by an iron bar, allowing him to walk only by shuffling. Eben had brought along thick rivets and a pair of smith's hammers.

"I welded this ring to his gyves, see?" Eben said. "We tie a rope to it. Won't take much of a tug on it to put him on the ground. Once we get these cuffs riveted on, we got him under control. 'Course then you still need to figure out what to do with him!"

"I got an idea on that," Gabe said. "Let's see how he likes his new jewelry."

Rothaus went back to whimpering and threatening, but in the end he lay still—mostly because Gabe had the muzzle of the Colt revolver stuck in his ear. Eben shut the shackles about the huge ankles. Gabe held one blacksmith hammer under the rivet while Eben struck with the other. When the shackles were secure, Gabe untied the lariat. They got Rothaus onto his feet and tied the rope to the iron bar. He stood as tractable as a muzzled dog, a defeated bully.

"Pretty slick shackles," Gabe said. "The blacksmith teach you that?"

Eben looked at him with one eyebrow raised in mild surprise at the question.

"Oh, yeah," Gabe said. "Well, he'd be proud of you, thinking up these iron hobbles."

"Maybe it was his idea," Eben said with a knowing smile.

"Your ancient Greeks," Gabe was saying, "they favored funeral pyres. Maybe the ground around Athens was too rocky to dig in. Or maybe they had a surplus of firewood."

"I'd prefer to be buried," Eben said. "Having your body burned on a pile of wood doesn't seem dignified. Bits and pieces left over. And all that ash and char. No, I'd rather be buried."

They were sitting together in the gathering twilight watching Rothaus dig graves in the clearing. So far he had managed to finish three side by side at the edge of the field. Gabe led him at gunpoint to collect three skeletons.

"You be sure to get it all," he warned the huge man. Rothaus was down on his knees in the grass gathering bones. "Every scrap of cloth. Every little finger bone. Unless y' want one of those graves t' be yours."

When the sun went behind the mountains and darkness began to creep across the valley, Gabe called a halt and locked the prisoner in the food cellar, together with a blanket and some cold food from the kitchen.

"I'll stand the first watch," Eben volunteered.

"And I'll let you," Gabe agreed. "Looks like we'll need at least two more days for him to finish burying them, wouldn't y' say?"

"And what then?"

"I'm still thinkin' about it," Gabe said. "Still thinking about it."

Dobé came to say goodbye the following morning.

"The ladies are getting anxious to be home," he said.

He cast a curious eye on the fresh mounds of earth out in the clearing and looked around apprehensively to see if Rothaus was in view. The prisoner was still locked safely away.

"We're going to stay until he's given every one of those poor souls a decent grave," Gabe explained. "Might take a few days, but that's what he's going to do. Then we'll meet you at the Surrey place. And we'll all forget about Mr. Rothaus."

"What's going to happen to him?" Dobé asked. "Going to hang him?"

"That's one idea," Gabe agreed. "That certainly is one idea."

It was painful for Gabe to sit there watching Rothaus dig holes while he could be with Catherine. He stared into space. He stroked his chin and thought he might need to shave before leaving and heading for the Surrey ranch. He fidgeted and sometimes paced up and down, wishing only to be on his way.

"Say, there goes another one," Eben said, breaking into Gabe's thoughts.

Gabe looked up and saw the horseman riding away from the place at a hard trot. The man glanced toward them but kept on going.

"Wonder where he's been hiding?" Gabe said.

"Don't know," Eben said. "But if he keeps headin' in that direction, he'd better take a long detour around the hacienda of *Señor Don* Galvez!"

From the hole came a clang of steel and an outburst of profanity as Rothaus struck rock. Gabe went to the tool room for the pick head. He put the handle in it and ordered him to keep digging. Eben went off in search of more skeletons.

"Get back to work," Gabe said.

Even though he was at a disadvantage from being shackled and waist-deep in a grave, Rothaus picked up a rock and hurled it awkwardly. It missed Gabe by several yards. The prisoner picked up a second chunk of stone and Gabe drew his Colt.

"Set down that rock," he ordered. "Right there. On the edge of the hole."

Rothaus glowered, but he complied.

"Blam!"

The .44 roared and the bullet sent fragments of rock flying in all directions, striking Rothaus and making him bleed. He whimpered and tried to rub his eyes with his manacled hands.

It felt good, the recoil and the blast of the Colt. Gabe recognized it as the first time he really felt victorious over Rothaus, the first time he felt he held absolute power of life and death over the madman. How much better would it feel, he wondered, to cock back the hammer and shoot him dead? Maybe this was part of being a real Keystone rider. Maybe being quick and clever and cunning and being polite to ladies wasn't all there was to it. Maybe a man had to like this feeling. Had to want it.

Eben came hurrying at the sound of the shot, but saw nothing amiss.

"You all right?" he asked.

"Sure," Gabe said. "Just helping our friend break up a rock. You find our next body?"

"The one hanging in the tree by the road."

"Fine. We've got another grave nearly ready. You might as well sit down and rest awhile. Then we'll take Rothaus over and make him pack it back here. If you feel like some target practice, go ahead and take a shot at him. I tried it, and it felt pretty good."

The digging and the search for skeletons went on into the next day. Then into the day after that. Eben and Gabe took turns, one of them watching the prisoner at his excavations while the other cast about in the grass and among the trees for more victims. Sometimes, in the trees looking for skeletons, Gabe could hear Rothaus shrieking and wailing, complaining of his sore back, complaining that the shackles wore his wrists raw, yelling for his men to come help him. But there was no one to come. Sometimes they caught a glimpse of the hag. She seemed to be the only living soul who had not lit out for parts unknown. Rothaus's reign was finished.

They asked him why anyone had ever worked for him; he replied by screaming and throwing dirt at them.

"You know," Gabe said to Eben, "I wonder if a few of these bodies weren't his own men. Not riders trying to save the ladies, but men trying to leave."

"Wouldn't doubt it a bit," Eben said.

"Back in civilization he'd get a firing squad. Hanging's too good for him."

"That what you want to do? Take him back to civilization?" Eben asked. "Dobé and at least one of the ladies would need to be witnesses. Long, long way to any kind of town. Even a justice of the peace."

"That was my thinkin'," Gabe said. "It's a problem. Wonder what a Keystone rider'd be expected to do."

"You want to get on to the Surrey place, I imagine," Eben said.

Gabe looked at him. For once there was not even a shadow or suggestion of a smile. The dwarf understood more than he realized. And he was right. Gabe wanted to be rid of this place. He wanted to be where Catherine Surrey was.

"Yeah. But I've got to think what Mr. Pendragon would want me to do. This job ain't finished yet. I wish it was, but it ain't. What I'd like to do is give Rothaus a bunch of Lucifer matches and lock him in that cellar full of blasting powder. Let him do for himself. Like the Greeks did with Socrates and that hemlock poison. No hanging, no firing squad, no prison. Just do it yourself."

"You wouldn't do that," Eben said.

"I wouldn't?"

"No. Look at what you've done on this job already. I don't

mean t' sound like a preacher, or like the blacksmith himself, but you've been fair to every man who stood in your way. That's what Pendragon sets store by. Fairness. You've proved your courage, proved you can be fair. Ever see that old needlepoint framed on Pendragon's wall? It says 'Above all, be just. Be brave, act courteously, and be just. All else follows.' "

"Never saw it."

"All the same."

Rothaus went on digging and complaining. They searched the valley for corpses until they found no more. When the giant patted down the last shovelful of earth on the last grave, he managed a weak smile. He looked at his captors through squinting eyes, sweat making channels in the grime on his face.

"Done," he announced. "Take these off."

He shook the manacles at them.

"What?" Gabe said.

"Take these off. Done. All done. Now you go away."

"No," Gabe said. "No. Now you need to dig one more grave. Make it a big one." Tears welled up in the killer's eyes and ran down his face.

Before the last grave was two feet deep he was sobbing bitterly. He snuffled and wiped at the snot running from his nose. His huge chest heaved as if every breath was painful to him.

Gabe prodded Rothaus with his .44 and told him to keep digging. When his shovel struck a rock, Rothaus went to his knees and clawed at the boulder with both hands, his tears turning the earth to mud. For a few minutes, he looked like an animal trying to burrow its way back underground. He heaved the heavy stone out of the hole and stood there with sweat and tears making furrows through the dirt coating his face and arms. Gabe had never seen a human being—if, indeed, Rothaus could be called a human being—look so absolutely miserable.

However, it did not give him any pleasure. The madman had it coming to him, yet there was no joy in seeing him suffer. The sooner it was over, the better it would be for both of them.

Gabe edged up to the hole and peered in to gauge the depth. He, too, was ready for all this to be over. The thing that had terrorized the whole region was nothing now, just a slumped, dejected, miserable pile of animal flesh. Gabe's hand itched and flexed, anticipating the hard bucking of the Colt against his palm and the sudden roar that would come with it. Another foot down and the grave would be deep enough. Gabe was not ready to be an executioner, but he couldn't think of any recourse. He wished Art Pendragon was there to tell him what to do.

And then something odd happened. Something very odd, indeed.

Rothaus, so tired he could hardly move, rolled the boulder away from the edge of the grave. Still weeping, he rested his hand on the shovel that lay beside the hole.

Neither Gabe nor Eben had seen the dog coming.

It was as if it had materialized out of air, a huge brute of mournful face and gray, shaggy hair. It was the sort of dog that should be back in the Old Country, chasing wolves or deer or guarding a castle.

The dog went for the grave and sniffed at the fresh dirt. With bristly head lowered to the ground, it walked around the hole. It licked Rothaus on the hand. Rothaus stared at the dog through squinty eyes, the rims fiery red from crying and from the dirt he had rubbed into them. The dog looked at Rothaus with eyes that were large and golden and looked unspeakably sad. And it licked his hand a second time. Then it walked off a dozen yards or so and lay down, watching Gabe with those big eyes.

"Damn," Gabe said.

Eben said nothing.

"Where'd he come from?" Gabe said.

All these graves, all this torture and suffering and killing. This valley of meadows and forests and running water, a whole valley used by one crazed tyrant as his personal butchering place. An entire world where such a man had no place to be, no reason to exist. If the world at large knew about him, it would demand that he be tried by jury, convicted, and taken out to be executed.

And a dog licks his hand.

"Damn," Gabe repeated. He put his hand to the butt of his revolver, but only to push it deeper into its holster. There was no question of chivalry here, nor any question of Christian charity. There was no sense of "thou shalt not kill" or even "vengeance is mine, saith the Lord." There was only the absolute certainty that he could not be the one to execute Rothaus. Not with a dog watching.

Gabe felt Eben's presence close to his side and looked down. The dwarf was looking up at him much the way the dog had looked at Rothaus. Eben drew his .38 revolver from its shoulder holster.

"You won't kill him, will you," Eben said.

"No."

"Then it's over. You're done here, rider. Nothing more to do. Your next problem will be waiting for us at the Surrey Ranch."

"So what do I do with Rothaus?" Gabe asked.

"Let me," Eben said softly.

Carrying his revolver, Eben went to the hole and ordered Rothaus to climb out. He marched the exhausted giant away from the graves and across the field of grass to the wagon they used to haul bodies and skeletons. He said something Gabe couldn't hear and Rothaus turned around and plopped down on the tailboard. There he sat with his shackled legs hanging down and nearly dragging in the dirt. Without a backward glance Eben climbed to the seat, took the lines, and drove away through the ranch buildings and across the ridge. It would be the last Gabe ever saw of Rothaus.

Gabe watched until the wagon was out of sight. When he turned and looked around again, the dog was gone.

"Dog or no dog, I should've shot Rothaus," Gabe muttered. "Right between the eyes. Justice."

But in his heart he knew he would not have done it. It made him remember Plato, who asked whether a man seeks justice willingly or out of necessity. Did he need to eliminate another human being, or did he just want to? If he really deserved to carry the Keystone *concho* maybe he'd know.

He went to the house, which would be empty unless the old woman was still lurking about somewhere. The first thing he did was to enter the cellar and tear away the fuse cords leading to the kegs of powder. Then he made his way through gloomy corridors to the vaulted, echoing dining hall where Rothaus kept his trophies and souvenirs. He tore a tapestry from the wall and spread it on the floor. He ripped down all the grim mementos, the crude drawings, the spurs and bridles, anything the madman had hung on the wall to remind himself of his killings. Gabe threw them all onto the tapestry and when he was satisfied that he had collected everything, he folded the corners together and dragged the whole lot outside to the empty grave.

He was tempted to return and set fire to the house itself, blow it up or burn it to oblivion, but what good would that serve? Maybe it could be claimed by some good person. Maybe he would claim it himself and rebuild the house, make it into a home for himself and Catherine Surrey. Together they could put a fence around the new graves and plant some flowers.

He pushed the tapestry bundle into the hole, then went to the shade of a tree where he rested.

The sun went on its arc across the sky. A few high clouds drifted west to east. The tree's splotch of shade shifted almost imperceptibly until the sleeping cowboy lay in full sunlight. Even then he did not wake up. It was the thud of heavy hooves and the jingle of trace chains that brought him out of his dreams into a fuzzy-headed wakefulness.

Eben had returned with the wagon.

The dwarf climbed over the seat into the back of the wagon and threw out the shackles and chains before leaping down to the ground. Then he picked it all up and threw it into the grave.

"Where's Rothaus?" Gabe asked without getting up.

Eben took the shovel and began filling the hole.

"Gone," he said. "You won't see him again."

"You shoot him?"

Eben paused on his shovel to study the concern in Gabe's face.

"No."

"Then what . . . ?"

"Evan Thompson has him."

"The blacksmith?"

"Yes."

"But how . . . where did you find Thompson?"

"Where he always is. Nearby. Closer than you'd think."

"I believe you. But it feels weird."

"When you get to riding for the Keystone, you'll get used to it."

Eben put down the shovel and went to the wagon. He climbed the front wheel and stretched to get something from under the seat. When he came back to where Gabe was sitting, he was carrying a wineskin and something wrapped in a bandanna.

"Evan Thompson said to give you this. He said you've done well."

They shared the blacksmith's wine. It was warm and sweet. When Gabe unwrapped the bandanna, he discovered a headstall of carved leather with fine silver buckles. Both sides were decorated by *conchos* the size of silver dollars, *conchos* stamped with the Keystone brand. And it wasn't a headstall that had belonged to some other cowboy. It was not a hand-me-down or something a man might win on a wager.

It was new.

And it was his.

CHAPTER FIFTEEN
QUEEN OF THE SURREY RANCH

Gabe and Eben stripped to the waist and hung their shirts on the wagon. Sweat poured from them as they shoveled scoop after scoop of dirt into the grave under the roasting heat of the midday sun. Sometimes they rested to drink from the canteen; during those moments without the sounds of shovels scraping and dirt plopping into the hole, a deep quiet returned to the meadow. The peace blended with the fresh green smell of clean grass and newly turned earth.

"A good feeling, isn't it?" the dwarf said.

"What?"

"To have it done. Over with. Letting this place get back to being what it was."

"I guess so."

"You did real well, rider. Real well."

"I don't know."

"I do. It's about patience. Courtesy, courage, loyalty, all of that. This wild country needs more like you. And that's the end of my speech."

"Good," Gabe said. "Let's get this hole filled up."

By the time they finished, it was too late in the afternoon to make a start for the Surrey Ranch. They would have to spend one more night in the valley. Neither of them felt even the slightest urge to sleep in the huge, silent house. When they explored the place they saw plenty of beds, some larger and softer than anything Gabe had ever slept in, but he opted for his bedroll.

He spread it out on clean hay he dragged out of the barn.

"Too dark in that house of his," Gabe said. "Makes me think of ol' Plato's cave. You never heard of it? Pretty interesting story. Let's rustle up a meal an' I'll tell you all about it."

With a whole kitchen to themselves—two kitchens, if you count the one on the upper floors used by Catherine Surrey, her sister, and her servant woman—the pair had very little difficulty "rustling" a meal. The only problem lay in deciding whether to eat tinned peaches or open a can of grapes, whether to open one can of tomatoes apiece or several, and whether to boil the potatoes or fry them. The buttermilk in the cooler had gone off, but the quarter of beef hanging there was still good for a couple of big steaks. Eben found an unopened sack of Arbuckle's and went to work cranking the coffee mill until he had ground enough for supper and for breakfast as well.

After eating their fill of meat and potatoes, the two retired into the open yard with their coffee mugs and a can of peaches apiece. The sun was down behind the mountain now and a small wisp of a breeze began drifting downhill as if the mountain had inhaled all day and was letting its pine-scented breath out again.

"About this cave of your man Plato," Eben suggested, using his knife to spear a slice of peach from his can.

"Cave," Gabe repeated. "Plato. Well, Plato was one of those old Greeks. Maybe you knew that. Anyway, he wrote about how some people live their whole lives locked up in chains. They're chained down to benches in a cave and all they see are these shadows on the wall. It's the whole world, so far as they can see. But!"

"But what?"

"There's some who can see something better. My mother's one of those. So's my older brother. They see the light like in the old gospel song. They see the light that makes the shadows.

And they're not afraid to look at it. Might hurt their eyes at first, but they go right on ahead out into the sunshine."

"This Missus Townsend," Eben said, "she one of those? Chained in a cave, I mean? Seems awfully brave, going all the way to the Keystone to get help and all, but I wonder if maybe she's scared of something at the same time."

"Might be," Gabe said. "I see what you're getting at. The idea of changing seems to frighten her some. But we ought not to be talkin' about ladies who aren't present. Let's just say I think she'll be real glad to get back into her own house and have her own routine back."

Somewhere in the distance an evening wren made its hymn to the departing day. A coyote barked three times and, hearing no reply, went back to its solitary search for food. Gabe and Eben sat together without speaking because there was no need to. Anyone passing by would have heard only the slurping of coffee and the clank of knife blades in tin cans. The two silent men were content to watch the light die out and the darkness slowly take hold of the hills.

On the following morning, the lady in question, she whom Gabriel declined to discuss, greeted the bright new sun with zest and joy. Her life had been returned to her. She had awakened to sunlight streaming through her own window. She put on her favorite dress to join her sister at the breakfast table; they discussed the day's business just as before, making lists of things that needed doing as they had done nearly every morning before Rothaus entered their lives.

"Do you know," Lynette said, "it is a pleasure to be holding my own teacup in my hand? Such a little thing, one's own personal teacup. I confess I never thought of it over all these months, but now that it is in my hand again, I have a sense of something being made whole. Do you know what I mean?"

Catherine did, indeed.

After breakfast, she and Catherine dressed and ventured outside. Some of the Surrey Ranch crew were hanging around the porch to await instructions, those who had either remained there under the tyranny of Rothaus's foreman or had returned from exile when they learned he was gone.

Catherine greeted them warmly.

She asked them to take stock of the Surrey's situation in order that she might know what plans to make for the next week or month.

"It doesn't seem so, with this warm weather, but winter will come before we know it. We need to be certain of hay and fuel, everything."

When she dismissed them to see to the chores, Old Tom lingered. From behind his back he brought out a small bouquet of wild roses.

"Awful glad you're all right, ma'am," he mumbled, handing her his tribute.

Young Philadra also stayed behind. Her pregnancy showed in her bulging figure and ruddy face. She attempted a curtsy and explained how she and the redhead cowboy, Andy, were sharing a room he had fixed up in the stable and would be married as soon as they could get to a preacher. Joshua, an older herdsman, stood farther apart so he wouldn't have to listen to Philadra talking about "women things." When she was gone, he came forward.

"Reckon somebody oughta see to gettin' some of them scattered cows back," he volunteered.

"Yes," Catherine said. "There must be a great many unaccounted for. I wish you'd make it your job to look into it, would you?"

There were two more ranch hands waiting to talk to her. They were young, rough-looking boys who had "gone over" to the Surrey after Rothaus's operation was brought to a halt. All they knew was cattle. Cattle and guns. All Catherine could tell them was to make certain the bunkhouse and stable buildings were clean and usable. Then they were to help round up whatever livestock they could.

Catherine and Lynette made an inventory of the root cellar and pantry. They inspected the house and outbuildings, writing lists of things that would need doing. Of primary importance was the matter of money, of raising enough of it to pay the crew. At the very least, they needed to assure the men that there was a plan to provide for back pay. By midmorning, the ladies agreed they had done enough to earn themselves a break; two hours later they were still relaxing on their shaded porch sharing their thoughts.

"This young man, Gabriel," Catherine said, "he should be arriving soon? Are we certain he completely vanquished Mr. Rothaus?"

"*Killed* him, you mean," Lynette sniffed. "You mean did he *kill* him? Let's not shrink from the word, Catherine. I can't be certain, of course, that he has dispatched our menace, no. However, from having been in his company through several dangerous moments—as I told you last evening—I can surmise that he has at least rendered Mr. Rothaus harmless. It seems incredible, but I'm forced to admit it could be true."

"And will he come here, do you think? What I mean is, if he decides his mission, or whatever you would call it, is finished, perhaps he will merely return home. There is no real reason for him to come here."

Lynette looked at her sister quizzically. Something soft and lingering had come into Catherine's voice when she mentioned the Gabriel person . . . Lynette had noticed it earlier, from the very moment when her sister first saw him.

"Why, Catherine!" she said. "Your voice! You sound positively winsome! I believe you would be disappointed not to see him again! And after only a dozen words to each other. Shame on you!"

She laughed as she said it, and Catherine responded with a little laugh of her own.

"And why not?" she challenged. "Why not admit it? I do like his appearance. I find him quite attractive to look upon. Strong, in a thin sort of way, and certainly capable. And from what you have told me, very intelligent. A cut above the 'ordinary' cowboy, wouldn't you agree?"

"Perhaps," Lynette admitted. "Then again, you didn't see him in his ridiculous apron, sweeping the kitchen and serving the Pendragons. You didn't see how eager he was to ride out from the Keystone as though he could be compared with someone like Link Lochlin. Or the one they called 'Pasque.' Or the heroic Mr. Owens."

"I didn't need to see any such thing," Catherine said, "for it wouldn't matter to me. I'm not one to hold myself above ordinary people. Especially one who has done us so much good! No, I will admit his attractiveness, and I may even shock you by saying I would welcome it if he were to ask me to go out walking or riding with him. When he arrives, of course."

"Walking or riding!" Lynette said. "Walking or riding! You mean 'courting'! I do wish you'd use the bare term for it. You want him to come courting you!"

"Why not? That day when he saw us off, when he was in such a hurry to make certain we were away safely, on that occasion I saw a little something in his eyes—he does have nice eyes, you must admit it—something I took to indicate he might be inclined to sit of an evening here on the porch with me. So there."

"Catherine Surrey!" Lynette exclaimed. "I do hope you are

not preparing to launch into some sentimental drivel about 'love at first sight'! You've been reading far too much English poetry, I believe. And not enough of your Bible."

"There's also love at first sight in the Bible, dear," Catherine reminded her.

A twinkle appeared in her blue eyes as she watched Lynette's face. Lynette was clearly straining to remember cases of instantaneous infatuation in her Old Testament. Bathsheba? David? Solomon?

Oh, bother it all!

"To return to your first question," Lynette said, "I'm sure he will come. I hardly think he'd return to the Keystone without some tangible recognition of his 'valiant' deeds, perhaps a letter attesting to the same. His one purpose in life is to be recognized as a Keystone rider. His one purpose."

She said "one" with pointed emphasis.

"You make him sound like a little boy who wants to be a grownup!" Catherine answered. "What I saw was a man already grown. A very competent man. You don't like him and so you see him as immature. Or not as serious as you would like him to be. But I liked him the moment I saw him."

"Well," Lynette replied, rising from her chair, "I'm going upstairs and see to my wardrobe. Everything is in need of airing and pressing. I have no time to sit here listening to mooncalf nonsense about Gabriel Allen."

The two sisters spent the afternoon apart from one another, but not because of any kind of ill feeling. When they came together again for supper the conversation resumed of its own volition, as if there had been no break whatever.

"I have been thinking," Lynette said. "I've decided to tell you what I overheard about Mr. Gabriel Hugh Allen. You are my sister, after all. You have a right to know. I say 'overheard,' mind you. I have no way of substantiating it."

"Go ahead," Catherine said.

"If you will listen to some advice from me," Lynette continued, "you will take this with a grain of salt. I cannot, and will not, forget the sight of him working as a common kitchen laborer. Fetching and carrying, waiting on table. A menial of the lowest order. I cannot understand how a man could do that unless he was born to the servant class. How could he even pretend to be one of that sort?"

"But dear, didn't you pretend to be *my* servant?"

Lynette sniffed and ignored the question.

"If you want to pursue this matter," she said, "I suggest that you confront Mister Gabriel with what I'm about to tell you and see what he says. There's something shady here. I don't think his motives are as he represents them."

Lynette told her sister what she had learned about Gabriel's pedigree and his actual relationship to Arthur Pendragon.

"It's all this secrecy, this mysteriousness," she said. "It seems strange, even in a country where most men have secrets, things in their past they've come here to get away from."

"I agree," Catherine said. "There is a mysterious secrecy about it. It's almost as if he didn't come here to help us but to find something, to make something happen."

Catherine had felt it the first time she saw him from her window. There was a fascination to him. It was like seeing a painted portrait that held the eyes and would not let you look away. It happened again when she saw him riding straight and tall on his way to confront Rothaus. And once more, after it was all over, when he came to see them safely away from that awful place. He was bruised and battered and noble. What powerful emotions rose in her bosom then! She felt pulled toward him, of that there was no doubt. It did not cross her mind to deny that feeling. Not once had she thought of him as an ordinary cowboy.

He was in no way ordinary.

And now! Now, according to Lynette, Gabriel is the nephew to Arthur Pendragon himself. And is the brother of a Keystone rider? When Lynette finished telling what she knew, what she had heard, Catherine sat quietly.

"Well," she managed to say at last. "Not such an ordinary man after all. All the more reason to permit him to 'court' me, as you say."

It was banal. It was a common, almost witless thing to say. It had the effect of triggering Lynette's worst fear, which was that her sister would dive headfirst into another sort of imprisonment immediately after having been delivered from one.

"Dear," she said. "Dear Catherine. For my sake, go carefully. Go slowly. You know I cherished my dear husband, Oliver, but . . . I do hate to say this . . . the truth is, there were times I wished I had been in less of a hurry to rush into marriage. There were! Sometimes, I doubted if what I had done was the right thing. I wish I had been able to wait a year before marrying him. A year to think. A year to grow."

"But that's you, Lynette! Not me!"

"Trust me," Lynette said. "If you think you are in love, wait. Be doubly careful. Marriage is a lifetime, you know. A lifetime! Promise me, you will wait—that you will ask him to wait—until you are sure who he is. And until you can be sure of your feelings. Is that too much to ask? I love you and couldn't bear it if you rushed into anything. Please. For my sake? I beg you, ask him to wait. If he asks you, let him wait."

"But a year!"

"A happy year, Catherine! A happy year! He will stay here, you two will have days and days to talk and to go riding and make plans and be together! It will be a happy year and the days will hurry by."

And so they came to an agreement, the two sisters of the

Surrey Ranch: if Mr. Gabriel were to come calling, if he had courtship on his mind, Catherine would diplomatically inform him he would need to be patient for a period of one year. Lynette saw it as a way of putting the Keystone rider's character and sincerity to the test, not to mention his patience. After all, hadn't he already passed several tests of his endurance?

Catherine, having read too many English poets, saw it as a terribly romantic interlude, a Grand Anticipation before the Great Event. It was like teasing a new beau, which was the sort of fun Catherine liked. Also, being who she was, she thought that Gabriel might laugh at the whole idea, boldly seize her up, put her on his saddle before him and ride away, one strong arm holding her fast as her hair flew wildly and her heart pounded. She did not reveal this romantic fantasy to Lynette. No. She kept it locked tightly beneath her own whalebone stays. After dusk, when she would lie uncorseted deep in the folds of her own bed, she would let it out and would visit it again.

Gabe and Eben came upon a rough camp, little more than an old tarpaulin pitched as a lean-to behind a circle of stones that held the smoldering remains of a campfire. Two blankets and two saddles lay under the tarpaulin. Two horses were picketed to a lariat stretched between a couple of trees.

They drew revolvers and rode cautiously into the camp. A light odor of tobacco showed that the occupants had been there recently. Probably heard them coming and hid back in the trees somewhere. Eben twisted in the saddle, looking right and left for signs of somebody. Gabe leaned over his horse's shoulder to study the ground for tracks. If somebody was sitting there smoking and heard horses coming up the road, which way would he run? *Probably* that *direction,* Gabe thought, spotting a boot track in the spilled ash from the fire. The boot print pointed at a thicket of chokecherry bushes.

He and Eben didn't need anything from whoever it was. Gabe was anxious to get to the ranch. Didn't feel like stopping for coffee or conversation. On the other hand, it was interesting that anyone would hide when they heard them coming. And if he and Eben were going to be riding on up this road, he'd like to know who was behind him.

"Hello!" he called, sliding his Colt back into the holster. "Anybody around?"

Silence.

"Anybody there?" he called out again.

This time the bushes moved.

Out stepped two men, their appearance as crude as their camp. It was obvious they were traveling "light," without the encumbrance of razors and soap. They looked sheepish as they stood in front of Gabe's horse.

"Y' the one what took care of Rothaus?" one asked.

"I guess so," Gabe said. He nodded toward Eben. "I had help."

"S'pose y' know we was workin' for him."

"Had it about figured, yes."

"We was goin' back, soon as you cleared out."

"Oh? Well, if that's what you want to do. None of our business, not any longer."

"Kill him, did you?"

"Rothaus?" Gabe glanced over at Eben and grinned just a little.

"Let's say you'll find fresh graves in that meadow back there. One of 'em is fairly good-size. You won't be seeing Mr. Rothaus again."

"Good!" the other one said. "Our ma, she says you was nice to her."

Gabe looked puzzled. "Your ma?"

"At the house. She hated him. Where's she gonna go, mister?"

"Ah. That woman. Good thing there's you two t' take care of her. Dunno know why she says I was nice. Hardly spoke to her."

"Still," one of the brothers said. "She thought you was all right."

"She sure hated him," said the other.

"I wish you luck," Gabe said. "We better be on our way."

"Anythin' we can do for you?" one of the men said.

"Do?"

"Make it up. Put things right. Ma, she always wants things put right."

"I suppose you could ride around hereabouts, see if y' find any Keystone livestock. You know the brand? If you find some, maybe push 'em back toward the Keystone range. Mr. Pendragon would make it worth your while."

"We'll do 'er," the first brother said. "We'll go see how ma is, then we'll do 'er!"

"Real cowboy work fer a change," the other said. "Damn. That'll feel good!"

As they rode away, Gabe turned toward Eben.

"You can holster the artillery," he said. "Danger's over with."

Eben looked down at the .38 in his hand as if he had just realized he had it.

"Yeah," he said. "I guess it sure scared them into line, huh?"

"Yeah," said Gabe. "Downright intimidating."

When they broke out of the timber where they could see the sage-dotted cattle range of the Surrey Ranch, Gabe recognized why Rothaus preferred his own dark and gloomy valley, why he took Catherine to his house rather than invading hers. The Surrey place would've been too cheerful, too bright for him.

A long humpback of high clouds rose behind the distant range of mountains, but the valley was washed in sunlight. A stream meandered through bright green meadows. Barn roofs of gray shingle were dull silver in the sun. Inside the picket fence surrounding the main house, a lawn of deep grass looked blue-green. There were a few pine trees in the expanse, and a few small groves of cottonwood, but otherwise the flat valley was a sprawling lake of grass around the island of ranch buildings.

Riding closer, they could see that Rothaus's men had occupied the place. Corral gates drooped open or were lashed shut with wire. Corral rails were broken. Pens for sheep or pigs, possibly milk cows, were knee-deep in bristling weeds. A haystack near a barn had collapsed and no one had bothered to rebuild it.

Anxious as he was to see the woman who had won his heart, Gabriel Hugh Allen lingered to take it all in. He was the sort of man to see potential in every circumstance, one who likes nothing better than an opportunity to fix things up and get them running smoothly.

Or as a neighbor once remarked to Gabe's mother, "he's the kinda kid who likes to plant flower seeds in a horse turd."

"A man could do a lot with this place," Eben said.

"Just thinking the same thing," Gabe agreed. "Just thinking the same thing."

"Some kind of storm brewin' in those mountains," Eben observed. "Might have rain tonight."

"Might," Gabe agreed. "Let's be getting on."

They followed the track down the hill to a pole barn and a corral holding four horses. While they were unsaddling, they saw Dobé hurrying toward them, followed by a man whose mustache stuck out beyond his cheeks. The waxed ends bounced up and down as he walked. He was a man in his middle years; judging by his girth, one could say he had not missed many meals in those years.

"Mister Gabriel!" Dobé exclaimed. "And Eben! How good to see you both! Just put your saddles in the shed there. Plenty of water in the trough for your animals. And you'll find hay just over the board fence."

Dobé wanted to conduct them to the house immediately.

"The ladies will be anxious to welcome you!" he said.

"Like to clean up first," Gabe said.

The cowboy and the dwarf put down hay for the horses, hung the saddles in the shed, and then stripped shirts and plunged their hands into the trough of cold water. While they shivered and scrubbed, Dobé introduced his companion.

"Mr. George Talboy," he said. "One-time roustabout. Former roundup boss. Recently appointed general foreman and ramrod of the Surrey Ranch. George came west with the ladies' father. That was back in the wide-open days. Been a king post of the ranch ever since."

"Not altogether true," George Talboy said. He drew one mustache through his fingers. "I pretty much let 'em down when Rothaus's men showed up. Miss Surrey, she told us all to kinda lie low and wait and see, so that's what we did. Didn't make any trouble, 'though I sure did want to. More than once. Glad it's over now. Damn glad. We sure owe you boys."

"Good to meet you," Gabe said. He wiped his face with his bandanna and ran a pocket comb through his hair. "Look forward to working with you, too. Maybe we can help get things fixed up again."

"Nice of y'," George said. "Darn nice. But we're pretty much on the way t' gettin' things back to normal. Whatever normal is! There's still cows t' round up. Unbranded yearlings runnin' around. Rothaus's men were too lazy to gather 'em. Fences and stuff needs fixin'. Few things like that."

"Later, later," Dobé interrupted. "All that can come later,

George. Mister Gabriel, you've got to tell me—how did it go with Rothaus? What has become of him? What finally happened back there?"

Gabe and Eben smiled at each other.

"You might say he dug himself a hole," Eben said, dusting his pants. "Several holes, in fact."

"Quite a few," Gabe grinned, putting his pocket comb away. "Why don't we go find Miss Surrey and her sister and tell everybody at once. Tell y' everything that happened."

"Yes," Dobé said eagerly. "Better yet, we'll lay out a good big supper so we can sit around the table and share stories! George here can fill you in on the state of things, the ladies can tell you their plans, and you can tell us what became of Mr. Rothaus."

"Sounds good."

"If you're ready, we'll go around this way to the house. The ladies will be on the porch."

George Talboy followed. He was watching the western sky. Those big puffy clouds could bring a downpour, he reckoned. Might be they'd drift on right over the valley and keep goin'. Or might be they'd open up like a busted grain sack and dump a whole world of rainwater.

CHAPTER SIXTEEN
KIDNAPPERS

"Catherine?"

Lynette discovered her sister standing at the window in the upstairs sitting room, her figure silhouetted against the darkening sky. Catherine did not turn as Lynette entered the room and lit the lamps.

"Catherine?" she said again. "Are you all right?"

The answer was a drawn-out sigh.

"I thought your cowboy was grand!" Lynette continued cheerily. "Such nice table manners! His mother certainly taught him well. That story of how she cured him from resting his elbows on the table! Very funny!"

"Yes," Catherine said.

"I have to admit I may have underestimated him. I can certainly credit his assurance that Mr. Rothaus is gone . . . that is to say, the assurance of him and the small man, Eben. Most mysterious, isn't it? Wonderful to think the horrid man will never bother us again. It was a nightmare. Now it's over."

"Yes," Catherine again replied.

"So tell me what he said to you afterward! After we excused ourselves to leave you two alone. I know you were going to tell him our plan. I'm so curious to know the arrangement! He'll stay here, of course. It's obvious from his interest in the Surrey Ranch. He wants to stay and build it up again. I was thinking perhaps he—and his little friend—might build a cabin or house of some sort to stay in. But I'm ahead of myself. Do tell me what he said when you told him!!"

Catherine turned with deliberate rigidity. Her skirts swept around; when they had ceased their pendulum sway she looked into her sister's eyes.

"Oh!" she said. And repeated herself, "oh!"

"Oh?"

"Oh, Lynette!! Lynette! Why did I listen to you, why?"

"I don't understand," Lynette said, clutching her hands to her bosom.

"A year, you said. Your idea, not mine! Make him wait a year!"

"Catherine, what happened?"

"I will tell you. And then I wish to be left alone."

"Is it something awful?"

"I will tell you," Catherine repeated. "When you left us, he waited for me to speak. We talked about one thing and the other. He stood closer to my chair. Then we sat together on the settee. I called him Gabriel. His eyes were shining so brightly! He took my hand, and I allowed it to him. It was evident. It was obvious what we were feeling for one another."

"And then?"

"I don't know. A sort of tension in the room. An expectation of something about to happen. A kiss, I suppose. Or an embrace. That kind of moment where you know something is about to happen. Yet you're frozen in place. I couldn't move. He only sat there with a shy smile like that of a schoolboy. When I saw how his eyes were shining, it nearly burst my heart. Well, I felt I had to break the silence somehow, and so I asked his intentions."

"Intentions!"

Lynette would have laughed had it not been for the look on her sister's face. Its sorrowful seriousness would make a bloodhound envious.

"He laughed—I love his laugh—and said he intended to court

me. Court me!"

"Wonderful!" Lynette said.

"Then I said I would need a year. A year to put my affairs in order. This date, a year from now, I told him, will be our day to look forward to. One year from this very day. Oh! What a huge mistake I have made! I told him I thought he might go and arrange a home for us. I told him you thought he was not . . . well, not a man of property. I told him you had suggested we postpone any formal agreement. You understand, until you were satisfied he was worthy of me. Worthy of me! I thought I said it jokingly! I smiled!"

"What happened?" Lynette asked. Her hands kept twisting damp wrinkles in her handkerchief.

"He withdrew his hand from mine. He said 'fine.' Just like that, 'fine.' Then, he rose and said good night, and left me there without so much as a backward glance. It was evident that he did not mean to come back. I'm up here because I had to be alone, but also to watch for him. He rode away not more than ten minutes ago."

"Rode away? In the dark?"

"Yes. I don't think he took anything with him. He just saddled his horse and rode off."

"What shall we do?" Lynette said.

"Do?" Catherine replied. Her eyes flashed with anger. "What is there for us to do? You've done enough, I should think."

It seemed to Gabe like he was back where he'd started all those months ago, when he stood on a hilltop wondering how he could ever become a Keystone rider. Trying to decide what to do. How to follow a vision he knew must be followed. He had come through all the fighting, wrestled with fear and a hundred decisions. He had succeeded, too: Eben said so. "You've done well," he said. But here he was again, wondering which way to turn. Back to his uncle, back to the Keystone and all it stood for, back among the Keystone riders, or back down to the Surrey Ranch and a year of waiting.

Lamps lit in the faraway windows of the Surrey Ranch were yellow specks in the dusk. Beyond the ranch lay the countless miles he had come and the challenges he had faced, now being cloaked in the coming darkness.

Ahead of him a range of ominous clouds rose like heaps of wet ash against the blue-black sky. The storm that George Talboy predicted was on the boil, churning and heaving just beyond the mountain. He felt the horse shivering under him. He dismounted and looped the reins around a bush so he could walk off a few yards. He needed to be alone; the animal's nervousness was an intrusion on his thoughts.

The time before, on another hill, many miles and months from here, watching storm clouds such as these, he'd been holding a plucked chicken in either hand. Now . . . he put his hand on the butt of the Colt revolver. Now, he seemed to hold two futures in his hands. He looked east away from thoughts of what was to come. His mind went searching among the twistings of his own back trail. He wondered if the Swiss brothers had found their countryman on that dairy farm south of the Espirita River. He thought of old Lou Barlow and wondered if he was still being cantankerous. And those two eccentric Scotchmen—Grit and William—did they move on, or were they still in their "wee hoose"? What about the Mexican, *Don* Galvez? Maybe Gabe would stop at the Galvez *hacienda* and stay a week or two, if his way back to the Keystone Ranch took him anywhere close to it.

From the corner of his eye he caught a flash of lightning. He turned toward the mountain as the peal of thunder reached him. A peal is what it was, a rising, rolling, booming swell of deep-throated thunder as if some giant hand was swinging the clapper of a bell of unimaginable size. Another long flash of light painted itself against the formation of clouds. Another long peal of thunder vibrated through his boot soles. Gabe felt the wind coming out from the storm. The first wind-driven drops of rain struck his face. The horse never had been much enamored of darkness in which lights flashed with loud noises that came out of nowhere and shook the ground; he pulled loose his reins and made for the distant corral. Gabe could only stand and watch him run. He would later discover the animal at the closed gate, standing and shivering in the cold rain, head hanging down until his nose nearly touched the mud.

The bursts of sheet lightning came closer and closer together until they lit the arching mass of cloud like a dance hall stage. The thunder's bass music rumbled beneath the lightning.

And the riders appeared.

The sky figures were formless and faceless. The horses plunging toward him might have been nothing more than storm clouds that looked like horses, the men who rode them part of those same cloud formations. Then Gabe could make out the hooves, the branded chaps, the flaring nostrils of the horses, the faces of the riders huge against the clouds. The sight did not frighten him, for he recognized who they were and he knew they had not come to harm him.

These were friendly images. They were riders he knew. They came on through the sky, horses flank to flank, the men shoulder to shoulder. Their bodies leaned forward eager for the adventure toward which they were plunging, eyes fixed on that distant moment and mouths set in hard smiles.

They were the riders of the Keystone, Art Pendragon's men, and Gabe knew he had earned his place among them.

Gabe saw Link Lochlin in the center, the leader. He recognized the black mustache and the way Link had of setting his hat square to the horizon. Next to Link rode Dick Elliot, the carefree, careless master of all horses. His horse was the largest and most powerful, yet it was under such perfect control that it was an extension of Elliot himself. And there was Will Jensen on the other side, Will with the smiling eyes and quick temper. Beside him rode the one they still called The New Kid, sometimes. Garth. Unpredictable, wild Garth. Then the Pinto Kid with his flashy silver ornaments and colorful vest.

The riders of the Keystone. Time stopped. The cloud apparition was so real to Gabe that he felt like he could mount up and ride with them. His hand opened to take the reins of his horse but closed again on drops of rain.

He saw more riders coming, riders also eagerly leaning forward, driven by freedom and exuberance. The faces were less distinct, but one looked like the rider he knew only as Sam. Another looked like Bob Riley, the steady and methodical Riley.

Rain slashed at Gabe with renewed force. With a final crash, the lightning ceased altogether. The ghostly Keystone images were swallowed up by darkness. Heedless of rain stinging his face Gabe went on staring into the sky, hoping for one more glimpse of the men who rode for Art Pendragon.

Then a question struck him with a force stronger than the wind-driven rain and just as chilling.

Where was Kyle Owen? And where was Gabe's own brother, the man known as Pasque? They were not among the riders. The vision was over, and they had not been part of it.

Gabe lowered his head, turned up his collar against the storm, and began the long soggy trudge down the hill toward the Surrey Ranch. The rain soaked his clothes and ran off the brim of his hat.

Pasque and Kyle. Even if the other riders were imaginary, why weren't those two among them? Gabe knew the answer. He knew it the moment he recognized they were not with the others. Kyle was living with the woman he married, the lady named Fontana. Pasque had gone to New Mexico and married Elena Victoria Godinez. Legends, both of them, among the men of the Keystone Ranch. They had gone on to new responsibilities now. Married and settled down, they no longer rode for the Keystone brand.

The horse waited at the corral. After putting the beast in the shed and unsaddling and rubbing it down with dry straw, Gabe went to the bunkhouse. He shivered out of his clothes and added an extra quilt to his narrow cot. He would get warm and he would sleep, and as soon as the morning was light enough to see by he would pack up his few things and he would be gone.

Gabe and Eben kept their voices low, although it was about time the men in the bunkhouse were getting up. Some were already stirring in their cots. Eben opened the stove and built up the fire under the cold remains of yesterday's coffee. They rolled some food into folded blankets, then rolled the blankets into their rain slickers to tie behind the saddle. All the rest went into saddlebags.

The sun turned the horizon crimson for a few moments before sliding up into a cloudless sky. The two men stepped into their stirrups and swung into their saddles.

"Looks like a nice day ahead," Gabe said softly.

"Sure does," said Eben. "Storm always leaves everything smelling real good, doesn't it? Fresh. Clean."

They rode slow and easy, following the wagon track toward the hill where Gabe had seen his phantoms, the hill marking the edge of the main ranch.

"Be interestin' to see what's become of our three Switzers," Gabe said.

"Hope they do well," Eben replied. "You won't find 'em at the river crossing, I'm thinking."

"*I* won't? Don't you mean 'we' won't?"

"Nope. I won't be there. I don't need to go back with you. Up at the top of the divide I'm headin' south. Goin' to meet up with Evan Thompson. He's a couple days away, I figure. Probably got another job for me."

"All right," Gabe said. "Well."

" 'Well'?"

"Well . . . it's been good riding with you. Wouldn't mind doing it again."

"Might be we will . . . say! Who's that, do you reckon?"

Eben was looking back down the long hill. Three horses had left the ranch and were coming toward them. So far they were just specks moving against the landscape.

"Hmmm," Gabe said. "Kinda early t' be out, unless you're goin' somewhere."

"Probably nothin'," Eben said. "Maybe the ladies sent them to do something up this way. Nothin' to do with us, probably."

At the summit of the divide, Eben reached up to shake Gabe's hand and Gabe reached down to shake his. They parted company as casually as if they intended to meet again that same afternoon.

"See y'."

"Yep. Thanks again. For riding with me, I mean."

"You're welcome. Another time, maybe."

"You bet."

Gabe watched the dwarf go. Somehow the little fellow on the big horse looked full-size as he rode away. The other horsemen had reached the base of the long hill and had stopped. They changed direction like they meant to meet up with Eben.

"How the hell we supposed to bring 'im back if he don't want to come?" one of the three Surrey horsemen said.

"I heard tell he's a dead shot, that's for sure," said the second one.

"He killed a buncha men gettin' here," the third one added. "The lady, she said 'bring him at gunpoint if you have to,' but I don't much favor our chances."

"So we tell her what? He won't come?"

"We don't know that, not till we ask him."

"Don't reckon he will. You seen him at the bunkhouse. A man like that? Man like that, he rolls his blanket and packs his saddlebags, he means t' go. He ain't comin' back 'cause some woman wants 'im to."

"Plus, there's two of 'em," the first man observed. "I'm thinkin' they got the odds goin' for 'em."

"Hell," observed the second man. "We can't just go back. The way I see it, we gotta go ask him, at least."

"Hey!" said the third. "What's that about?"

He pointed to the two figures atop the divide, one of whom had separated and was heading south down the slope.

Number One, who had keener eyesight, squinted hard and looked.

"By God," he said, "I think the little fella is ridin' off alone. Headin' south, I'm thinkin'."

"There go the odds then."

"Too bad it ain't him she sent us t' bring back. A little dwarf wouldn't give us no trouble."

The Idea did not come to them immediately. They were the sort who have trouble thinking of an idea unless it's been thrummed into their heads by someone else. To put it another way, if one were to say they had to come up with an original idea or die trying, they'd be among the expired. Nevertheless, The Idea managed to permeate the skull bone and brain mass of Number Three.

"Say," he said slowly, since he was as clumsy at expressing

original thought as he was at having it in the first place, "I betcha . . ."

The other two looked at him expectantly, like watching a man tipping back in a flimsy chair.

"Bet what?" Number Two said.

"Well . . . I betcha if we was to grab the dwarf and hightail it for the ranch with 'im . . . I betcha that lanky cowpuncher'd come after him. Y' know. The way a cow comes after her calf."

"What if the cowboy rides off instead?"

"Nuthin' lost. Then we let the little guy go an' figger out somethin' else."

As a strategy it seemed simple and natural. The three Surrey riders put quirts to their horses and headed to intercept Eben. Eben saw them coming fast and calculated they had some message for him, maybe something for him to carry to the blacksmith. Maybe the ladies had decided to offer him a job at the ranch. They were short-handed, after all. Eben reined in and waited. He found himself quickly surrounded and disarmed. They tied his wrists to his saddle horn. Then the three headed back toward the ranch with Eben in tow. They looked back to be certain that Gabe had seen them.

Gabe had indeed witnessed the whole thing. He was uncertain what it meant. Like Eben, he first imagined some sort of message was being delivered to his small friend. His next thought was that some emergency had arisen and Eben's help was urgently required, but what kind of emergency could it be? Maybe he ought to turn back and find out. But why wouldn't they come and tell him? Why grab Eben and ride away?

Then he thought of Catherine. And then of Lynette Townsend. That was the answer. One of them, or both of them, wanted him back on the ranch. They had sent these three cowboys to get him. They knew he wouldn't ride off without knowing Eben was all right. It was cunning. Underhanded, but cunning. Probably hide Eben somewhere until they'd said their piece and persuaded him to stay on the Surrey for that "year of waiting" both women seemed so set on. But he was a Keystone man now. His job wasn't over with until he had reported back to Art.

A realization slapped him across the face. He'd finally done something wrong. No Keystone rider would sneak away like that, no explanation, no goodbye. It was cowardly and it was wrong. This was the penalty. When Eben was taken by those three men, it was his fault.

Gabe lashed his horse with the reins and used his spurs with unprecedented fury, recklessly turning straight down the slope in pursuit of the three cowboys. Whatever they were up to, he was going find out. He would stop them before they reached the buildings even if he had to put a bullet into one of them, or into a horse.

His horse stumbled, recovered, kept plunging forward. Strings of drool flew from its mouth and streaked Gabe's chaps, and he felt the horse's sweat making the saddle slip, but he rode on, rode rough with spurs driving hard and the ends of the reins slashing one shoulder, then the other. At a shallow arroyo the horse slipped and nearly went down but recovered and clawed his way back into a hard run. Now they were close enough that he could see one of the cowboys holding Eben's reins, pulling his horse along as fast as he could. Eben was swaying and jolting, holding on for dear life. He yelled at the men to rein in. Gabe yelled for them to stop. They kept on going even though it was clear he was going to overtake them.

Gabe sat up straight in the saddle and drew his Colt. He held it up so they would see it when they looked back. And still they kept going, dragging Eben's horse behind them. Gabe could see the little guy bouncing up and down and leaving daylight between his Levi's and the saddle leather, hands frozen onto the saddle horn.

Now Gabe's anger at himself overcame his reason altogether. Unable to think straight, he thumbed back the hammer and fired over their heads.

Frightened, Cowboy Number Two pulled a gun and twisted around. He snapped off a shot at Gabe.

It turned out to be an unlucky shot. The lead slug caught Gabe in the bicep of his left arm just below the shoulder. His arm jerked upward hauling the reins and dragging the horse's head sideways. Going too fast to recover, horse and man went into the ground. Gabe came out of the saddle and headfirst into a tombstone-size piece of granite.

The Surrey Ranch men stopped long enough to see if Gabe was still alive, then raced to the main house where they reported that they would be able to bring Gabe back, but they would need a wagon. They would also need to catch his horse and shoot it, since it had a broken leg.

"Th' other, we got him back all right. That dwarf fella. He's all right. We got that little gun off'n him. Might be best not t' give it back t' him, not right away. We'll be takin' a wagon t' get your Keystone man now."

The women kept fluttering in and out of the room, hovering around the unconscious Gabriel, bringing whatever silly comforts they thought a wounded cowboy might require such as larger pillows, their father's Bible, constantly refreshed pitchers of cold water for when he woke up, and a lamp with a flower-embossed glass shade, which they hoped would soften the light for him. Eben anxiously monitored the bandages for signs of fresh bleeding. The wound in the upper arm was serious, but not worrying; as he cleaned the blood away, Eben had seen the slug lodged in the muscle. With his small fingers he was able to pluck it out with having to dig for it. A dose of alcohol, a tight wrapping, and Gabe's arm was on the way to recovery. His head injury; that was a different matter. Eben didn't like the shape of the bruise, nor did he like the fact that his friend had been sleeping motionless for two days. Eben slept on a settee near the bed, his senses tuned to awaken him at Gabe's slightest moan or movement.

The return to consciousness of Gabriel Hugh Allen was neither dramatic nor momentous. One morning—the fourth morning since the horse had sent him headfirst into the rock—he was simply awake. He managed a bit of a grin when he saw Eben's concerned little face peering at him.

"You all right?" was Gabe's first question.

"Me? Sure, I'm all right. You're pretty bunged up, though."

Eben helped Gabe sit up against the pillows and held a glass of water to his lips.

"Thanks," Gabe said. "Arm hurts."

He put a hand up to his head and winced when his fingers touched the lump beneath the bandages.

"Ouch. Head, too."

"It oughta," Eben said. "Horse tossed you headfirst into the biggest rock around. Turned out to be harder than your head, which is sayin' a lot."

Gabe grinned. "Hungry," he said.

As soon as Eben passed the word that Gabriel was awake and wanted to eat, the hovering sisters returned, followed by a cook and a kitchen boy. They brought soup and stew, bread and buttermilk with them, but hastened to let the patient know that he had only to request anything he wanted, whether it be steak, venison, or quail, and it would be whipped up quicker'n he could say "scat."

The lady Townsend stood behind the cook. Gabe tried to read the expression on her face. She sort of looked concerned, but she seemed to show a kind of satisfaction, too. There was an almost imperceptible pursing of the lips as if she was thinking everything would be fine now that her sister's true love was back where he belonged. Riding off like that. Probably got what he deserved.

Catherine stood behind Eben's chair as if trying to use the dwarf as a kind of shield. Her face wore a look of guilt mixed with hopefulness.

Gabe ate the soup and tried the buttermilk, then asked for steak. Without further conversation, the cook and the boy vanished out the door with the lady Townsend following close behind to give them the benefit of her counsel and guidance. Feeling awkward where he was, Eben stood up to leave, but Gabe stopped him with his one good hand.

"Stay here," he said.

Catherine understood what it meant. Gabriel did not want to be alone with her. Whatever she needed to say, she had to say it in front of both of them.

"I'm so sorry you are hurt," she began. "Please believe me, I had no idea it would turn out this way. You left without a word! I was so unhappy to find you had gone, when I didn't know when you would be back, or where you were going . . ."

"Goin' back to the Keystone," Gabe said. "I owe Mr. Pendragon an accounting. That's the way it works. This thing isn't over until I tell him everything that happened. His riders don't just do a job and then go off on their own somewhere."

"And afterward. You'd come back to me?"

"I won't promise. Can't promise anything until I find out if I'm gonna be a Keystone rider or not. I can promise you I'll think about it for a year. Like you said. Or like your sister said. I don't know which one's making up the rules. I might come back. Maybe Mr. Pendragon will have a job for me. If he doesn't, maybe I'll drift around some."

"But . . ." Catherine glanced at Eben in embarrassment. "What about us? Can you give me any kind of assurances? Will you write to me, at least? There's a Mormon town, Coal Springs, where we can get mail once a month."

"You don't want letters. You want me here. You made it plain enough. You want me to sit right here while this year of yours goes by."

"Yes! Of course we do. Lynette and I agreed it would be the best thing. You, and Eben of course, could put up a house anywhere on the Surrey you wanted to. I don't care about your real name or whether you're a Keystone rider or not. I don't care if you have property. You could be an ordinary cowboy, for all I care. Just stay. Stay until we know, until we're sure of each other."

"There's the problem," Gabe said. "It's like Plato said, once a couple of people begin to talk about both sides, they find out where the problem really lies. You don't care if I go back and report to Mr. Pendragon or not."

"No. I don't, not really. I want you to stay."

"So there's another problem. I do care. All that time I worked in the kitchen, I had to care who I was. Otherwise it wouldn't have meant anything. I had to keep knowing I was good enough t' be a Keystone rider even if I was scrubbin' pans. Knowin' I could do any dirty job they gave me. Mr. Pendragon treated me as more than kitchen help. So did Link."

"I know. I understand."

"That's why I'm goin' back. Because now I can be one of them. And they oughta know it. I owe it to 'em."

"Yes."

She was fighting to keep tears from starting.

"You can come with me, if y' want to. When your sister showed up at the Keystone and asked for a rider to come help her, I took off my apron and I came. Now's your chance to do

237

the same. Just hand this place over to your sister. Come with me. You'd learn to care whether I'm a Keystone rider or not, just like I care. You'd find pride knowing I can fight for the brand. Like my brother did. You might not care about my name, but I sure do."

"Your brother shouldn't matter now. Whatever he is or whatever he did, you can't let his life run yours for you."

"You can't let your sister run yours."

"I can't go with you. Not right now."

"And I can't stay here right now."

Catherine Surrey was at a loss for words. He was looking at her but she could not meet his gaze. She didn't know how to explain to him what she needed and wanted.

"I'm sorry you were hurt," she said at last. "I'm sorry I sent the men to bring you back. Lynette said something to suggest that they do it any way they could, but we didn't think they would resort to any violence. Certainly not kidnapping."

She looked at Eben for some sign of forgiveness.

"They took it on themselves. They hoped that if they made Eben come back with them, you'd follow. I'm sorry. I'll speak to Lynette. Some sort of punishment needs to be arranged."

"Leave the men alone," Gabe said. "They're not the ones to blame. What do you say, Eben? You're the one they grabbed."

"I'll go along with you, rider. Leave 'em alone. No harm done to me. I'll just need t' get my gun back."

"There you are," Gabe said. "No harm done. Now. My head's hurting me something fierce. Soon as I get that steak I guess I'll take another nap. We'll be leaving in the morning. Again. And this time you know why."

Chapter Seventeen
TRAIL CUTTERS

"What's the matter with you?" Eben asked. "We been gone better'n two hours. An' you're still fidgety as a preacher in a cat house."

Gabe had twisted around in the saddle to check their back trail. The dwarf couldn't begin to count the number of times Gabe had done that.

"I'll feel a whole lot better when we've got the Surrey Ranch about a day and a half behind us," Gabe replied. "There's just no telling what those women might think of next. This arm's got me on edge too, bouncing in this sling. Can't seem t' get used to this horse. Every time my arm gets comfortable, he finds us a rock to trip over. Or else jams one foot down hard and gives me a jolt."

"You don't need t' ride with me, y' know," Eben said. "I'm all right. You oughta be heading east. I'll find the blacksmith on my own."

"I suppose so," Gabe said. "Still and all, I'd feel better tagging along awhile longer. There's no rush to get to the Keystone."

He grimaced as the obstreperous horse put a foot down wrong and jolted his arm again.

Gabe didn't ask Eben to tell him exactly where they were going. But Eben kept riding like he had some particular destination in mind, so Gabe let him set the pace and direction. Toward noon of the second day, the small man began to look around

more and more. A couple of times, he left Gabe sitting and resting while he rode to some high point or up along the banks of
some creek. Looking for a sign. They stopped to eat, and Eben
went off by himself to a grassy patch of ground where he just
sat cross-legged and stared south. It seemed strange, but to
Gabe it was as if the little man was getting himself back in
touch with the land. Maybe he needed it after all the time they'd
spent with humans and human problems.

Gabe was also feeling the freedom, relaxing into the long
rhythm of a day in the saddle. Each morning he felt less anxious,
less guilty about leaving Catherine Surrey, more certain that he
had done the right thing.

Late one afternoon Eben stood in his stirrups and pointed.

"There!" he said.

They were riding on one of those magical gateways into the
southwest, one of the routes through the hills the Spanish called
entrada or *paso*. Magical, because they are places where a traveler
realizes he is coming into a different land. On this high sandy
ridgeline the land abruptly took on a different shade of green;
the heavy shade of ponderosa forests gave way to the dusty haze
of piñon groves. Instead of seeing everywhere the low-growing
juniper scrub of the northern foothills, they now saw individual
desert cedars dotting the landscape, like green gumdrops scattered on sand. There was less gray; in the north the cliffs and
outcroppings were somber granite plastered with lichen, but
now cliffs and canyon sides were red sandstone darkly streaked
in desert varnish.

"Makes a man want to keep traveling south," Gabe said.
"Maybe clear to Mexico."

"Pretty country," Eben agreed. "I guess nobody'd stop you if
you were t' ride south. Least I wouldn't. Y' could stop in and
visit your brother, maybe."

"No," Gabe said. "It's a temptation, but I can't do it. I've either got to back trail myself to the Surrey place and talk that woman into goin' with me, or else just get myself back to the Keystone. That's where I'm goin'. It's sure pretty here, though. I feel like that man in the Bible, lookin' into the promised land and not allowed t' enter."

"Moses?"

"That's the *hombre*. You expectin' to meet up with Evan Thompson somewhere around here?"

"Was. Except we're runnin' late. By a week or two. But it was supposed to be right around here."

At the top of a hill they came to a campsite that had been used by untold generations of travelers, from the earliest Indians and trappers to Anglo mapmakers and cattle chasers. The view reached out in all directions to take in mountains, plains and woods, and canyons all the way to the misty horizon. Piñon trees offered dry limbs of pitchy firewood. The level sand promised a night's rest uninterrupted by those pebbles and pine cones that seem to come alive and crawl under a man's bedroll when it's too dark to find them.

"No water," Gabe observed while trying to unsaddle his horse with one hand. It wasn't pretty to watch.

"I'll look around," Eben said. He took the canteens and headed down the side of the hill toward a showing of cotton-wood tops.

He came back with water and a piece of metal rod bent into the shape of a J. He handed it to Gabe. The rod was twice the thickness of a man's thumb.

"Heavy," Gabe said. "Thick. Puts me in mind of a rifle barrel, but that ain't what it is."

The short leg of the J was forged flat, tapered like a wedge. The end of the long side was abrupt and jagged.

"Figure it out?" Eben smiled. He was unpacking the coffee pot.

"A big old hook, I guess," Gabe said. "Maybe the eye of it was broken off. Not that old, though. Look here. The rust is just starting to take hold on the broken end."

"Nope," Eben said. "Not a hook. Belonged to Evan Thompson. That's a link for his chain. Looks like he had it ready to weld closed, and it broke. See?"

Gabe saw. It was half of a broken link.

To make one of these, the blacksmith would heat a steel rod, then hammer both ends of it flat. He'd heat it again and bend it into an oval with the tapered ends overlapping. Finally he'd weld the tapers together with his hammer. The weld would be along the side of the link where it would be strongest.

But this link had broken before the blacksmith could finish it.

"Figure it's a flaw in the iron?" Gabe asked. "Maybe he didn't see it had a crack in it?"

"No flaw," Eben said. "Steel can have a mind all to itself. A smith never really knows the strength of the steel until he tests it. Pass me that saddlebag with the coffee in it, will y'?"

"Woulda been a heavy link. Like a wagon link, maybe."

"Sometimes, a rod just doesn't want t' be bent into the chain," Eben said. "Or so he's told me. Y' never know what might be inside a piece of steel. Or what kinds of fires it's been through. Every piece is a little different."

"Where'd you find it?"

"Down there at the spring. I figured I'd find some kind of sign around here. Near the water, if there was any water."

"A sign?" Gabe said. "From Evan Thompson, y' mean?"

"Yeah. He was here. He's gone east. But I know where's he's headed."

"I guess maybe we missed him because of this," Gabe said,

touching his bandaged arm. "If I hadn't got shot, we'd of been here a week ago. Good thing you know where he's gone. I guess maybe tomorrow I'll be leaving you. You'll be all right and it's time I made tracks for the Keystone."

Eben squatted by the fire and used his sheath knife to cut the tops from two cans of beans, which he placed near the flames.

"I'll go along with you a day or two," Eben said. "Not all the way. Probably leave y' at the Galvez *hacienda*. Maybe at the salt works. I'll turn south again somewhere around there and find Thompson. We'll see."

The next day they rose early, in the last remnants of darkness. They watered their horses and set out toward the Mexican's ranch, the *hacienda* of *Don* Gregorio de Galvez. The late afternoon sun was hot when they arrived at the *don's casa*. The buildings and grounds were completely deserted. There was ample water in the *acequias* for their horses and themselves, although it was evident that the ditches had not been cleaned recently. They found leftover hay in one of the empty barns and enough straw for bedding. But no tack hung beside the stalls. There were no saddles on the racks, no pails or feedbags lined up next to the stall doors.

Searching the equipment sheds and the yard, they found the wagons and carts gone. No sign of horses anywhere. They entered the open door of the *casa* and walked through the great house with their bootheels echoing on the tile floor, but not a chair, bench, bed, or mirror did they find. The same was true in the small huts where the *caballero's* workers had been housed. Eben found a candle holder hanging from a beam in one hut, but it was the only remnant of furnishings anywhere on the place.

There was no sign of violence, no bullet holes in the walls, no scorch marks from fire, no indication of any sort of attack by outsiders. Just the silent doors standing open.

"Pulled stakes, I guess," Gabe said.

"Looks that way. Maybe the *don* had a good crop of calves and headed back to Mexico with 'em."

"That's what I'd say happened."

"At least they left some clean straw. We can bed down in that."

"Can't help but wonder, though," Gabe said.

"Y' remember what he said. About wantin' to get back to his own country, I mean?"

"So that's what he did?"

"That's the way I figure it. Took his cattle and everythin' else he owned and went south."

This supposition was confirmed two days later when they arrived at the salt works.

"Yeah, the Mex hauled freight," Smith told them. "Heard he was goin' down into New Mexico. Hired all the extra hands he could find. Culled his herd and pulled out. Filled every wagon on the place with furnishin's and such. Bought a couple of old wagons off me and a whole lot of salt. Yeah, he's long gone."

"How's my little *compadre* doing?" Gabe asked. "The Castillo kid, the one I called *'conejo'*?"

Smith spat on the ground.

"Hell. That damn Galvez. He got wind of how good *Señora* Castillo could cook. And damned if he didn't come and hire her right out from under me. Oh, he gimme a couple of Mexican gold pieces in return. But without her around, the food just ain't so good anymore. The kid went too."

"Sorry to hear that," Gabe said. "I sort of planned on staying until suppertime. But we'll keep moving on. Make a few more miles before dark. Wanted to stop by and see how you're doing, though. Business coming along?"

"Yeah, pretty good."

"Trooper, he manage t' find customers did he?"

"It's workin' out. Ain't been that long. But he got as far as that Mormon town on Soda Creek. Not the Springs. That other town. Anyways, he give 'em a bag of salt for free. Just like you figured. Damned if they didn't show up here a couple of days ago, packin' cash money for a wagon of salt."

"Glad t' hear it." Gabe grinned.

"Stay a spell?"

"Need t' be movin'. We'll let you get back to what you were doin', but good luck to you. *Adios!*"

There was no need to turn off the trail and ride down into Colonel Grumm's camp. He was dead and his men were scattered, and the atmosphere of death still hung over the place. They traveled another hour before making camp. For the next two days they searched the creek bottoms and thickets for cattle carrying the Keystone brand.

"I think those Swiss boys did a pretty good job of rounding everything up," Gabe said. "We might as well pack up and ride on."

"Swiss? Or Swedes were they?" Eben asked.

"I don't know! Always did get those two mixed up. It's like Dutchmen and Germans—you hear them called both until you don't know which is which or why."

Despite not finding any cattle, the search was not a total loss. They dined on wild grouse they had scared up out of the creek bottoms. In a cottonwood grove Gabe shot a deer, and they dried the venison in the smoke of a cedarwood fire. It was lazy work, spending the clear, dry mornings exploring the range and sitting around in the late afternoon tending to the fire while their horses grazed.

"That shooting thing," Eben said one evening. They were

lounging against their saddles with little to do except feed twigs and sprigs of green cedar to the slow fire.

"What shooting thing is that?" Gabe said.

"I'm thinkin' about you and the rider they call Link. He know who you are? About bein' nephew to Mister Pendragon?"

"I suppose he did," Gabe said. "Maybe."

"But you two blowin' up those bullets. Seemed silly. And didn't really prove anythin', did it? Seems like all y' did was get rid of ol' Grumpy's ammunition."

"Worth doing." Gabe said.

"Didn't prove you could outshoot Link."

"Nope."

"Didn't prove he was better'n you, nor you bettern' him, neither."

"Nope. Although I think he is."

"So what was proved?"

"I'm not sure," Gabe said, breaking a stick and throwing it on the fire.

"It showed what kind of a man Link is," Gabe continued. "Most people, they look at a man's clothes or his job or how young he is or how old he is and make up their minds right then and there."

"You're right," Eben said.

"Take that lady Townsend for instance. She made up her mind I was a kitchen boy and that was it. Until she decided I might be good enough to court her sister if I'd wait a year."

"Y' gonna do it? Wait a year, I mean, then go back t' the Surrey place?"

"Dunno. Anythin' can happen in a year's time. But we're talking about Link. A man like Link—or Art Pendragon, come to that—he'll let another man show what he is. Doesn't judge a man until he's seen what he's made of. You ought to know what I mean. Being kind of short."

"I know," Eben replied. "Like you did. I'm small, but you never treated me that way. Want to say I appreciate it."

The lanky Keystone rider and the dwarfish blacksmith's assistant would take leave of one another at the river crossing. They arrived to find the shack deserted and the three Swiss brothers long gone. Some recent traveler had built a stone fire circle at the edge of the river and used porch planks as firewood. Cattle rubbing on the back wall had knocked one corner of the shack off its flat rock, and now the whole building was leaning. One heavy winter snow would knock it flat.

"Not much in the way of bein' carpenters, were they?" Eben observed.

"Let's hope they do better as dairymen," Gabe smiled.

"Camp here tonight?" Eben asked.

"No, I don't think so," Gabe said. "Lots of daylight left. A man could make another five, ten miles. Might stop at where those two crazy Scotchmen live."

"Well," Eben said, "you go on. I guess I'll cut loose of y' right here. Accordin' to Mr. Thompson's sign, he'll be downstream where this river joins into the *Río Cruzados.* I'm thinkin' maybe he'll be there helpin' *Don* Galvez. Makin' new horseshoes for the teams, maybe fixin' a wheel or two, makin' new trace chains or tugs. That sort of thing."

"Someday you gotta tell me how you know all this stuff about Thompson all the time," Gabe said.

"Maybe. Someday."

Eben stayed long enough to share an afternoon meal with Gabe, although it was nothing more than a chunk of trail bread and some jerky. When they finished, they divided up the remaining supplies.

"Got enough ammunition?" Gabe asked. "I guess mine wouldn't do you much good, not with that .38 you carry."

"Got plenty," Eben said. "Thanks."

"Want some more of Smith's coffee t' take with you?"

"Nah. You keep it. Might stunt my growth."

"I still owe you for a horse and saddle," Gabe said. "That one you brought me at the Keystone. I either owe you or Evan Thompson. Soon as I get on a payroll, I'll figure a way to send some money to you."

"Don't y' *dare* to do such a thing!" Eben smiled. "The ol' fur trappers used t' say, it's 'on the prairie.' Thompson wouldn't take a cent of your money, and me neither. Besides, someday he might need a favor from you. If he does, then maybe him and you'll be quits."

"Whatever he needs," Gabe said. "Let him know I'd drop everything and do it. Thanks."

Gabe sat in the saddle and watched Eben ride away down the river. When the dwarf turned for a final farewell wave, Gabe wished he was going along with him. Another year of riding free. Back to being a grub rider. Another year of drifting, taking jobs where you could, making your camp wherever nightfall caught you, riding up hills to see what you could see or following wagon tracks to see where they went.

The horse jerked its head up and down impatiently. As Gabe leaned forward to pat him on the neck his eye caught a dull gleam. It was the silver *concho* attached to the headstall, the *concho* with a letter K inside a keystone. Until he reported back to his uncle and explained everything, he was still riding for the brand. If there was no place for him at the ranch, he'd go back to drifting. Maybe south, or maybe out into Kansas. But until he was told different, Gabriel Allen rode for the Keystone.

The two Scots greeted him in their usual way, a .60 caliber rifle ball fired over his head. Afterward they admitted that warning shots to visitors no longer seemed necessary. Over a supper of thickly sliced roast washed down with homemade "poteen" liquor, they told Gabe they hadn't been bothered by rustlers since he left. But old habits do die hard.

"Besides that," pronounced Grit McByre as he toasted their guest in highland firewater, "we've a few neighbors hereabouts who'd nae ken wha' tae make of it if we were nae t' shoot a wee bit o' lead o'er their heads frae time t' time. Och, they'd tak' it we'd gone ill."

William Willis came from the stove carrying hot potatoes in a folded towel. He dumped one onto Gabe's tin plate.

"Now there's a fine 'tatie for ye," he said. "And ye'll help y'self tae anither slab o' that fine beef yonder. Grit, ye lazy fou, fill th' man's glass for God's sake."

"It's good beef," Gabe said. "That's for sure. Best I've tasted in months."

"Which gaes t' remind me," William said. "Aye, we'll say it now an' again come the mornin' when we're sober. There's a wee herd o' your own cows here."

"Keystones?"

"Aye, that's the mark on th' brutes. Grit and me came upon 'em doon along yon rye. Four heifers and twa . . . what d'ye call 'em, cow bairns?"

"Calves? Yearlings?"

"Aye. They're nae branded, but they stay alongside their dams who are. Ye're free tae take 'em with 'ee when 'ee go."

"And there's only the six animals hereabouts? You haven't seen any more anywhere?"

Grit and William looked at the heaped platter of roasted meat.

"Nae," said Grit.

"Nae," said William. "Just our own auld milch coo."

Gabe had already seen the cowhide drying on the back wall

of the woodshed near the pig sty. But among all the old unwritten rules of the west, high up the list was the rule saying you never discussed cattle brands while eating beef.

He might have been happy as a grub rider. It had been a good life for him, moving from place to place, taking adventure where he found it and lodging where it was offered, but as he drove the small herd toward the Keystone, Gabe realized he was equally happy to be a cowhand again. He let them move at a slow walk, sometimes leaving them on their own while he rode in and out of canyons or into creekside thickets to search for more Keystone cattle. He found only two, an old cow with the brand on her and a good-size yearling bull as yet unbranded. The way the male hung around her, Gabe knew she was his mother. He urged them out of the draw and folded them in with the other six.

Two more days went by, as he drifted slowly eastward. Gabe rode easy in the saddle, smacking his good hand against his chaps or whistling in his teeth from time to time to keep an animal from getting too far from the bunch. As nightfall approached, he scouted out a place with good grass and water and let them stop there. He got himself some supper, then took his arm from the sling to exercise it. Another few days and he wouldn't need the sling. Remounting, he rode a big slow circle around the bunch, calming them with his voice until one by one they bedded down on the grass. Then he could picket his horse and lie down in the grass himself.

Wrapped in his blanket with his head pillowed on the saddle, he watched the stars come back to life in the gunmetal sky. Somewhere a night bird sang its serenade to the darkness. Somewhere a coyote yapped, then yapped again at its own echo coming back across the low hills. The reborn stars gathered into familiar constellations wheeling in ancient patterns across the sky and Gabriel Hugh Allen closed his eyes and slept.

At daybreak he pulled his picket pin and moved the horse to better grass to graze while he had breakfast. He boiled some coffee and fried up the eggs and thick bacon the Scots had sent with him. The morning was icy, crisp, and still. As the sun climbed the sky, its warmth awakened a breath of breeze that stirred the grass. Gabe ate and packed up his camp, then rode out to collect the cattle. They had been up and grazing since first light, each one wandering off in its own direction.

"Kinda like us, huh, horse?" he said.

He wished he had named this horse. But he was just one of those horses that no name seems to fit. Or to put it another way, "no name" seems the most fitting name for it.

The cattle gave him no trouble so long as he let them amble along at their own pace and grab a mouthful of grass from time to time. One cow who had her calf with her took the lead in a natural, matter-of-fact way and the rest followed her. The bull yearling stayed in the rear; Gabe kept a watchful eye on him. Sometimes, a male youngster gets to feeling his oats for no apparent reason at all and starts making trouble for the whole bunch.

Trouble did come because of that male, but not the kind of trouble he had anticipated. It began in the afternoon when Gabe started feeling a prickly sensation on the back of his neck like he was being watched, that little ripple of shivers a man gets without knowing quite why.

"Kind of like one time at a barn dance," he told the horse. "Had a social misfortune concernin' the stitching on the seat of my pants, and all the rest of that evening I just couldn't shake the feeling people were staring at my backside. You ever feel like that?"

Either the horse had never known the experience or wasn't in a conversational mood that afternoon, for he said nothing.

251

"I guess you've never worn trousers at a dance," Gabe went on. "Maybe I can think of another example."

The little hairs right under Gabe's neckerchief continued to stand on end. Then, just as he was beginning to think he ought to look for a place to camp for the night, four cowboys caught up to him. They got between him and the cattle and they turned in a line, forcing him to stop. He noticed one of them was carrying field glasses. Gabe thought he recognized him as one of the men from Colonel Grumm's place, but he didn't let on. Even if he was one of Grumm's former men it wouldn't be an issue until he made it one.

"Afternoon, gents." Gabe grinned amiably. "Anythin' I can do for you?"

"That depends," said the leader, a tough-looking man wearing two revolvers. He sported one of those oversized Texas hats favored by performers in the so-called "wild west" shows. "Got any idea whose cattle those are?"

"Got a real good idea. Keystone Ranch. You can see the brands. Like this one."

He touched the Keystone insignia on the halter.

"Ride for the Keystone, do you?" said the man under the big hat.

"That's right. Mr. Pendragon's been sending men out t' bring in strays. Some have strayed a right smart distance from home."

Gabe didn't come right out and say he suspected the cows had help "straying," but the notion did seem to hang in the air. He looked at Grumm's man as he said it.

One of the four wheeled and rode among the cows, looking at brands. Gabe and the others sat their horses and watched him without comment. Gabe used the time to size up his visitors and put his own nicknames to them. The one whose skinny arms and legs stuck out from his sleeves and pants legs he dubbed "Bones." He decided to use the handle "Confederate" for the one who had been with Colonel Grumm, and he named the one who was inspecting the cattle "Plug" because of the narrow brim plug hat he wore.

Or, Gabe thought, *because his face reminds me of the rear end of that plug horse I had.*

As for the leader of the four—his most outstanding feature, and outstanding was the word for it, was his nose. Gabe thought of calling him "Boxer" because it looked as if he'd been in a few fights; in spite of having been broken and bent on more than one occasion, it still stuck out from his round head like a tomato glued onto a watermelon. Moreover, the man seemed to have done what he could to accentuate the size of his proboscis: he wore his hat down across his eyebrows so that you first saw the hat brim and then the nose, and beneath that appendage he sported a thick mustache that looked as if it had never been trimmed. With the mustache, his nose looked like a tomato sitting in a bed of lettuce.

Gabe couldn't help himself. He had to call the man "The Nose."

Plug came riding back and pointed to the bull calf.

"No brand on that one," he said.

"Mebbe we'll have t' take it," The Nose replied.

"That yearling's still keeping company with his mother," Gabe explained. "His mother's that lady with the dewlap and white forefoot. She's branded.

"And anyway," Gabe continued, "maybe I missed it, but did you ever tell me who you are? Not that it matters, of course. Not until you start talking about 'taking' cattle. That makes it a point of curiosity with me."

Gabe grinned affably.

The Nose grew more grim and serious.

"I don't hafta explain nothin'," he said. "But seein' the Keystone sign on your headstall there, I'll favor you. We're trail cutters for the stockmen's association hereabouts. We're jus' comin' back from inspectin' herds further north and happened t' spot you and these cows walkin' along."

"Is that right," stated Gabe.

More likely they'd been watching him until they were sure he was alone and not part of a bigger trail crew, but he said nothing.

"Yeah, that *is* right. We got an outfit—a dozen men or more, plus two wagons—holdin' our herd just behind them hills there."

"I see," Gabe said.

He knew about cutters. Big trail herds moving up from Texas sometimes went across local grazing land where local cattle would join in and walk along. Cutters were generally men from the area who rode out to the trail herds to cut the locals out and head them home again.

What Gabe saw here, however, was four "trail cutters" carrying fat bedrolls behind their cantles. They had bulging saddlebags, probably stuffed with food and extra clothes and the like. They carried gallon-size canteens slung to their saddle horns and were wearing their revolvers. Any kind of a roundup crew would leave blankets and slickers at the wagon, along with cumbersome gun belts and big canteens. He figured these men were not part of any "crew" at all. But it was best to go easy until he knew more.

He saw the Confederate pluck at the leader's sleeve and the two rode off a little distance for a private consultation. They spoke in low voices, turning several times to look in Gabe's direction. *Interesting,* Gabe thought. *I'll bet the Reb is filling his boss in on our little set-to back at Grumm's place.*

When they returned The Nose wore a smile on his face, a smile he evidently intended to be disarmingly friendly. But he was unaccustomed to making such expressions: his smile looked more menacing than his frown.

"It's gettin' late," he said, showing yellow teeth under the mustache shrub, "and we had us a long day. So why don't you just go on along your way and we'll go ours."

He wheeled his horse as if to leave, and then as if having an afterthought he turned about again to face Gabe. His artificial smile now had a sneaky look to it.

"By the by," The Nose suggested, "y' mebbe oughta get a brand on that bull calf. Never know, he might get a urge t' stray. Might come visitin' our herd, or somebody's."

"Good advice," Gabe said. "I'll see what I can do."

It was a spring creek, narrow enough to step across. It ran deep among arched willows, cutting itself down into the dark earth. Gabe tried the water, and found it cold enough to hurt the teeth and clear as glass. Somewhere upstream in a shadowy tunnel of willow branches, it made soft burbling echoes where the current dropped over an ancient rock or root.

For thousands of years this creek had been meandering back and forth between the bluffs, depositing silt until it had laid down a level bottomland a hundred yards wide. The tall grass grew thick and moist in centuries of silt and Gabe's cattle attacked it as if they had never known anything but sage and cactus. Gabe left them there and rode up a hill to collect firewood branches.

Once he had a fire blazing brightly in a circle of stones, he began to jury-rig a branding iron.

From a saddlebag he took a piece of broken horseshoe he had found back on the trail, along with a foot-long chunk of old rusty wire he had coiled up and saved. Down by the little creek he cut a thick piece of willow. Then he carefully split the end of it far enough to hold the broken horseshoe. He wrapped wire around the end of the stick and showed it to the horse. It looked like a primitive spear except that it had a curved piece of metal

255

instead of a sharp point.

"That's our running iron," he said to the horse. "Now we'll stick it in the fire to heat it up while we go catch that bull calf."

The horse went back to grazing. If he had any interest in running irons or catching cattle, it didn't show.

"That's why you never get anywhere in life," Gabe said as he wrapped wet willow leaves around the shaft of his branding iron and propped it up with the metal point in the coals. "Not enough curiosity."

He blew on the coals and added fuel until the metal began to turn red. Now all he had to do was rope and hogtie the bull calf and drag it to the fire where he'd use the running iron to draw a facsimile of the Keystone brand into its flank. It wasn't going to be much fun, especially without somebody to hold the calf's head and feet while he did the branding, but he figured he could do it.

Roping the calf took next to no time at all. The horse seemed to get some satisfaction out of dragging it toward the fire at the end of the lariat. But getting it to the fire was the easy part. Being larger than most calves, he gave Gabe a considerable struggle when the cowboy grabbed him around the neck and tried to reach over to get hold of a leg and flip him. And doing it with one bad arm took a lot of the fun out of it.

"Come on, now," Gabe panted. "Just lie down here for me."

Gabe was very glad there was no one watching him pushing and straining and trying to twist the calf's legs out from under it. In a corral, maybe with some pretty gals watching, a cowboy would take pride in quickly flipping his calf and tying its legs without so much as losing the ash off his cigarette while doing it. But here was Gabe, his shirttail flapping loose, his hat trampled into the grass, hair in his eyes, sweat drenching his shirt, wrestling a dumb animal out in the middle of nowhere.

"I bet this doesn't make sense to either one of us," he panted, addressing the aforementioned dumb animal.

"Look at it this way," he said, stopping to breathe a minute. "You're the cow, I'm the cowboy. A Keystone cowboy, by golly. So this is what we do. Got it? Why don't y' just lie down and let's get it over with."

In the end, human intelligence and guile won out, not to mention cunning and leverage. Gabe wrestled the calf down until it was lying on its side with all four feet tied securely. He untied the lariat from the saddle horn and fastened one end to the pigging string holding the calf's feet together. Holding the lariat, Gabe could move around and still keep the calf from getting up. If it did manage to get back onto its feet, it would be easy to jerk it down again.

The horse assumed that its services were no longer required. It headed for the creek where it grazed upstream until it was out of sight among the willows. Gabe knew it wouldn't leave the grass and water. He'd catch it up later on, before dark.

It was time to address himself to the bull calf.

"Now you went and wasted so much time," he said, "we'll need to heat the iron some more."

Unlike the horse, the calf had plenty to say. It bellowed and kicked, twisted and struggled against the rope.

"You know," Gabe explained while he fanned the coals and watched for the metal to begin glowing again, "if we were to follow ol' Plato's advice and go to a system of 'community of property' there wouldn't be a need for brandin'. I guess in Plato's time anybody who wanted a steak for dinner could just help themselves to a piece of you. I'm not sure how that would work. Probably wouldn't involve you bein' burned with hot irons an' me covered in sweat and calf slobber."

The branding didn't go too badly, despite needing to have both knees on the calf's flank while he burned the K and keystone into the hide. The animal bucked and kicked and squirreled around trying to get loose. And because of the short handle of the running iron, the stink and smoke of burning hair and flesh clouded into Gabe's face and brought tears to his eyes.

Gabe rose from his work disheveled and panting. He was tired out. He reeked with the stench of scorched hair. He tossed the running iron aside and bent down to release the piggin' string holding the calf—and realized he was no longer alone. The four so-called "trail cutters" were sitting on their horses no more than twenty yards away. They had come up on his blind side while he was struggling with the calf, the soft grass along the creek muffling their approach.

Gabe fixed his arm in the sling again and waited for them to speak.

"Remember us?" said The Nose, sneering.

"Looks like he's been runnin' a brand," Bones said. "I'd say we got him red-handed. He's holdin' everything a rustler needs, rope, piggin' string an' all. Runnin' iron's still warm."

"Yep, sure looks like it," The Nose said. "Boys, we got a cow thief here. We got all we need t' hang him, right now. All we need's a tree."

"Saw a good tree just over the rise there," the Confederate said.

He urged his horse close enough that Gabe could smell the sweat and feel the animal's warmth. Gabe saw the Confederate's right hand dangled down alongside his leg, holding a big cavalry revolver uncocked.

"I'll trouble you t' hand me up that Colt's you're carryin' now," the Confederate ordered.

Out of his line of vision Gabe heard the unmistakable clack and snick of a cartridge being levered into a saddle carbine. Plug Hat most likely had it trained on him.

"Well," Gabe said to the calf, "looks like you ain't the only one in trouble. Remember what I said about community property? If we had it, we wouldn't be in this fix we're in."

He addressed The Nose, but he made no move to surrender his Colt.

"You got any authority to be hanging people and collecting property hereabouts?" Gabe asked. "Some kind of papers, maybe? Stock detectives and trail cutters always carry their authority with them. Saves them from getting called cow thieves themselves."

"Heck," said the brutish man, "I reckon I went an' left my papers back at the wagon. Boys, one of you get down and turn that calf loose and get that lariat. We'll use it t' hang him with. Pick up that runnin' iron, in case somebody might ask us for proof why we hung 'im."

CHAPTER EIGHTEEN
ANOTHER GRUB RIDER

"Maybe we could talk it over," Gabe suggested.

The Confederate brought his horse uncomfortably close, the big shoulder nearly nudging Gabe's chest. But Gabe held his ground.

"Nuthin' t' talk about," The Nose growled.

"Ah," Gabe said. "We disagree, see? That means we've got somethin' to talk over. Nice evening. No reason t' hurry into a decision t' hang me. We could maybe talk about findin' a definition of justice. Or price of cattle, whatever you want. Let's make us a pot of coffee and kinda get acquainted before you string me up."

The Nose leaned a forearm on his saddle horn and glowered at his captive.

"What the hell you talkin' about?"

The three "trail cutters" behind the leader's back were laughing at Gabe's suggestion like it was a big joke.

"Shut up!" The Nose barked at his men. "I'm thinkin'."

Silence followed. Gabe thought he heard sounds in the willows along the little creek. Must be his horse splashing through the water. Probably decided to cross to where the grass, at least according to the old proverb, was greener.

Gabe wished he could join the horse. His rifle was in the saddle scabbard.

"Price of cattle," The Nose rumbled. "Y' said 'price' of cattle."

"That I did," Gabe smiled. "Always a good topic for discussion. Talkin' about cattle prices will get the conversation going every time, I don't care where you are. Fer instance, some men hold with the notion that these new beef breeds make prices go up for all kinds of beef anywhere in the market. But there's others who think the fancy breeds drive down the price you can get for an ol' longhorn steer. What do you think?"

"Shut up!" The Nose said. "What I want t' know is, have y' got any money t' pay for that calf? Seein' as how you already run a brand on 'im, mebbe y'd want t' buy it. Mebbe the famous Keystone spread'd pay y' back the money, if that's where you're really from."

His laugh was evil.

"Or mebbe," he said, "mebbe one of them famous Keystone riders'll come along and help you. Hell, we hear them riders go everywhere. Might be one comin' right soon now! Hah!"

"There you are!" Gabe said. "There's another topic t' discuss. It'd be more friendly over a cup of coffee, but I'll start anyway. What I'm thinkin' is this: I might be carrying money, or I might not be. Either way, I don't believe in payin' for property I haven't taken. And I don't like the idea of buyin' property from someone who doesn't own it. What's your thinkin'?"

"We ain't discussin' nothin' because you ain't in any position t' argue, Mr. Keystone cowboy. And now y' went and made me mad 'cause y' called me a rustler again. So here's how it's gonna be. We're takin' all these cows and all the money you're packin' with y' and your outfit t' boot. If'n you're real lucky and behave yourself, we're gonna let y' live awhile longer."

"Outfit?" Gabe said.

"Yeah!" came the voice of Plug Hat from behind him. "That's right! We're takin' y' right down t' yore drawers! I got dibbies on that gun o' yourn. Who wants his hat?"

"I mean t' hunt up his horse and git his saddle," said the

Confederate. "Mine's got a cracked fork. I'm claimin' his hat too."

"I'm fer them britches and shirt," Bones put in. "These here I got on ain't got enough longitude t' suit me."

Plug Hat was dismounting. Gabe saw him let the hammer down on the saddle carbine and return it to the scabbard. He was anxious to get Gabe's gun belt before one of the others grabbed it.

Leading his horse by the reins, Plug Hat was advancing on Gabe when a new voice entered into the discussion. It originated from the direction of the willows along the creek.

"I'd like for you gents to grab some sky!" the voice ordered. "Now!"

It was stated with authority.

"You heard me!" the voice repeated. "Get those hands way up, unless one of you wants to get ventilated!"

Gabe did not wait to see the source of the voice. He ducked beneath the neck of the horse and grabbed the Confederate's arm, dragging him out of the saddle. Gabe pulled his revolver and administered a bone-breaking slam to the side of the man's head. Sliding his left hand out of the sling and ignoring the stab of pain, he got hold of the reins and used the horse as a shield.

Plug Hat reached for his saddle carbine. But he froze when Gabe yelled "No!" At that range Gabe couldn't miss, and Plug knew he'd never get the carbine clear of the leather. His comrade, the one Gabe dubbed Bones, was sitting motionless in his saddle. His hands were raised as high as they would go.

The Nose, however, was not to be intimidated by the fact that two guns were trained on him.

"Throw down now!" the new voice ordered.

Gabe still couldn't see who was shouting from the willows.

The Nose proved foolish. Brave, possibly, but foolish nonetheless. It's possible to be both. Instead of lifting his hand from the butt of his revolver to hand it to the man who had the drop on him, he jerked it free of the leather and cocked the hammer. Evidently he intended to make a fight of it. Gabe heard two distinct sounds. One was the clack of The Nose's revolver being cocked and the second was the sharp *splang*! of a .30-30 carbine discharging. Whoever the new stranger was, he had made good on his threat to provide The Nose with additional ventilation.

Nose slumped, tilting sideways. He fell to the ground with his foot still caught in the stirrup. The horse stood with its eyes showing white and nostrils flared, but stood.

"Get down," Gabe stated.

As Bones dismounted he held his gun hand so high in the air that the cuff of his sleeve rode up to his elbow. Plug Hat was careful not to make even the slightest move toward his saddle gun. He kept his hand well away from his revolver.

"Throw those guns," Gabe said. "Do it."

And they did.

"Step back!" came the new voice, much closer now. "Get clear of those horses."

Gabe saw his visitor for the first time. A young man, about his own age. He wore no hat, but a line across his forehead showed white skin above and tan skin below, indicating he had recently been the owner of one. He wore no gun belt. He wore no boots. All he was wearing, in fact, was long-handled red underwear. The underwear was faded and baggy; being soaked in the creek had not improved its fit, either. It sagged precariously from his shoulders and shanks. Other than a wet union suit, the only thing he had was the .30-30 he was holding. But the rifle wasn't his. It was Gabe's.

"Hope y' don't mind," he said. "I borrowed this Winchester off a horse I found grazin' back of the willows there. I guess it's yours."

"Glad you did," Gabe said. "You could've even got into the

saddlebag and helped yourself to my spare shirt and pants while you were at it. None of my business, but it looks like you might have lost your clothes somewheres."

"These polecats are wearin' 'em," the stranger said, pointing with the rifle. "That one I had t' shoot, he's wearin' my gun belt. That horse there, with the Lazy A brand? That's mine, too."

"I see," Gabe said. "So, first thing we need do is get your clothes and belongin's back to you. Then we can work out what to do with these three gents."

Before long the three surviving rustlers, wearing only their long johns, were hogtied and tethered to a tree.

"Name's John Waters," the stranger said, offering his hand.

"Gabe. Gabriel Hugh Allen," Gabe said. "At least that's what my mother told me to say."

"She oughta know."

"So how'd you happen to run afoul of these coyotes?" Gabe asked.

"Happened a few days ago," Waters replied. "I'm just ridin' along, mindin' my own business when they came catchin' up t' me on the trail. Said they were range detectives lookin' for cattle thieves. Said I was trespassin' and all that. The skinny one, he was ridin' a horse that was about played out and had a bad limp, so they said they'd let me go if I was t' trade horses. With four guns on me, I figured I'd make the trade. But they didn't stop with the horse. They stripped me right down t' my union suit. Left Skinny's horse behind, but I didn't have any way t' rope him or bridle him. He went wanderin' off and there I was, tryin' to walk and catch him up and me in just my socks. Socks don't last long in this kinda country, neither."

"Catch that horse?" Gabe said, stirring the beans.

"Yeah, finally. Got lucky. But I had t' ride just holdin' onto his mane and kickin' him in the direction I wanted him t' go. Started trackin' these four. I'd just got close enough t' see 'em when they stopped t' talk t' you. Says to myself, 'that *hombre* with the cows, he's gonna be in trouble.' Sure enough, next day they had you. I couldn't figure out why you'd taken time t' stop and brand that yearling, but it looked like it gave me a chance. I figured I'd sneak up the creek through the willows and maybe grab one of 'em if he came down for water or somethin' like that. I had a club. And a big rock. T' hit him with, you know."

Gabe dished up bread and beans and bacon. John Waters pitched into it as if he hadn't eaten in three days. Which he hadn't.

"So," he said through a mouthful of food, "what'd I find back in the bushes but this horse carryin' a good Winchester .30-30 in a saddle scabbard! All loaded and everything! 'I bet he won't mind me borrowin' it,' I says to myself. And you were there for the rest of it."

"Awful glad you did borrow it," Gabe said. "Glad you stayed, too. Pullin' down on those four took starch, even with a rifle. Help yourself to coffee."

"Glad I run acrost you," Waters said. "I reckon we're even."

"Why don't we take turns watching these *hombres* tonight," Gabe said, "and then come mornin' we'll decide some appropriate fate for 'em."

"I'll agree to that," John Waters said. "You want t' pass me that can of peaches, if you ain't gonna eat 'em?"

The corpse wasn't going to keep very long in the heat, so the following morning Gabe and John Waters suggested to his gang of accomplices that they lug their companion up the hill and bury him. Mr. Colt seconded the suggestion, and Mr. Winchester cast the deciding vote.

While John Waters guarded the burial proceedings, Gabe

saddled up and rode a sweep on the other side of the hills just in case The Nose had been telling the truth about a herd and wagon. But if there had been, they had vanished completely, along with all their tracks.

"We're not that far from the next town," Gabe said. "I vote for herdin' these cattle robbers along and turn them over to the first lawman we run across."

"I'd a lot rather turn 'em loose buck naked," John Waters suggested, "but then there's always a chance they'd make it t' rob another day. They might turn out to be prominent citizens, too. Then we'd be in trouble. Between the two of us, I think we could handle 'em. We got plenty of artillery now."

"All right," Gabe said. "Town it is."

They tied the rustlers' clothes and boots into a blanket and lashed it across the back of a saddle. Then, with wrists bound to their saddle horns, they rode alongside the cattle where Gabe and John Waters could keep an eye on them.

"Shouldn't be too long," Gabe said.

"Nope," said Waters. "When we get there, I want t' buy y' a big steak."

"Yesterday you said you were riding along minding your own business," Gabe said. "Mind my asking what that business might be? You've got the look of a cowpuncher."

"You guessed it in one," John Waters said. "Cowpuncher it is. I'm young, but was a top hand back before the Lazy A went bust. Been on the trail maybe two months. Most of the summer, seems like. Driftin' from range to range and workin' for my meals."

"Ridin' the grub line," Gabe said. "I know that trade. A man gets plenty of fresh air and exercise between meals."

"Amen," John Waters said. "Been there, have you?"

"Had some experience with it."

"Couldn't help noticin' you wear a cavalry Stetson."

"Took it off a man," Gabe said. "He ruined my hat, so I took his. You in the cavalry?"

"Nah. Nearest I ever got was my father. He rode with the Eighteenth Kansas awhile."

"Long Island, Kansas?"

John Waters looked at Gabe like he was trying to remember something.

"You know Long Island? Well, that settles it. You're him," he said.

"Him?"

"You're the kid from school. At Long Island. I been thinkin' that ever since I saw you. You're the one who was always sayin' things from literature. Plato and them classics. Your mother was our teacher back when we were kids. But your name wasn't Gabe. I'd bet my shirt on it."

"I thought I'd known you from somewhere, too."

"Lemme see," John Waters said. "I bet I remember the name of every kid I was ever in school with. Yours was . . . don't tell me. Somethin' unusual. Sounded like 'gear' or 'gar' or somethin' . . . Garth! That's it. Garth."

"Gareth," Gabe said. "There's not many of us around. Like I said, my mother told me to call myself Gabe. Her brother's the owner of this big ranch, the Keystone. But I'd never met him before I went to work for him. He didn't know who I was and she didn't want to have any favors done for me. I kinda got used to the name Gabe. My uncle, he went to Wyoming, about the time I got myself born in Kansas, where my mother stayed. At Long Island. Then we moved to New Mexico country. Soon as I got too growed up to stay home, I thought I'd ride the grub line, find the Keystone Ranch, see about a job."

"That's your relation? Art Pendragon?"

"My uncle. But that's enough talkin' about me. What about you? Headin' for a job, are you?"

"Hope to be. Nowhere in particular, though. From all I heard about Pendragon, I'd admire to work for him."

"Been a long time between paychecks?"

"Seems like long."

"Well, I owe you," Gabe said, "that's for sure. Maybe you'd help me push these cows along to the Keystone. I can guarantee you'd get a few meals and a place to throw your bedroll awhile. Afraid that's the best I can offer, seein' as how I don't own the place."

"Good enough for me," John Waters said. "Let's get shut of these prisoners and head for the Keystone Ranch."

Toward noon the next day they were intercepted by a well-mounted, armed group of male citizens who turned out to be local ranchers and shopkeepers on the lookout for a gang of cutthroat rustlers who'd been terrorizing travelers and other folks. They had ridden out to find these rustlers and invite them to a community get-together involving hemp and a high crossbeam.

Gabe looped a leg around his saddle horn. A canteen was passed around. A couple of the citizens rolled cigarettes and smoked while they conferred as to the fate of the cow thieves. In the end it was determined they would take them to a local justice of the peace. But they'd need the testimony of John Waters.

"Seems right," Gabe said. "John won't mind stayin' a few days. Provided you feed him. If it's all the same to you, I'll just keep moving these cows toward home."

"Sure," the leader agreed. "One witness is all we need. Although you'd be more'n welcome t' put your cows in the town corral and stay over awhile."

"Thanks," Gabe said. "But I'd rather be gettin' on. If there's any kind of reward being offered for this gang, you give it to

John here. And for God's sake, feed the man! He hasn't got enough meat on his bones to keep his underwear up. John, when you're done here, you catch up to me. Or meet me at the Keystone. Just about anybody can tell you which way it is from here."

The small herd walked and walked. They walked across flats where the grass was turning autumn brown, across low hills of sage and sand where they scared up grouse and sent jackrabbits zigzagging for cover. They ambled down into swales and drank among stunted cottonwoods and drooping willows. After the creek bottoms they plodded uphill again, sometimes following deer trails where cedar and pine trees grew.

A single cowboy rode behind them, occasionally slapping his coiled lariat against his chaps. A Keystone cowboy. Nephew of Art Pendragon. Brother to the rider called Pasque. In days to come, before the time of the mythic West drew to its inevitable close, he would win his own name. And when he had his name, he'd make the long ride back to the Surrey Ranch and see whether that woman was ready to share it.

"He who endures to the end of every action and occasion of his entire life has a good report and carries off the prize which men have to bestow."

Plato, *The Republic*, Book X

AFTERWORD

Followers of the Keystone Ranch series will recognize that *The Grub Rider* follows the Arthurian legend of Sir Gareth, also known as the kitchen boy Beaumains. Those who remember the ultimate fate of Gareth will recognize that this story brings us one step closer to the final tragedy of the Keystone. However, at least two more parts of the legend remain to be written, including the story of how Art Pendragon came into the Wyoming Territory in the first place and became a leader of men in the region.

Given world enough and time, as the poet said, Art's tale will be next.

James C. Work
Fort Collins Colorado

ABOUT THE AUTHOR

James C. Work has published seventeen books, six of which are Arthurian-theme western novels in his Keystone Ranch series from Five Star. His anthology *Prose and Poetry of the American West* won the Colorado Seminars in Literature Annual Book Award. His essay collection *Following Where the River Begins* won the Charles Redd Award. He served on the Executive Committee and was President of the Western Literature Association as well as serving as Executive Director of Colorado Seminars in Literature. He retired as Professor Emeritus from Colorado State University, where he taught the literature of the American West and co-founded the university program in nature writing. Other than westerns, two of his recent books include *Windmills, The River and Dust* (Johnson Books), a collection of personal essays; and *Don't Shoot the Gentile* (University of Oklahoma Press), a humorous memoir of his early teaching experiences in southern Utah.

The employees of Five Star Publishing hope you have enjoyed this book.

Our Five Star novels explore little-known chapters from America's history, stories told from unique perspectives that will entertain a broad range of readers.

Other Five Star books are available at your local library, bookstore, all major book distributors, and directly from Five Star/Gale.

Connect with Five Star Publishing

Visit us on Facebook:
  https://www.facebook.com/FiveStarCengage

Email:
  FiveStar@cengage.com

For information about titles and placing orders:
  (800) 223-1244
  gale.orders@cengage.com

To share your comments, write to us:
  Five Star Publishing
  Attn: Publisher
  10 Water St., Suite 310
  Waterville, ME 04901